RISE OF THE STRONGEST SOVEREIGN

BOOK 2

RISE OF THE STRONGEST SOVEREIGN

BOOK 2

KAZ HUNTER

Podium

This book, like all things, is dedicated to Lucas

Cover design by Xiaoraini

ISBN: 978-1-0394-5457-6

Published in 2024 by Podium Publishing
www.podiumaudio.com

RISE OF THE STRONGEST SOVEREIGN

BOOK 2

CHAPTER ONE

Level: 20]

[Name: Jason Lee]

[Skills:]

[Monster Trainer: Tame a wild monster of an equal or lower power.]

[Pocket Dimension: Create a pocket dimension where you can store your unneeded monsters.]

[Rapid Heal: Heal a tamed monster! Warning: Overuse of this skill will have consequences.]

[Dual Leveling: A designated tamed monster will level up along with you! This will not decrease the XP that you receive. The monster may be in a pocket dimension at the time.]

[Interrogation: You may now speak to monsters you have not tamed, though they may not be willing to talk.]

[Random Strikes: You may now spontaneously tame a monster in the midst of combat. This is random and is not affected by any factors.]

[Brief Acquisition: Gain temporary control over a hostile mob. The duration of this will depend on the strength of the monster, as well as your level compared to its level. With this skill, you can tame monsters of a higher level than with your basic Monster Trainer skill.]

Dark energy flickers around me as I dive through the portal, following the lizardmen. My Phoenix flashes through the dimensional rift behind me, flames trailing off its red and gold wings. It lets out a powerful shriek, and in front of me, the lizardmen quail. There are twenty of them in all, each armed with a shield made out of wood and leather and a rusty sword.

"Alright!" I cry out, holding up my sword. Light flares from its blade, making them shriek and draw back. "Surrender now!"

Behind me, the portal flickers and closes, leaving nothing but a bare, cold wall of stone. I pause as the lizardmen suddenly sense that I'm in a slightly worse position than before. One of them, just a bit taller than the others, climbs up onto a small boulder and opens his mouth.

"*SCREEEEEEEE AK PA LIIIIIIIIIIIIIIIIIIIIIIIIIIIIII!*"

I'm not tremendously fluent in lizard speech, so I'm not quite certain if the battle cry was an eloquent, well-rehearsed speech or something more akin to "Kill him now!" Either way, the result is the same, as all twenty lizardmen beat their weapons against their shields and rush at me.

That was their first mistake.

For that matter, it turns out to be their last and only mistake.

My Phoenix screams and flashes forward, cutting loose with an immense blast of flame that sears across the first wave of the monsters. They turn to ash and crumble into dust under the intense flames, and I step forward to meet the second wave.

The first lizardman to attack leaps forward, bringing his sword high overhead. I simply step forward and duck under it, then drive my blade up into his gut. He falls headlong, and I spin as another one of the monsters tries to bash me with his shield. It hits me firmly, knocking me backward slightly, but I just kick it in return. The lizardman is staggered, and that's enough. I lunge past his guard and drive my sword into his chest, and he falls to the ground, dead before he hits the stone.

Suddenly, claws latch down on my shoulder, and I feel cold steel pressing against my throat. Thinking quickly, I send a mental command to my sword. It shrinks down into a dagger, and I stab backward, spearing him in the gut. It's not a well-aimed attack, so it doesn't kill him right away, but it does make the thing let go of my shoulders. I spin around and slash the dagger through his neck, then kick him as hard as I can, sending him staggering backward.

[Random Strikes: You have turned a lizardman to fight on your side!]

There's a sharp squeal from off to my right, and I spin to see one of the lizardmen cleanly take off the neck of a fellow combatant. It's not exactly how I foresaw the battle going, but I'll take it. He gives me a nod before jumping at another of his fellow cold-blooded soldiers, and I turn my attention back to the battle at hand.

It takes precious little time to carve through the remaining monsters. The one who turned to my side doesn't last long, perhaps a minute, and suddenly turns to attack me once more. I thank him for his help by cutting off his head, a quick and easy death in repayment for services rendered. My Phoenix blasts through another wave, and suddenly, the only soldier left in front of me is the leader himself.

A loud hiss echoes from his maw as he opens his jaw wide and steps down off the rock, backing toward a tunnel.

Master!

It's the voice of my Phoenix, echoing in my head.

"What is it?"

I do believe he's trying to lure you into a trap! I can see something just inside the entrance . . . but I can't quite see what.

"Thanks." I give a nod to the bird. "Skill: Interrogation."

There's a sharp *ping*, and the words of the lizardman suddenly become a great deal clearer.

"Come closer . . . Come closer . . ."

"Hey," my voice emerges as a series of hisses and squeals, "talk to me."

[ChaosRider: Wait, what??? Jason can talk to lizards now????]

[DarkCynic: He can talk to *any* monsters. Pay attention.]

[ViperQueen: But only for a few moments! SHHHHH!]

"You can speak my tongue. Interesting," the lizardman hisses softly. "Then you already know I'm leading you into a trap. I wonder . . . Will you spring it anyway?"

"I'll answer that question when you answer one for me." I keep my weapon as a sword of light, though I discretely—I hope—draw out my Shadow Dagger, keeping it behind my back. "The dungeon just closed up."

"That is not a question."

"Alright, then. How do I get back out?" I ask. "Who can open up dungeons?"

The lizardman laughs. "The boss, and only the boss. He's deep within . . . waiting . . . watching . . . And I doubt that he's going to be willing to work with you."

"Then I'll go find him and convince him," I answer with a chuckle.

"Oh, I don't think that that's likely." The lizardman laughs. "If you kill him, well . . . A dead boss can't open a thing. A live boss will only want to crush you and grind up your bones."

"We'll see about that." I shrug. "If you'd like to help, I'll consider keeping you alive."

"And have *my* bones be ground up?" The lizardman laughs again. "In your dreams!"

With that, he steps back into the entrance of the tunnel. There's a *crack* and a roar from within, and a massive, scaly fist explodes out. It latches around the lizardman and yanks him into the darkness beyond. His long scream echoes through the halls, until it ends with a loud *crunch*.

With that, something begins to rumble. The ground trembles, and I hold my breath. Something dark moves within the shadows . . . Something big . . . Something evil.

[GoldenShield: What do you think it is? I'm starting a poll!]

[Giant Lizard: 75%]

[Giant Snake: 15%]

I shake my head as I glance at the poll, but I keep most of my attention focused upon that darkened entry point. Suddenly, a head appears . . . followed by a body . . . followed by the aforementioned scaly claws.

As the thing crawls out and begins to circle me, I'm honestly not sure who to call the victor from the poll. It has the body and head of a snake, but it walks on long, spidery legs with matching deadly looking claws. Venom drips from long fangs as it circles all the way around the entrance, the tip of its spiked tail just meeting its long, scaly head.

"Huh." I take my stance. "You're a bit smaller than I expected."

The monster hisses at me. I don't bother trying to translate it. These sorts of bosses really only ever say one thing, and I'm not in the mood to hear it *again*. It lunges forward, opening its jaws wide, and I race up to meet it.

Just as the monster snaps at me, I jump up into the air, sailing over the jaws. Teeth slam together just underneath me, so close that I can feel the breath of air from their passing. I slam my Shadow Dagger into the corner of its mouth and pull with all my might. Unfortunately, the dagger meets bone, and instead of cutting it wide open, I'm suddenly yanked along for the ride as it begins to rage about the area.

[ShadowDancer: Now *that's* my Jason! What a move!]

[IceQueen: Are you *sure* that was intentional?]

"I have this all under control!" I grunt as the head slams into the craggy ceiling. A few stalactites break away and fall to the ground to shatter, and the monster spins and comes crashing down along with them, intending to batter me to pulp on the stone below.

I decide not to give it that chance.

I wait until the last moment, then throw myself to the side. The snake's head slams into the ground, and it staggers, stunned. I take that moment to leap up onto its back, draw up my sword, and slam it down—driving it all the way in to the hilt.

The lizard-snake, as you might expect, does *not* take kindly to that. It also remains a bit less dead than I had originally hoped and starts writhing back and forth in pain. I'm thrown from its back, and the thing's tail whips around and whacks me firmly in the chest. I go flying across the small arena to smash firmly into the wall.

Boom!

Dust and gravel explode outward from the point of impact, and I groan and slump to the ground. There are a number of large cuts across my body, though they're all surface level. I *did* mention that the tail is covered in spikes, right? It looks sort of like a porcupine, if porcupines were lizards. The lizard-snake, getting its bearings, spins and charges at me, and I prepare to defend myself.

Now, at this point, I have nothing more than my Shadow Dagger up against a hundred-foot-long lizard-snake that survived getting stabbed in the back of the neck. As it opens its mouth wide, I draw back my arm and fling my remaining dagger with all my might into its gullet.

Gulp!

The monster swallows it without flinching, though it *does* pause for a brief moment. I appreciate the reprieve, but I'm now down to having no weapons, save for a bow and arrow—which I don't really enjoy using in close-quarters combat, which means I don't ever use it. I have only my wits and my Phoenix to help me survive.

Thankfully, I think that's enough.

"My faithful companion!" I hold out my arm. The Phoenix flies down to land on it with a *squawk*, and I nod at the lizard-snake. "Shall we take this monster down?"

Yes, Master! The Phoenix sounds eager. *But . . . how?*

"The only way you *can* take down something like this." I bounce on the balls of my feet. "From the inside."

Are you sure this is a good idea, Master?

"Just make sure I don't get bitten by the fangs."

The Phoenix, despite his hesitation, is a loyal bird. As the lizard-snake charges forward and opens its mouth wide, I rush forward and dive straight into its gullet. Flames from the Phoenix scorch past on all sides, burning the monster's fangs and making it scream. With a *squelch*, I enter the snake's head, sliding down toward its stomach.

Now, this happens in the movies really quite often. It obviously happens in real life too, since I'm telling you about it. But what they don't tell you in the movies is how bad it smells. I mean, just think about a burp or a blob of puke. Not pleasant.

As I slide down the monster's throat, I find myself immersed in bile. My exposed skin starts to burn from the stomach acids, while the stench filling my lungs makes me gag. Still, I hold steady, feeling around for my dagger. *I know it's here somewhere . . .*

The stomach of the monster constricts around me.

Come on . . .

It tightens even more.

Somewhere . . .

Whatever air may have been left in my lungs is being forced out. Black spots begin to flicker across my vision.

Then, suddenly, my hand touches black steel.

A moment later, light breaks through, and I explode from the guts of the monster. For being disemboweled, it actually handles itself quite well and turns and throws itself at me one final time. My Phoenix fires a great deal of cleansing fire into its throat, peeling away scales and scorching the monster quite intensely. I brace myself and prepare to carve it up with my dagger yet again . . . But thankfully, there's no need.

The whole thing falls to the ground with a mighty *thud* that shakes the cavern. I let out a long breath and step back, and my chat room explodes.

[ChaosRider: THAT WAS EPIC, Jason! What a way to start off this dungeon!]

[RazorEdge: I'll give it to you. I thought we'd seen the last of you, but you pulled through mighty well.]

[LunarEclipse: Course he did! He's Jason! He's the best of the best!]

[ViperQueen: I don't know. John's not half bad, either. I'll miss him while he's away.]

That last one makes me sigh. I'll miss John as well. Friends are a rare commodity in this strange new world, but he certainly qualifies as one. He last told me that he was going to visit his sister but that he'd be back soon. I square my shoulders, though, and retrieve my sword from the corpse of the giant lizard-snake.

"Well, I sure hope you all enjoyed that show." I give a bow to the audience. "Look forward to lots more as I, Jason Lee, continue to explore and conquer the dungeons of this new world!"

That makes the chat explode, and I turn and walk into the darkened tunnel. I'm not sure exactly how large this dungeon will be, but I know I need to get a move on if I'm going to get to the boss and force him to open the portal back to New York.

This is indeed a strange new world . . . And I'm going to tear down everything that seems to be working to destroy it.

CHAPTER TWO

The tunnel is a long one, dark and winding . . . Though, considering that it was the den of the giant lizard-snake thing, I suppose I shouldn't be surprised. I shrink my sword back down to a dagger and carry one in either hand as I slowly walk along, keeping my eyes turned forward, alert to any and all forms of danger. Only the light from my blade, as well as from my Phoenix's pale flames, casts any illumination on the area around us.

Master, I sense a chasm up ahead.

"Thanks," I murmur, then glance up at the bird. "By the way, what's your name?"

I have no name.

"Wonderful!" I beam with joy. "Bjorn already had a name, and I can't even begin to pronounce the name of my squirrel. What do you think would be a good name?"

I am not qualified to answer that question. I am your servant. I will answer to whatever name you desire.

"Alright, then." I run through a handful of names in my head, then turn to the chat. "Why don't we hear from some of you? What do you guys think we should name this wonderful, fiery companion?"

[Poll:]

[A: Flamer McFlame]

[B: Burnie]

[C: Frank Firebird]

[…]

The list goes on for some time as everyone adds in their favorite name and then begins to vote. In the end, Flamer McFlame winds up winning with almost 60 percent of the votes.

[LunarEclipse: Flamer McFlame it is!!!!]

[IceQueen: Woo-hoo!!! Hopefully this one will be luckier than Garg.]

"Guys," I raise an eyebrow, "I don't want to crush your spirits, but I'm not naming him Flamer McFlame."

[ShadowDancer: WHY NOT?????]

The same sentiment is echoed a dozen times over, and I sigh. "Because, in the middle of battle, that name is *much* too long to be calling out for assistance."

[DarkCynic: Too true.]

[ViperQueen: It doesn't roll off the tongue well, does it?]

[GoldenShield: I still think it would be good.]

"I like Burnie," I say, after I scan through all the options for a moment. "Burnie, how would you like that to be your new name?"

As I said, Master. I serve you. Tell me what to answer to, and I will do it. Though I would appreciate not being called Flamer McFlame, I will do so if you so desire.

"Burnie it is!" I clap my hands and grin. The chat begins to congratulate both me and my Phoenix, but my attention is drawn forward. Ahead, I can see the tunnel coming to a close, and I steal forward as quietly as I can. Soon, I come up to the exit, and I peer out into a chasm, just as Burnie indicated.

The thing is immense, rising dozens of feet above me and hundreds of feet below. I can't see what's at the bottom; it could be sharp rocks, or a stream, or simply an infinite void. Those *are* prone to crop up every now and again. In any case, Burnie flies out and spits a fireball down the length of it, illuminating the long and winding way.

The walls of the chasm are pocked with deep hollows, inside which I can see glowing eyes. Here and there, narrow rock bridges and archways stretch across the gap. They don't seem like they were man-made; they seem more like natural structures. I pause for a moment, and then, as the fireball flickers out, it reaches the end, where I glimpse a large, iron door.

That's my target.

"Alright, guys." I prepare to go charging headlong into battle. After a moment, I sheath my Shadow Dagger. When I'm carrying both, I have a tendency to throw one or the other, and with the chasm below, I really don't want to lose one of my weapons. They weren't easy to come by, by any stretch of the imagination. "Time me. Who thinks I can make it all the way to the end in fifteen minutes?"

[ChaosRider: I DO!!!]

[ShadowDancer: I'm going to guess twenty.]

[Originalgoth: I'm going to hope he falls and dies.]

[IceQueen: Hey, not Originalgoth again!]

I roll my eyes. Originalgoth has been pestering me in my chat ever since day one, but every time I ban her—I assume it's a her, but it's impossible to know that for sure—she just reappears. Same chat handle, same annoying attitude, so I figure it's easier to just put up with her shenanigans. In any case, as I look for a path down the chasm, I don't really find anything except sheer walls, some of which might be rough enough to climb.

I don't know about you, but I've always hated climbing animations in games. They're terribly unrealistic, and in real life, it's so slow. Plus, I don't have any skills that let me go faster, so . . .

"Alright, Burnie!" I race toward the edge of the chasm. "I'm going for it! Everyone else, time me!"

[DarkCynic: Wait, what's he doing?]

[IceQueen: He's . . . He's really . . .]

I leap out into midair, sailing toward one of the alcoves. Burnie flashes down out of the sky, meeting my foot right at the midpoint. I land and push off once more quite lightly, hardly touching him at all, and spring onto the mouth of the cave. Burnie flies up behind me, and we face the interior.

Rrrrrrrrrrrrrrg!

The chat explodes with comments about the cool trick, but I'm not really given any time to read them as the creature inside, a lizard-cat, leaps forward and rakes at me with its claws. I duck under the first three blows—which is *usually* all that monsters can throw before they run out of moves—and take a step forward.

Wham!

I'm thrown backward with all the force of being hit by

a semitruck. I should probably clarify that the monster is a cross between a *lion*-sized cat and a lizard. Anyway, Burnie flies down and catches me before I fall off the edge, and with that, I leap forward once again.

This time, I'm ready. The lizard-cat lunges, and I drop to the ground, sliding underneath the raking claws. I land a few cuts across its belly, drawing blood, and come up behind the thing. Quickly, I grab its rather scaly tail, brace myself, and pull with all my might.

The monster is lifted from the floor and slung back into the nearby wall. It lands and pounces, but I keep a tight hold of the tail, side-step it, and yank on it with all my might. A great number of bones pop up and down the length of it, and I sling the monster around to throw it into the wall at the back of the cave. A shockwave explodes outward from the point of impact, and it drops to the ground, groaning and swaying on its feet.

"I've got you now!" I spring forward. The monster looks up, and I drive my dagger into its throat. It drops to the ground, bleeding on the floor, and I race back to the alcove entrance. "What's my time?"

[RazorEdge: You're at 1:04.]

[ViperQueen: You're not going to be able to fight every monster if you want to actually hit the time you were wanting!]

"Right you are," I nod, trying to think. I'm not too far away from one of the bridges, so I call out Burnie again. He swoops down, and I step back, then rush forward and jump once more. For a moment, I sail through the air, then land on Burnie and bounce to the bridge.

When I land, the whole structure shakes, and I steady

myself. Growls and snarls echo from either end, and I glance over my shoulder to find another of the cat lizards dropping down from a lair, using its claws to climb the rough patches of the wall, to land on the bridge as well. Two more do the same thing at the far end, and I frown.

"Alright, Burnie! Do your thing!"

Burnie shrieks and dives from the top of the ceiling, where he had apparently hidden to lie in wait. He fires an immense blast of flame at the two monsters in front of me. One of them takes it dead-on and is blasted off into the abyss. The other one is merely a bit scorched and charges at me, snarling and slashing, while the one behind me does the same thing.

Quickly, I turn my dagger into a sword, then charge up to meet the first one. It snarls and leaps to meet me, and I nearly duck underneath it. But sensing that this might be the case, it keeps its own claws low and prepares to carve me to bits. Instead, I stay upright, brace myself, and slash at the monster with every last ounce of strength I have in me.

The sword connects with its face. It doesn't break bone, but it does succeed in knocking the monster back, gaining me a few seconds. As it recovers, I spin around to find the other one lunging. It lurches up onto its back legs and proceeds to try and claw me to shreds. I narrowly parry the claws with my sword, then duck as the one I hit in the face manages to recover and lunges at me anew.

[ShadowDancer: Go, Jason!!! Pinwheel!]

[ViperQueen: Taking on two at once. Not too shabby!]

[DarkCynic: I'm going to record this and put it on the internet!]

For a few long moments, I fight desperately against the

raging cat monsters. They lunge and spit and hiss and slash, and I cut and dice and stab. They're fast and they're tough. My blade can hardly even score their flesh, it seems like. But I *can* hurt them, and that's the important bit. And, best of all, there's a rather handy environmental factor that might just help me.

I block the one standing in my way, then turn and dodge-roll underneath the claws of the second one. Claws rake down my back, which stings, but I ignore it. Sometimes you just have to muscle through a bit of discomfort for the sake of a victory. I stab the creature in the left rear leg and then stand up and throw all my weight into a massive punch on the right-hand side.

The creature staggers. It's not much, but it's enough. The bridge we're standing on isn't wide, and it starts to slip. Immediately, it digs its long claws into the stone, and I spin out of the way and slash it across the back left leg. That makes it lose its balance entirely, though its two front legs do manage to hang on. The bulk of its body swings off the edge of the bridge, where it simply dangles, snarling, as it tries to climb back up.

I'm given no quarter to celebrate this victory as the next cat races forward, lashing and snarling, well aware that I intend, and have the capabilities, to kill it. It slashes high; it slashes low. All the while, the other cat slowly starts to get a grip and pull itself back up onto the bridge. I need to end this, and I need to end this now.

"*Arhhhhhhh!*" I grit my teeth and rush forward, drawing the sword behind my back, preparing to inflict a devastating blow. It sees this, of course, and crouches down, preparing to spring up and block me, just like it's done a dozen times already.

Thankfully, I only did that in order to serve as a distraction.

Right as I go to swing, I shrink the sword back down to a dagger. Thus, as I attack, the blade is a great deal shorter than where it was supposed to be. The lizard-cat leaps up to block, only to find itself catching air, and over-extends itself. I suddenly find myself with a rather nice view of its belly and step up and slam the dagger deep into it. A flick of my wrist causes the dagger to expand back into a sword, and the tip is driven out the far side.

The cat lets out a gargle and falls. I yank the sword free and only narrowly dive out of the way. It hits the bridge hard enough to shake the stone, then slides off, falling down into the darkness below. By now, though, the other cat has nearly pulled itself back up.

Nearly, though, is a long way from being ready to fight.

I rush forward and stab my blade down into its right paw, making it howl with fear and pain. That claw comes loose, leaving it dangling from a single paw. For a moment, it stares at me with nearly unbridled hatred and anger. I decide not to leave it in suspense for a long time.

As it plummets into the abyss, it lets out a long, drawn-out roar that gradually fades away. I don't hear a *thump* or any other sound of impact from below, which makes me suspect that the chasm really is more akin to an abyss than a simple cave. Oh, well. Doesn't really matter what's at the bottom; if it's deadly, I just have to avoid falling down there.

I quickly race to the end of the bridge, where I time my jump to leap over to the next pocket in the stone. This time I jump upward, angling toward the stone, and bounce one foot off the rough patch of rock, bounce a second time off Burnie, and then land in the entrance of the cave. Inside, several lizard-monkeys stare out at me, hissing and chuckling.

"What's my time at?" I give my sword a twirl.

[RazorEdge: You're at 5:17.]

A few moments later, bits and pieces of lizard-monkey rain down into the cavern, and I move on. Coolly, though quickly, I work my way across the next bridge and then the one after that. Soon I find myself on the final stretch before the great iron doors. There are no more bridges, only a wall of rough stone marred here and there by the monster-inhabited recesses. Growls and howls fill the air, and I take a deep breath.

"One last time call."

[RazorEdge: 14:31.]

[ShadowDancer: You're going to be close!!!]

[FireStorm: What do you mean, close? He's not going to make it.]

[ChaosRider: You just watch him. I bet he does!]

I take a deep breath, judge several distances, and then rush forward. Burnie flies along at just the right height, and with that, I launch myself over the abyss.

For that last hundred—maybe two hundred—feet, I dash across the open void. My right foot plays against the chasm wall; my left foot finds its purchase on the back of my noble bird. I pass by several darkened alcoves full of snarling monsters, but I ignore them all. They're too small for me to bother killing just for the sake of it, and beating the clock is more important. My breath comes in gasps as I close the last little bit, and—knowing that if I miss a single step, I'll fall to my death—I throw myself forward.

[RazorEdge: 14:56 . . . 57 . . .]

[IceQueen: AHHH! There's no way he makes it!!!]

[RazorEdge: 58 . . .]

I give myself one last burst of energy, leap off the wall, and fling myself at the door.

[RazorEdge: 59!!!!!]

Wham!

I slam into those iron doors with enough force to dent them—albeit not much, it's still cool. They resound with a great *bong*, and the chat explodes with cheers.

[RazorEdge: HE DID IT!!!!!!!!!]

[ChaosRider: I knew he would!!!]

[FireStorm: I stand corrected! I don't know anyone else who could have done *that!*]

[Originalgoth: I bet *I* could have.]

I chuckle and take a moment to catch my breath. Burnie flies down and lands on my shoulder, and we both wave and bow to the invisible crowd watching us. Once my heart has stopped pounding, I slowly turn toward the iron doors.

"This looks an awful lot like a boss room door." I smile, grabbing hold of the handle. "Time to get out of here!"

CHAPTER THREE

The doors crash open as I fling them aside with all my might. A deep, resounding *boom* echoes through the area beyond, an area lit by soft, glowing lights. I slowly step through, waiting for the doors to slam shut behind me. They do no such thing, and I lift my sword to let the light cast out a bit further.

The glowing lights, such as they are, come from pools of water. Well, I suppose it would be more accurate to say *the* pool of water, since there is really only one, as the dozens of smaller pools crisscrossing the long, vast cave in front of me are all connected by small channels carved through the stone. Bridges run across the channels, while small fins and tentacles splash merrily from the liquid.

"Huh." I slowly lower the sword after a moment. "This *doesn't* look much like a boss room, after all. Guess we've got a bit longer to trek."

[ChaosRider: So you mean we have to watch you slog through even *more* monsters? How awful? Sarcasm intended.]

[ShadowDancer: You've got this! You're going to do great!]

[ViperQueen: This room may not be a boss chamber, but *that* certainly looks like one.]

The final comment is accompanied by a screenshot of my own vision from several seconds earlier. On the left is what I had seen originally, while on the right is a zoomed-in version. A moment later, a third, even more zoomed-in version appears, and I nod slowly.

Off in the distance, so faint that it looks more or less like it might be a pinprick of light reflecting off one of the pools, is a little speck. Zoomed-in, while admittedly it's a bit pixilated, the speck can be seen as a door, flanked by a torch on either side. I can't tell many more details than that, but it certainly looks foreboding and ominous, which increases the odds that it is, indeed, the boss chamber.

"Alright, then." I smile and start walking forward. "We have a goal. Let's get there."

Master?

I frown and turn as the voice echoes in my head. Thankfully, his words are displayed as subtitled text to my audience, so it doesn't look like I'm crazy and just talking to the air.

"What is it, Burnie?" I hold out my arm. He flies down and perches on it, rather like a falcon, which is sort of cool. I approach the closest pool, wary of anything that might come out.

I may not be of the greatest use here. When put head-to-head, fire rarely wins out over water.

"Very true." I give the faithful bird a nod. "In that case, why don't you go take a rest? I might need you for the boss battle."

Burnie flies up into the air and performs a short spin. I

open up my pocket dimension, and with another twirl, he flies inside. There's a pause, and I hold out a hand.

"Alright, poll! Which one of my pets should I bring out?"

[ChaosRider: Uh . . . Bjorn, obviously!]

[FireStorm: Yeah! Because wolves prey on things in the water, like fish!]

[ViperQueen: Also . . . What other creatures does he have? There's that annoying squirrel, and then a horse, but nothing that's really going to help him here, you know?]

[FireStorm: Fair point.]

I chuckle as I look over the chat, then give a nod. "Alright, Bjorn! Come hither!"

Bjorn steps out of the portal, noble and strong. He looks over at me and gives a nod, then slowly turns to regard the chamber. His fur ripples a bit in the soft wind that blows across the waters. I allow the portal to close behind him, and he lets out a snarl.

I can hear them. They're mocking you.

"Oh, are they now?" I give my sword a twirl. "And what exactly are they saying?"

Now *that* gives Bjorn pause for a moment. *It's hard to translate into human speech, but . . . They're commenting on the number of appendages that you, and other land-dwelling creatures, possess.*

"Four?" I blinked in surprise.

Which is less than an octopus's eight, a squid's ten, and a kraken's however many it happens to need.

"Huh. Never thought about it that way." I twirl my sword one more time, then start walking forward. "Well, Bjorn, shall we go show these calamari just what we landlubbers are made of?"

Yar, Master.

The chat breaks into laughs over that, and Bjorn chuffs quietly under his breath to me. And with that, we head for the first pool. Now, strictly speaking, do we *need* to go to that first pool? Maybe not; we could easily walk around it and make for the closest bridge, but I want to see what we're up against.

As it turns out, we really have our work cut out for us.

We come racing up to the waters, only for a great deal of said water to be ejected up into the air. Both of us draw up short as tentacles and blobs of luminescent flesh come rising up. For a long moment I struggle to comprehend just what I'm looking at, until the mass resolves itself into two separate creatures.

First, there's a giant octopus, pulling itself up out of the waters onto the land.

Second, there's a jellyfish, which seems to be the actual source of the light, which floats up into the air as if it were some sort of a balloon. The stingers and barbs across its tentacles glisten with venom, and I hold up my sword defensively.

And with that, the octopus attacks.

All things considered, the octopus is probably about the size of a car. Not terribly large, but bigger than it should have been. It streaks across the ground, eyes bulging, and lashes out with several tentacles at once. Bjorn howls and leaps into battle, grabbing hold of one of them while I step up and slash at the other.

Of course, both of us are thwarted almost immediately. Several tentacles wrap around Bjorn's neck, holding him fast and dragging him to the ground, while two more dance nimbly around the hilt of my blade and latch down upon my wrist.

Quite suddenly, aware that it holds both of us, the octopus seems to sense victory. It hefts up the mass of its body, revealing the telltale beak that the creatures are known for. As it starts to drag me closer, I fight enough that it thinks I'm actually worried, all the while allowing it to bring me in. Bjorn senses this and does the same thing.

[ChaosRider: Fight, Jason! FIGHT! You didn't defeat an undead jarl just to be taken down by a squid!]

[IceQueen: It's not a squid, and he'll pull out of it! He means to do this, I'm sure.]

[RazorEdge: Why would he *mean* to do that?]

I smile at the chat but don't want to give anything away. As the monster opens up its beak—which is probably a foot wide, or so—to start chomping on us, the two of us spring into action.

Because after all, while water does tend to win out against fire, ice has a strong tendency to defeat water. And Bjorn, of course, is a Frost Wolf.

Bjorn tilts his head back and howls, and a great, freezing blast of wind roars through the cave. The tentacles around us freeze, and I smile. The body of the octopus starts trying to thrash away, but it freezes solid after a moment as well. Quickly, with my free hand, I draw out my Shadow Dagger, stretch forward, and drive it into the beast up to the hilt.

Crack!

The whole thing shatters into tiny pieces an instant later, with octopus ice tinkling to the ground all around. I smile and step back, give my sword a satisfied victory twirl, and then sheath my Shadow Dagger once again. I look across the whole of the cave, watching as the ice grows to cover each and every pool and crevice in the entire room.

[ChaosRider: WHOA!!! That's so epic!]

[ViperQueen: Better watch out, Jason, or you'll make things too boring for us.]

[ShadowDancer: Uhh . . . What's happening?]

I frown in thought as, quite unexpectedly, the frost growing across the surface of the water suddenly reverses. It thaws out, the tentacles and fins go back to splashing . . . and out of every pool, more of the jellyfish rise up. I turn my attention to the closest one, which—while it hasn't made a move against me yet—is still certainly hanging there. The long tendrils still extend down into the pool, which are now pulsing with energy, likely keeping it warm and preventing anyone from simply using a frost creature, or some other form of ice magic, to do exactly what Bjorn nearly did.

"And there's how we make it a bit more interesting!" I smile and charge at the jellyfish. "Let's see how good the defenses on this thing are!"

Now, at that moment, it's probably hovering a good five or six feet off the ground. Certainly well within range of my blade. As I swing it up, though, several long tendrils flash up, moving to intercept.

ZZZZZZAP!

A great deal of electricity pulses through the tentacles as it meets my blade. I find my hand letting go of the sword against my will. It clatters to the ground, and my arm, numb, falls to my side. I frown and take a step back, only to feel something prick the back of my neck.

ZZZZZZZZZZZZZAP!

Electricity pours through my body, and I fall to the ground. More of the tendrils wrap around me and start pulling me toward the thing. I try to move but find myself completely unable do so much as twitch a finger.

[Condition: Paralyzed.]

[Duration: 0:00:59.]

Now, fifty-nine seconds isn't bad, to be certain, but I have two very distinct suppositions about the monster. First, it won't take a full fifty-nine seconds to eat me. Second, if it does, it'll likely just shock me again. Bjorn tilts his head back and howls, blasting the creature with icy air, but it simply generates a bit more heat to fight back against the attack.

[ChaosRider: Alright, Jason! You got the octopus to lure you in. Now you're doing it to this thing too!]

[ViperQueen: . . . I'm not so certain that this is intentional.]

[IceQueen: Of course it is! It's Jason! He's about to wow us with some sort of daring escape!]

[Originalgoth: This will be . . . interesting.]

[GrendleH8tr: Keep your head about you, kid. You'll make it through.]

I smile, at least inwardly, at GrendleH8tr's appearance. I don't know who he is, but he always seems to pop in when things are at their darkest, and he always has a good bit of advice to go with it.

Use my head.

Think, Jason, think!

I can't move; I can't even call my other creatures—otherwise I'd just call Burnie, who could likely make short work of these things. What can I do?

Suddenly, the thought pops into my head, and I form a mental command.

Use Skill: Brief Acquisition.

There's a flash of light, and the jellyfish suddenly drops me. I land on the ground with a great deal of force, and a soft, blubbering noise flickers up inside my head.

Hello, Master. Sorry about that. What can I do for you?

I try to answer, but I find that I still can't speak, and mental commands only work for skills, not talking to monsters. It's not terribly epic, but I wait until the paralysis wears off, and climb slowly to my feet.

"Thanks for letting me go." I give a bow. "Do you have any tips for . . . I don't know . . . defeating the rest of these jellyfish?"

Of course I do. All I do is think, and I have plenty of ideas. Your best bet would be to use our own weapons against us.

I frown in thought. "You mean . . . the lightning?"

Yes, Master!

[Warning: Brief Acquisition will expire in 10 seconds.]

"Then do you think you could do that? Send a bolt of lightning through the pool?"

Of course, Master!

The resulting blast of lightning is, in every sense of the word, spectacular. Lighting erupts downward from my tamed jellyfish and streaks across the surface of the water, leaping and flashing from wave to wave, arcing from tentacle to tentacle. It blasts up the next jellyfish, who freezes, and seems to serve as an amplifier as the blast goes on. I watch, rather in awe, as the entire room is suddenly bathed in light from the crackling, deadly electricity.

Wait . . . you're . . . you're not my master!

The jellyfish turns against me, and it suddenly lifts its tentacles to strike at me. By now, though, it's too late; the effect, which has begun to resound and amplify, comes streaking right back. It gets caught up in its own wave of destruction and is soon flickering and pulsing with deadly light, just like the rest of them.

And then they all explode.

All in one moment, one single instant, every single jellyfish detonates rather like a light bulb popping. There's not really all that much substance to a jellyfish, so it doesn't exactly splatter loads of gore or anything. They all just flicker and collapse back into their pools, landing with odd splashing sounds.

Of course . . . That's when I remember that they were also the source of light.

The splashing of the tentacles intensifies. Fun fact: octopi are apparently quite poor conductors of electricity. I hold my sword higher, casting long rays of light across the expanse, though it's a poor substitute for the previous lighting.

[FireStorm: That was epic! And now he has to fight his way across in the dark!]

[ShadowDancer: Yeah, which means we won't be able to see it.]

[IceQueen: You can always use a light filter on your display.]

"Not to worry, everyone." I give a nod toward that distant pinprick of light. "I've got a destination in mind. I just have to get there. You'll have plenty of light to see me soon enough."

CHAPTER FOUR

The trip across the rest of the cave isn't a difficult one, really. Bjorn tilts his head back and howls once more, a long and powerful call that chills my very bones. Thankfully, it also chills the water, and a layer of ice grows across the floor, freezing over the rest of the pools and the channels. It doesn't seem to actually kill anything inside the water, but I ignore the immobilized monsters as I stride toward my destination. They're too small for me to worry about killing every single one.

The boss, on the other hand . . . Him, I'm going to need to teach a lesson.

Now, at this moment, I'll fully admit that I don't know exactly what I'm going to do with the boss. The lizardman at the beginning was right. If I kill it, then it won't be able to open up a portal to let me out. On the other hand, if I *don't* kill it . . . Well, bosses aren't exactly known for their cheerful and helpful personalities. Due to the issue of volatility and temperament, I know I'm not going to be able to figure it out until I get into the boss room and see what I'm up against, so I don't worry about it all that much. One thing at a time.

The chat begins to buzz with speculation as I slowly approach the doors at the far end. It's definitely a boss chamber; I'm sure of that now. For starters, the doors are a whole lot larger than I initially thought them to be, almost fifty feet high, and the torches on either side are made out of enormous bones, each one probably a dozen feet long. The doors themselves are made out of bronze, I think, and are covered in runes that seem to be in some sort of lizardish writing. You know what I mean? Sort of like Viking runes or dwarvish runes, but they just look like something with claws scratched them into the surface.

Anyway, I stand there, and a poll flickers to life in the chat.

[Poll: What do you think this boss will be?]

[A: Lizard thing!]

[B: Giant octopus!]

[C: Giant jellyfish!]

[D: Something entirely unrelated to the rest of this dungeon!]

I chuckle, particularly at that last response, and then make my final approach to the doors. "After you cast your vote, put up any specific guesses you have in the chat. Level, power, name, and so on. Whoever gets the closest, I'll send a personal call-out to!"

The chat practically explodes at this point, and I pause as I put my hands on the doors.

[RazorEdge: OOOH! It's going to be a giant octopus, nine tentacles, Rank C!]

[LunarEclipse: No, it's going to be a giant cat, Rank E.]

[ViperQueen: You guys are all wrong. Giant lizardman, Rank S!]

"Rank S?" I lift an eyebrow. "That'd sure make for an interesting fight." I take a deep breath, then brace myself and push. "Here goes nothing!"

The doors rumble and grate open at my touch, stone against stone, propelled by some unknown force. Inside lies only darkness. I take a deep breath and draw out my sword of light, holding it high as I venture inside.

"Bjorn, you might want to get back in the portal." I give a nod to the wolf as my sword begins to show the interior of the room. It's large, with a circular base and sheer walls rising up into the darkness. That likely means that something's going to come dropping down from above. "Burnie, I could use your help right about now."

The two creatures switch places. Burnie flutters over and lands on my shoulder, while Bjorn vanishes. I close the portal to my pocket dimension then take a long look around.

Suddenly, though, torches flare to life, and the doors slam shut. There are four torches, spaced out evenly around the room. The walls are covered in scratch marks, *big* ones, and I slowly tilt my head up.

"Right now, it's looking like ViperQueen is the closest, though I do rather hope he isn't Rank S."

[Originalgoth: Why's that? You *scared?*]

"No, not really." I shrug. "But S-Ranked monsters are going to be *tanks*, and I'm getting sort of hungry. Should've eaten something before coming in here, but I didn't even think about it."

The chat chides me for my carelessness, and I laugh a bit. Suddenly, there's a long, mournful sort of call . . . followed by a loud scrape. I look up, and something *big* comes falling out of the darkness.

With a massive *boom*, a lizardman almost thirty feet tall comes crashing down in front of me. He's wielding a sword and shield, just like all the others, but . . . Well, his shield is the solid iron door of a castle, while his sword is . . . honestly, sort of hard to describe. It looks like several suits of armor, maybe three or four, were dumped together into a mold and half compacted, half melted into a vaguely sword-like shape. It certainly doesn't look like the sharpest weapon I've ever faced, but with the size of his muscles, any hit from it is still going to hurt quite a lot.

"Alright." I take my stance and hold my sword of light firmly. "Surrender now, and I promise no harm will come to you!"

The giant lizardman doesn't really seem to take any notice of my words. Instead, he simply lets out a hiss, holds out his shield, and charges forward.

Now, I'll certainly give this to the creature: he's a whole lot better than the other ones. He keeps his shield in front of him while preparing to strike; it's a better tactic than I've seen before. I have to admit that his technique is flawless, even as I scramble to dive out of the way. As he reaches me, he lunges forward with the sword, and the blade passes narrowly behind my head as I roll underneath it.

I come up behind his guard and stab him in the leg, but I'm only able to make a small wound before he spins out of the way and shield bashes me. Now, if you're keeping track, you recall that his shield is *big*, so when that hits me, I feel it. I'm picked up off the ground and flung backward across the arena, where I hit the wall with a resounding *boom*. My health bar drops down into the yellowish-green, and I climb back to my feet.

The lizardman is already charging me once more. This time, he opens his guard, then performs a great sweeping attack. I jump up into the air, narrowly sailing over the weapon, then charge forward once more. Unfortunately, he seems to anticipate this attack. Maybe he was trying to lure me into attacking, even. I don't know for sure, but I suddenly get a face full of castle door and get slammed back into the wall yet again. Since I'm so close, it hurts a lot more this time, and my health bar drops all the way into the orange.

I gasp and pant as I slide down off the wall. The lizardman sneers, then charges forward once more. I can see victory in his eyes, and I know I don't have long. I have to think.

I have to fight.

"Burnie!" I call out. "I need a distraction!"

Burnie, who had been hovering nearby, watching, swoops into action. He lets out a massive blast of flame that scorches across the lizardman's eyes, momentarily blinding the great beast. He still attacks, but I dive out of the way, and his mighty sword slams into the wall instead of me. With him stuck for the moment, I race forward, jump up into the air, and bring my sword crashing down onto his wrist.

My blade hits his bones, and his scaly flesh, and sticks firmly. I grit my teeth, change the sword into a dagger to get it free, and then perform the attack a second time, growing it back into a sword. This time, as I bring it crashing down, my aim and strength are truer.

Whack!

Bone is cut from bone; my blade carves straight through tendon and sinew, and with that, I cut his wrist clean off. The lizardman staggers backward, staring down at the mutilated stump, and then snarls.

Suddenly, I notice his health bar dropping. Lights flicker across his wrist, and his hand regrows! It cost him . . . I don't know . . . maybe 10 percent of his heath? All in all, though, it seems like a fair trade-off. He quickly reaches out, grabs hold of the sword once more, and yanks it out of the wall again.

[IceQueen: Now *that's* going to make things tough, Jason! What will you do now?]

[ShadowDancer: This might be the end!]

[ChaosRider: Nah, we all know it's not. Don't be dramatic. Cut him to bits, Jason!]

I give a nod and a smile. "ChaosRider, I think you've got the right idea."

With that, I charge forward once more. Burnie dives down out of the sky and unleashes another blast of fire and flame, making the monster stagger once more, and I dive around behind him. There, his tail is whipping about, helping maintain his balance. I decide to rectify that situation and bring my sword crashing down. The blade cleaves cleanly through the tail, and the monster staggers forward, off-balance. It starts to flicker and regrow, but at the expense of more of its health, and I smile.

I have it now.

The monster whips around to face me, but by then I've dived forward, underneath his legs. When he turns, I simply find myself right underneath his arms, well inside his guard.

Before he knows what's happening, I leap up and bring my sword crashing down on the hand holding the shield. This time, there's almost no resistance; I simply cut clean through. The hand falls to the ground—I do as well—and the shield falls with a resounding *bong*.

Crack!

That, of course, is the sound of the monster kicking me in the chest. I'm thrown back into the wall once again, so hard that stone is shattered into dust and gravel beneath me. My health bar drops to just a sliver of red, and the monster snarls and charges forward. He doesn't seem intent on re-growing the hand, but simply prepares to slash at me with the sword.

"Alright, guys," I grit out. "Time to pump this up!"

I dive forward, narrowly passing underneath the blade, all the while opening my inventory. A Pumped! drink falls into my hands . . . Well, my left hand. My right hand is still rather busy holding my sword. I stare down at the drink for a moment. Then, as the monster lifts up a foot to stomp me, I get an idea. I pause and wait until he brings the foot crashing down, jump to avoid the shockwave, and then reach out and use the scales of the monster to pop the cap off. It's particularly epic, I think, and I chug the bottle as the monster spins around and tries to bisect me once again.

My health bar starts to rise once more as I finish the bottle and toss it to the side. The lizardman seems tired of playing around, and draws up the sword for a massive, overhand strike. He flings the blade down, and I only narrowly dodge out of the way. The shockwave from *that* lifts me off the ground and throws me down, and I groan as I stand back up. The monster snarls and charges forward to meet me, and I grit my teeth.

Suddenly, though, I have an idea.

"Burnie, on me!"

I charge forward, duck under the blade once again, and reach the long, curved wall. I leap upward, landing my right foot on a protrusion, and leap off, up into space. Burnie swoops into position, catching my left foot, allowing me to jump upward once more. My right foot finds purchase on the wall again, and quickly, we start to climb.

It sounds easy, but in reality, it's anything but. The monster continues to snarl and attack. Once, as I go to land on Burnie, he stabs upward with the sword, and I'm forced to land on *that* instead. It does look particularly epic, but it nearly causes me to fall.

In any case, I'm soon more or less at the level of the monster's head, which was my goal. Burnie swoops into position one last time, and I launch myself into space, sailing across the distance. My foot finds purchase on the back of my faithful companion, and . . .

This time, I drop right onto the back of the creature's neck.

My blade flashes in my hand, and I cut through the monster's neck in a split second. The head tumbles to the ground, leaving the body to sway for a long moment before falling as well. I leap forward, landing next to the head, while the body hits an instant later.

Boom!

As the shockwave and the dust fade away, I slowly approach the head, where a faint sliver of health still remains.

"Skill: Interrogation," I command, then kneel down next to the creature's eye. "Correct me if I'm wrong, but you aren't going to be able to grow a new body without depleting your health."

The head lets out a soft hiss before answering.

You . . . You come into my home . . . And you insult me.

"In all fairness, your minions were coming into my home first." I shrug. "I was just returning the favor. Now, all you have to do is open a portal for me to get out, and I'll let you go. No muss, no fuss. You can go back to mucking around in your lonely little dungeon, and I'll be on my way."

And let you continue to slay my friends? The head seems to laugh. *I don't think so. You will die here with me—from starvation, if nothing else.*

"Alright, then." I slowly stand up and hold out my hand. "In that case, you leave me no choice."

[DarkCynic: What's he going to do???]

[RazorEdge: Ahh, this is going to be epic!!!]

"Skill: Monster Trainer."

Light flares across my palm, and a great deal of energy wells up inside of me. I've only done this a few times, and never to a boss. The monster's eyes open wide in horror, and I smile grimly.

[Lizard-Giant is resisting your efforts to tame it.]

"Come on," I whisper under my breath. "I know you're a boss, but you have *no* health left."

[Lizard-Giant is still resisting your efforts to tame it.]

You will fail. The lizard chuckles. *This is . . . entertaining. You will die here, Jason Lee.*

[Lizard-Giant is massively resisting your efforts to tame it. Failure imminent.]

I grit my teeth. I have to succeed. I have to! I . . .

CHAPTER FIVE

Lizard-Giant has been tamed.]

The message seems to come as just as much of a shock to the lizardman as to me. I allow the energy to die down, and the lizard head blinks at me several times.

"Alright." I nod at the thing. "Open a portal."

Right away, Master. But . . . The creature seems to pause. *If you heal me, I do believe I can assist more.*

I shrug. The monster seems to be tame, and given how well Bjorn and Garg behaved after they had been tamed—considering that prior to their taming, both of them saw me as little more than a snack—I don't see any reason *not* to trust him.

[ChaosRider: JASON TAMED A BOSS!!!!]

[ShadowDancer: Yeah, but like . . . What's he going to do with it? You can't exactly have a boss walking around the streets of New York. Way too big.]

[IceQueen: He *does* have a pocket dimension, remember?]

I open up my inventory and find a few small healing

items, some painkillers and bandages and such things, and apply them to the creature. His health bar begins to rise, and the eyes flicker closed. A moment later, the body flares with light and vanishes, as does the head. I'm left standing there, dumbfounded, and fury begins to flood my veins.

[LunarEclipse: Hahahahahahahaha! He tricked you!!!]

[Originalgoth: Serves you right, I'd say.]

[DarkCynic: So . . . What happens now?]

My mind begins to race. Burnie flies down to land on my shoulder, and we start trying to think about things. Well, I do most of the thinking, but Burnie puts on a thoughtful expression, which helps. Suddenly, though, I hear something skittering from above, and look up to see a small creature darting down the wall.

It isn't more than a foot tall, and as it reaches the bottom and rushes over to me, I have to blink a few times to see what I'm looking at. It's a lizardman, alright, but . . . Well, aside from walking on its hind legs, it's hardly more than just a lizard. I bend down, and it climbs up my arm onto my other shoulder.

Here I am, Master! Fully restored! It'll take me a while to grow back to my full size, but now I can help you!

I laugh at that and slowly put my sword away. "Can you fight?"

Maybe if we get attacked by an anthill or a swarm of butterflies. For clarification, not horribly mutated ones or anything, just . . . normal ants and butterflies and things.

"Good to know." I start trying to think. "Will you grow and level up on your own, or should I use my Dual Leveling skill to help you?"

That would certainly be helpful, Master!

"Skill: Dual Leveling. Target . . ." I pause. "What's your name?"

You can call me . . . Krak!

"Alright, Krak. You're the target."

[Dual Leveling will now allow Krak to level up alongside you.]

"Wonderful." I give a nod to the creature. "So how *can* you help me?"

Well, first and foremost . . .

There's a flicker of energy, and a portal forms in front of me. Lightning crackles around the edges of it, and I slowly walk forward. The hairs on the back of my neck prick up, but that's hardly unusual, and a moment later, I step through.

I know I've said this before, but the trips through portals are tremendously unpleasant. It feels like you're being sucked through an interdimensional straw. You feel like your insides are being turned outside and directions go all wonky, and then in the end, you get spat out the other side not knowing if the flesh currently making up your head used to be in your feet, or if the nerves in your eyeballs used to be located in your stomach. Anyhow, I braved it well enough, and a few moments later, I found myself standing on the streets of New York, right about where I had been standing a few hours earlier.

HONK!

The noise of a horn blares through my ears, and I leap to the side as a garbage truck barrels down the road. Of course, that puts me in the path of a taxicab. Jumping out of the way of *that* throws me into the path of a motorcycle, and jumping out of *that* puts me directly in front of a city bus.

Quite unfortunately, at that moment, my foot slips in a pool of monster bodily fluids, and I fall smack into the windshield of the bus.

Crash!

I tumble through the front window and land on the floor, where I groan and slowly rise back to my feet. The bus driver, an elderly man with a grizzled beard, gives me a scowl.

"You still have to pay fare, you know."

I blink in surprise, then open up my inventory. "I've got an ancient obsidian shadow sword I pulled from an undead—"

"Got three of those already." The driver snorts, pointing behind his seat. I almost point out that one of them is a *runic* obsidian shadow sword, not an *ancient* obsidian shadow sword, but I'm not sure the point would land well. "I need money. How far are you going?"

I rub the back of my neck. "Uhh . . . Next stop?"

"That'll be five dollars."

I sigh and fish around in my pockets until I find my wallet, but he simply shakes his head again as I pull out my silver card.

"The credit card companies all got crushed by the monsters. Cold, hard cash."

I admit I'm a bit flabbergasted. I wasn't exactly carrying a lot of cash when the apocalypse went down, and since then, I've been more interested in picking up weapons than money. Suddenly, a man at the back of the bus stands up and gives a small bow.

"I'll cover this good man's fare." He strides forward, a warm smile across his face. Still, though, his eyes . . . They seem cold, hard, and calculating. "There you go! Five dollars. And, on top of that, I'll fix this window for you."

[ChaosRider: WAIT! Is that really him?]

[IceQueen: NO WAY!!!]

[ViperQueen: Are we about to see the most epic team-up of all time???]

I blink in surprise at the chat, then stand back as the man reaches past me and taps the place where the window had once been. With a flash of light, the glass shards are swept up off the ground, and the window re-forms. He then pulls a *thick* wallet out of his pocket, withdraws ten dollars, and a few minutes later, the two of us are standing on a street corner not far from the ruins of the MOMA.

Or, I should say, what *used* to be the ruins of the MOMA. Now, it's actually looking quite well put together, as if it hadn't been blown up just a couple days before. The bus rumbles away, and the man and I turn to face one another.

He's tall—almost seven feet, I'd say—and is wearing a suit that would mark him as a CEO, or at least a board member, of some high-level company. His eyes are still roving over me, and I hold out my hand.

"It's good to meet you, Mr. . . ."

"Wang." The man shakes my hand and gives a small nod. "Mr. Wang."

"It's good to meet you." Krak crawls up onto the top of my head and stares across at him, while Burnie flies in circles about my head. I mentally order them both into the pocket dimension, and after a few moments of hesitation, they agree. I raise a questioning eyebrow. "I have a distinct feeling that you're about to propose something. Who exactly are you, and what can I do for you?"

Mr. Wang smiles, then starts walking down the street. I

follow, growing more and more confused, and he spreads his hands.

"Tell me, Jason Lee. What exactly do you see here?"

I shrug. "I see a city that's getting back onto its feet."

"Precisely." Mr. Wang gives a nod. "The apocalypse has come and gone, and the world shrugged with indifference. Do you have any idea how that came to pass?" Before I can answer, he holds up his hands, which he seems to regard with some delight. "People like me."

"People who can fix things?" I raise an eyebrow.

"Precisely." Mr. Wang lowers his hands once more. "When the portals first opened, the majority of people were given no powers. Of those who were allotted abilities, the *vast* majority were given the ability to crush. To destroy. You can tame monsters and use them as your lieges, your companions in battle. Harold could manipulate flame and fly. John was exceptionally strong and had some physical alterations that added to this effect."

"But you were given the ability to fix things."

"Yes," Mr. Wang explains. "Things. There were, of course, many healers—people with the ability to heal other people; warriors who could rush onto a battlefield and help their comrades. Me? I have the ability to fix anything that was native to Earth to begin with. Your Elven Bow? Can't do a thing with it. On the other hand, that crack in the sidewalk?" He points down to a simple spiderweb crack running across the sidewalk. With a flash of light, it heals.

"What are you saying?" I ask after a moment. "I don't really see where this is going."

"Where this is going, my good friend—or at least, my

new acquaintance . . ." He chuckles softly. "Is that I would like to form a partnership, of sorts. I am utterly useless inside the portals. Less than useless, really, I'd only get in the way and become a damsel in distress in constant need of rescue. You, on the other hand, are largely useless outside the portals. Certainly, you can kill the monsters that venture out into the streets, but you have no concept of our new world's economy, our culture, our government—any of it."

"It's only a few days old," I point out. "Are you saying that you *do?*"

"These sorts of things are formed by the people who make them so," Mr. Wang points out. "I have been, and intend to keep, making them just the way that I please. You need someone like me, and I need someone like you."

"How exactly do you mean?" I frown in confusion. "It's easy enough to see why I need you. To be frank, I really could use a few extra bucks, but what do you need *me* for?"

"The dungeons on the streets are numerous, open for a few minutes, and are often dealt with by half a dozen upstart warriors," Mr. Wang explains. "There are quite a few of you around, and more every day as more and more people flock to New York. On the other hand, there are other dungeons, secret dungeons, that require a bit more care. A bit more . . . specialty."

That gets my attention. I stop walking, and he stops as well.

"What are you saying?" I ask quietly. "Secret dungeons?"

"The stock market just got back online this morning. It's taken a hit, but it's holding on." Mr. Wang's voice is quiet. "Those stocks are what keep our world moving, what give companies their relative value. Now, in the past three days, I've made a small fortune going around to an assortment of businesses and patching them back up. However, I'm running into a small problem. A large number of these businesses have dungeons opening inside their factories, their warehouses, their basements, their closets, and so on. While I can repair the damage, I *can't* do anything about the dungeons themselves. That's where you come in."

"You want me to go clear out the businesses of your clients." I start to understand. "Give me a list, and I'll see what I can do."

"Not so fast." Mr. Wang smiles. "Stocks, remember? If word of an infestation leaks out, the business in question will take a nosedive. I'll provide you with the names of the businesses as they're ready to be taken care of. At that point, with your reputation, they'll see no loss in stocks. And in fact, with a bit of marketing on my end, their business may actually soar as people see that no harm comes to their product lines or their data analysis, or what have you. Once you're done with a company, everyone will know that they're safe. Both of us stand to make quite a good living from this arrangement, I do believe."

"It does sound better than just running around the streets waiting for portals to open up." I think for a moment, then look upward. "Well, what do you guys think? Should I go into business, or just stay on my own?"

[A: Go into business!!!: 80%]

[B: Stay on your own!: 18%]

[C: Go into business but make it clear that you're still your own man!: 2%]

The third option, despite starting out lower, quickly begins to outpace the other two and soon holds almost 90 percent of the votes. I give a nod of approval, and I hold out a hand.

"I agree with these stipulations. If I take a job from you, I'll complete it. That's a given. However, between jobs, if a boss appears to threaten the city, or if a Rift opens, or if some other unspecified sort of threat emerges, I'm free to go take care of it first."

"But of course." Mr. Wang gives a nod. "We're business partners, not master and slave. I'll draw up a contract and have it out to you by the time you finish your first dungeon—if, of course, you do wind up performing as well as your following claims that you perform."

"I won't let you down." I give him a smile.

"In that case . . ." Mr. Wang pulls out his phone and scrolls through his list of apps. "Allow me to start up the bidding. We'll see who's the most desperate to get your services. I'll set the time at one minute."

There's a long pause, during which Mr. Wang's phone emits a long series of beeps and bings. When one minute has elapsed, he gives a satisfied nod of his head and lowers the phone.

"It looks like Sampson's Fish Packing, down on the waterfront, would like to hire our services for ten million."

My jaw drops. "Ten *million?*"

"I know. It's small fish, pardon the pun, for your skills, but once you've done one or two, your fame and reputation will grow. In the meantime, here's a hundred dollars to get you through" Mr. Wang hands me a crisp new bill as if it were no more consequential than a candy wrapper. "I'll send the address to your chat interface. When you're done, report to my penthouse."

"Where is it?"

"I don't know. I haven't purchased one yet. One more thing, take this Dungeon Positioning System." Mr. Wang gives me a small smile. "Good day to you."

He walks away, and a notification appears in my vision.

[Waypoint added: Sampson's Fish Packing.]

[Time to arrival: 30 minutes walking, 5 minutes biking, 2 hours by cab.]

"Well . . ." I shrug, then turn toward the waterfront. A man not far away is selling bicycles, and I make my way toward him. "I guess we have our next job! Get ready, everyone! You're about to see some more cold, cool battle!"

CHAPTER SIX

After paying the man for the bicycle, I head out, riding down toward the shore just as fast as my legs will pedal. Thankfully, I've gotten a whole lot stronger, so it's a pretty fast trip. The Dungeon Positioning System interface that appears in my vision guides me along the way with ease, though I do run into some issues when I'm taken on a detour around a bit of demolition being performed by an Enraged Behemoth. That part isn't an issue, of course, but it takes me through a crowded marketplace, where I nearly bowl over quite a number of old ladies trying to buy groceries.

In any event, I soon arrive at Sampson's Fish Packing, which is indeed down on the waterfront. Several long docks extend out into the bay, where a handful of boats are docked. I can see them all piled high with crates of fish, waiting to get inside. Just outside the front door, there's a rather pudgy-looking businessman in a well-pressed suit, fidgeting and waiting for my arrival. I come flying up on my bicycle, and he holds out a sweaty hand.

"Welcome, welcome!" He beams from ear to ear. His voice shakes a bit, and I shake his hand. "We're glad to have you here at Sampson's, where our feat is to make fish good to eat!" He pauses, then quivers. "No, that's not right. Our feet walk to get fish to eat . . . We . . ."

"Don't be worried." I smile and give the hand another squeeze and shake. "My name is Jason Lee. Yourself?"

"John! John Cunningham." The man seems to gain a bit more of his composure. "My apologies for my state. You see . . . Ever since this thing opened, it's been a proper wreck around here. The factory is still working well enough, mind you, but . . ." He sighs. "You might just want to come take a look inside."

I nod and follow, and he leads me through the front doors and into a lobby. Stuffed and mounted fish hang on the blue-green walls, while paintings of calming ocean waves set the scene. A set of double doors at the back of the lobby leads to a sterile white hall, with dozens of doors branching off in just about every direction. Workers bustle to and fro, some wearing messy butcher's aprons, others wearing greasy uniforms, and still others dressed in lab coats. A few of them give me excited-looking nods and a thumbs-up, but the majority seem to think it's just another day at the office.

In any event, Mr. Cunningham doesn't say a word until we reach a set of doors at the very end, where he leads me into a large, open sort of room. It's a packing line, where the fish are off-loaded and brought into the processing rooms. Dozens of roller belts are set up to take the fish from the docks and inside. However, at present, only two of the lines—one on either end—are being used. A crackling portal stands across all the lines in the middle of the room, though nothing seems to be coming out.

"As you can clearly see, this portal is ruining our business." Mr. Cunningham wrings his hands. "We haven't missed a delivery yet, but we're starting to fall behind, and if we don't get this taken care of soon, we won't be able to bring in enough supply to meet all our deliveries. On top of that, if the fish out on the boats start to spoil . . ."

"Not to worry." I smile and clap my hand down on his shoulder. "I'll get this taken care of. Don't you worry."

"That's a great relief." He sighs deeply. "You really think you can do it? Several of our workers have gone inside, and not a single one has come back out."

"I'm a professional." I smile at him. "Been on the job for as long as portals have been around."

"That's only been . . . Oh, I suppose I shouldn't complain." He gives me a nod. "I'll be in my office whenever you're done. Thank you, thank you dearly, for your help. If there's anything at all you need, please let one of us know. And, on top of that, if you could bring our lost workers back out, I'd greatly appreciate it."

"If they're still alive, I'll make sure they make it back," I assure him, then square my shoulders. "Alright! Are you all ready to do this?"

[ChaosRider: YEAH!!!! JASON, GO!!!!]

[DarkCynic: Pack these fish up and ship them out!]

[ViperQueen: Bring home the bacon! Well . . . the fish!]

[Originalgoth: I hope you wind up swimming with the fishes instead.]

I roll my eyes, then start forward. If I ever get a chance to talk to Originalgoth in person, I'll . . . Well, it probably depends. If she's an old lady or something who's just angry because her kids sent her off to a nursing home and always forget to visit, I'll probably just give her a stern talking-to. If instead he's a guy in his mid-twenties with a chip on his shoulder? That's another matter entirely.

As I reach the portal, I pause for a moment for dramatic effect. Glancing over my shoulder, Mr. Cunningham is watching me closely through a window. I give him a wave, then take a deep breath and step forward.

Once more, I get sucked down the interdimensional straw, and with a loud *pop*, I come flying out the other side. Quickly, I look around, trying to get my bearings and taking in the same thing that the workers saw when *they* all came through.

The first thing I notice is that the air is *cold*. Not just a little chilly, or mildly unpleasant, but *cold*. I can see my breath in the air. The second thing is that the whole thing is made entirely of ice. It looks like I'm in an ice cave of some sort, really, with sunlight filtering through a ceiling that resembles frosted glass. Shadows move over top of it, thumping along slowly and steadily, as heavy footfalls send tremors through the room. I give a nod, then turn my attention forward.

I'm standing on what amounts to a small chunk of ice, maybe five feet across, which is surrounded by a frosty body of water. About fifty feet away is another shelf of ice, which then extends through the remainder of the cave, all the way to the darkened tunnel that marks my exit. In between me and the shelf of ice are five small blocks of ice, bobbing about, slowly moving back and forth through the water. On top of simply moving, they're actually rolling a bit, which does *not* make me confident that they're going to serve as solid pillars to jump on.

"What do you think?" I murmur softly. I don't know who I'm talking to—mostly myself—but the livestream responds instantly.

[FireStorm: Just go for it! You're *you*, Jason! You'll come out alright!]

[ShadowDancer: Ooh, I know! Use Burnie again! He'll do well here!]

[GrendleH8tr: This is gonna take some thought, kid.]

I agree with GrendleH8tr, and I crouch down for a moment. There's almost certainly something in the water, though I'm not sure what it might be. A giant fish is always a possibility. Sea serpents are an option, as are eels or another kraken or octopus. Or a crab. In any event, it's almost certainly *some* sort of a sea creature. That's probably where the workers went, down into its belly. Or bellies, I suppose. There could easily be more than one, though for the sake of the workers, I do hope that each individual worker only got eaten by one apiece.

"Alright, now. Can't bring out Krak, since he's cold-blooded. Burnie isn't going to like this; too much water. Bjorn . . . Bjorn?"

My pocket dimension crackles and starts to open, but before much can happen, something surges up from beneath the water. I stand up and make myself ready, but I have to admit, I'm really not prepared for what comes next.

With a mighty splash, a monster erupts from the waves and lands on the ice. It stands a bit shorter than myself, maybe coming up to my shoulder. Though it takes me a few moments to figure out just what I'm looking at, I'm soon able to recognize the rather distinct features of a goblin. Green skin—this one has rather light-green skin, almost like it's covered in a layer of frost—a flattened head, long pointy ears, and beady eyes. And, of course, a spear. I'm not sure what it is with goblins and spears, but that seems to be the only weapon they're really capable of wielding.

"*Ki krakaw!*" the goblin cheers as he stabs at me with the weapon. I dodge to the left, then spin and kick it firmly in the gut. No time really to do much more than that. It's lifted off its feet and flies back into the water, and I give it a nod.

Of course, this victory is short-lived. Quite suddenly, a great many lassos flash up out of the water and land firmly around my torso. They're all quite flimsy, and I could almost certainly have broken out of them if given a few seconds to do so, but unfortunately, the goblins on the other end give me no such time. I'm yanked off the ice an instant later, tumbling headlong into the waters.

Bubbles and foam churn around me as I'm yanked downward. Thankfully, my monster-hunting expertise kicks in, and I quickly get my bearings. There are six of them pulling on the ropes, drawing me down into the darkened depths of the place. A few others swim alongside, gripping spears. My lungs burn, but I force myself to relax, letting them tug me along.

[LunarEclipse: Come on, Jason! Fight back! We know you can!]

[Moneybags: Please don't lose our investment! Fight!]

[DarkCynic: Hey, is Moneybags actually Mr. Cunningham?]

[Moneybags: It's no crime to watch while your workers do their jobs.]

I smile at the chat. I'd wave, but my hands being tied down prevents that. In any case, a few moments later the goblins all turn and pull me up under a deep shelf of ice. There, a bit of light trickles from some glowing stones, and I'm thrown up into a chamber full of air.

"Ahh!" I inhale deeply. "That's nice."

The goblins leap up after me and start tugging me down the chamber floor. I think I glimpse some cages at the end, but I don't have time to figure that out. I flex my muscles and strain with all my might. The cords around my body break, rather like string, and I leap back to my feet.

"*Yaw!*" A goblin behind me rushes forward and drives his spear into my side. It *hurts*, and I stagger a bit while the others circle around me. More spears flicker in the low lighting, along with some knives that appear to be made out of ice. They're in *very* close quarters, which makes fighting them difficult. I feel another spear hit me in the left leg and then a third in the gut.

"Not . . . today!" I grit my teeth, then draw out my Shadow Dagger. I stab it through the throat of the closest goblin, and it drops, giving me a bit more room. My other hand grabs hold of the spear in my gut and pulls it free—and if you think that's pleasant, I've got some oceanfront property in Arizona to sell you. I stagger a moment, then with all my might I whirl around, using the shaft of the spear like a club.

Goblins are blasted back before my might, battered into walls, and smashed to the ground. None of them die, but it gives me a moment of breathing room. I let the spear drop to the ground, draw out my Photonic Dagger, and with the two weapons hand in hand, I go to work. Two of them spring at me, and I stab them both at the same time, one in the chest and one in the gut. As they fall, I put the blades together and leap at the next one, cutting its head clean off. The rest of them charge me all at once, and I spin, grit my teeth, and throw myself into their midst.

Goblin limbs fall to the floor while goblin blood mixed with my own blood drips freely across the ice. Within moments, I've cut through the last of them. They're not terribly tough, but when there are a lot of them, they can sure be difficult. As the last one hits the ice with a dull *slap*, I gasp in pain and slump against the ice. I'm bleeding from half a dozen wounds, and my health bar is ticking steadily toward zero.

"Alright, everyone. Time for a quick pick-me-up." I open my inventory and snag a Pumped! drink, open it with my teeth, and chug the liquid as fast as I can. When I finish, I find that the bleeding has stopped and my health bar has stabilized. I let out a long breath and look for another one, only to find that I'm out of the energy drink. For that matter, I'm quite low on pretty much all my healing items. I've not exactly been doing a lot of looting since the Statue of Liberty. Mostly just fighting.

"Well," I groan and force myself upright once more, "that's nothing that a little bit of rest won't cure." I turn toward the cages, which I expect to find empty. To my surprise, though, I find that there are actually three people, quite alive, all watching me. One of them seems to be a butcher, one of them an accountant, and the third is dressed as one of the fishermen.

"Are you here to save us?" The accountant, a man in his thirties, seems hopeful. "I'd love to get home to my family!"

The other two nod, though they both appear so

shell-shocked that I don't think they'll be doing a lot of speaking anytime soon. I walk over and heft up my daggers and use them to cut open the locks, which are simply made out of bone. My daggers cut through *that* just about every few minutes, seems like.

"Let's get you guys out of here." I give a small nod to them. "Your boss was the one who sent me here. We're going to get each and every one of you back to Earth, just as quick as we can."

CHAPTER SEVEN

s this . . . Is this real?" The fisherman steps forward, trembling. "I've had dreams about escaping, but . . . I didn't think . . ."

"I'm real, alright." I give the three of them a nod. "I need to heal a bit, and we need to find a way out of here, but I'm real."

"There's a door." The butcher, a rather large man, points to the rear of the cave. "It doesn't look like one, but they've been able to get it open well enough. I can't help you on the healing items, but maybe we can find something."

I give them a nod, then return to the ice goblins, hoping to get a bit of health off the scattered corpses. A quick loot reveals some goblin teeth, goblin claws, a handful of trinkets and totems, and a large number of goblin spears and goblin blades. I ignore it all, then rise and walk to the rear of the cave.

[Riftwatch: A Mysterious Benefactor has sent you a gift!]

"A gift?" I feel my spirits rising. "Now what could that be? Open!"

With a flash of light, a loot box appears in my hands. It's styled like a medicine bag, and I pull it open. There's another flash of light, and a large crate—far larger than the original loot box—appears in front of me. My fingers are strong enough to simply rip it open, and I find myself looking at a crate containing nothing but Pumped! drink.

[Contents:]

[Pumped!: 10]

[Pumped! Cherry: 10]

[Pumped! Lemon-Lime: 10]

[Pumped! Root Beer: 10]

[Pumped! Grape: 10]

"Now, this is what I'm talking about." I quickly glance at the bottles. The original Pumped! simply gives more health. Cherry gives about the same amount of health but also increases stamina. Lemon-Lime gives about twice as much health and adds damage resistance. Root Beer gives about as much health as Lemon-Lime and adds a 5 percent chance that creatures fighting you will become Intimidated. Finally, Grape gives only about half as much health as the original but repairs damaged limbs. I grab one of the Grape and one of the Lemon-Lime bottles, chug them both, and sigh in contentment as my health rises. It's not quite back to full, but it's a whole lot closer than it was. The rest of the bottles go straight into my inventory.

"Are we ready to go now?" The fisherman is starting to regain his nerves. "I'd like to get moving, if we can."

"We're ready." I walk up to the rear of the room and place my hands against the stone. For a moment, as I push against it, nothing happens. I grit my teeth and push harder, and something cracks softly within the ice. There's a rumble, and ever-so-slowly, I'm able to force the door aside.

Truth be told, I likely *could* have just thrown it open, but there's no telling what's on the other side, and I do have other people to take care of now. As the door opens with a *boom*, I step through holding my Photonic Dagger outward, letting its pale gleam fill the area. There's a long and narrow tunnel that turns sharply to the left after about thirty feet. My breath puffs out in front of me as I start forward, carefully feeling my way along.

"Stay close to me," I murmur. "I don't know what we're going to run into, but I imagine that we'll encounter *something* before the end of this tunnel. Certainly before the end of the dungeon."

If I could do so, I would take the workers right back to the start and let them out before heading back to clear out the dungeon, but that just isn't a possibility. They are stuck with me all the way through, whether I like it or not. I reach the bend in the tunnel, where it begins to spiral upward, and follow it. Goblin claws had broken up the icy floor, making it far less slick than it could have been, which I appreciate. Soon, after making at least three turns, I come to a small, wooden door. I crouch down and put my ear up to the wood, listening through it just as carefully as I can.

Inside, something tinkles softly. The wind whistles, swishing here and there, though I can't tell exactly what that means. I let out a long breath, then stand up.

"Stay back here until I've cleared this out," I order. The three workers nod, and I grip the doorknob, give a sharp twist, and throw it open.

Inside, I find a small antechamber. On the other side, two large, wooden doors bar my path, but at present, I don't really have time to think about what they might contain. At a glance, I can immediately see that this place was *not* built by the goblins. Ice pillars, carved smooth as marble or glass, stand around the edges of the room, while a red carpet stands just in front of the doors. There are even a few paintings hanging on the wall, paintings of an icy landscape and mountain ranges. Of course, all these details are rather secondary compared to the ice wraith floating in the air just above the red carpet. It hisses at me, and I brace myself and slam the door behind me.

The thing seems to be an undead porter, perhaps, though it's hard to tell for sure. The face is shrouded in shadow, with only the two eyes peering out like blazing beacons. Below its neck, it has only a vague form roughly shaped like a torso, with no distinguishable arms or legs. Moving just as rapidly as I would expect from a wind-monster, it charges headlong at me, flashing through the air across the distance in the blink of an eye.

I brace myself and lunge forward with both of my daggers, but they pass harmlessly through the creature. It hits me an instant later, and that's when I discover that it's made of both wind and ice. I'm lifted off my feet and smashed back into the door while the form of the wraith breaks apart and swirls around for a few moments. The tiny ice particles form a cloud, which then condense into the form of the porter, as I'd seen before.

"You are not the goblins," the porter hisses. "You have killed them?"

"Will you mourn for their deaths?" I raise an eyebrow.

The thing laughs. "Hardly. Nor will I mourn for yours."

With that, it flashes forward once more. I push myself off the door and throw myself into its midst, throwing a punch as hard as I can. Once more, it passes through the wraith without a hint of resistance. When the thing hits my torso, though, there's a *great* deal of resistance, and I'm lifted off the ground like I'm just some sort of plaything.

The porter throws me across the room and smashes me into one of the icy pillars, then tosses me up onto the ceiling. There, icy brackets grow across my wrists and ankles, and the wraith withdraws. Both of my daggers clatter to the ground a moment later, and it laughs up at me.

"You are weak." It chuckles softly. "You will fall before me. Unless, of course, you would like to turn. Become like me. A life of immortality."

"You're not living any sort of a life." I grit my teeth. "You're a puppet, doing the will of some dark ice lord living in this compound somewhere. And you're only going to be immortal until I find a way to kill you."

"Perhaps." The ice wraith smiles. There's a hissing noise, and the ice starts growing across my arms and legs a bit faster. "On the other hand, perhaps I *will* kill you, and perhaps . . . just maybe . . . your little friends you came here with will be willing to join me instead. Can you take on all four of us?"

I grit my teeth, then flex my muscles as hard as I can. The ice around my arms and legs cracks . . . And then, with a loud *bang*, I come tumbling to the ground.

When I hit the floor, a low *boom* echoes through the air, and a shockwave rolls through the walls. The paintings quake a bit, and the porter gives them a sharp glance. That gives me an idea, and I slowly climb back to my feet.

"You like those paintings?"

The porter's voice doesn't relay his obvious concern. "I painted them myself, back when I was still mortal, like you."

"Indeed." I stroke my chin. "Then, since they remind you of your old life, you wouldn't mind if I took one? Or . . . I don't know . . ."

The wraith doesn't wait for me to finish but charges forward at me once again. This time, as it comes, it swirls around to form a knife's blade pointed straight at my heart. I dive forward, narrowly passing underneath it, and charge at the closest painting.

Almost instantly, the wraith swings around and charges at me once again. I feel ice across my back, pain lancing through just about my whole body, and I'm thrown headlong into the wall just next to the target painting. I ball my hand into a fist and throw a punch at it, but the wraith intercepts the hand before it can strike home. A ball of ice forms around it, holding it fast, and prevents me from moving it even an inch forward.

So I throw my second fist.

The wraith, quick as a wink, flashes over and wraps around my other hand, then shoves me backward. As I stagger and get my bearings, it forms into an icy spear and drives forward, hitting me right in the chest. Thankfully, my extra damage resistance from the Pumped! helps me survive, but the wraith nonetheless manages to drive me back into one of the pillars. Ice cracks, and I groan in pain.

"Go . . . away." I grab hold of the spear and cast it to

the side. As soon as it leaves my hand, it whirls back around my head, forming a sphere of ice that clogs my nostrils and mouth. I can't breathe; I can barely see. I can hear the thing laughing in my ears and decide not to give it the satisfaction of winning.

Quickly, I whirl around and smash my head into the pillar. It sees this and detaches before I can strike home—but then, I was hoping it would do just that. I swing my head out of the way of the pillar before I dash my brains out, turn, and bend down to snatch up my daggers, which are still lying on the ground.

"What do you think you'll do with those?" The porter laughs as it takes on a humanoid form once more, just a few feet in front of me. "I'm far too fast for you, and you have no way of harming me."

"Don't I?" I raise an eyebrow, then throw both daggers. I throw one to my right and the other to my left. The blades carve through the air, and the wraith freezes. It's not much, but it's a moment of indecision, and that's all that was needed. In the end, it flashes off toward my Photonic Dagger, stops it firmly, then spins around and goes after the Shadow Dagger.

The Shadow Dagger, though, has already sunk into a lovely painting of a snowy cedar tree.

The wraith howls in pain and falls apart for a moment. The Photonic Dagger falls to the ground, and I scoop it up and throw it once more. The wraith tries to react, but it's much slower and can't prevent the blade from damaging a painting of a large, towering mountain. It shrieks again and falls apart once more, only slowly pulling itself together after several long, painful seconds.

Those seconds are all that I need.

I rush to the third painting, one simply depicting a wide, snowy landscape, and tear it off the wall. I slam it to the ground, smashing it, and the wraith emits one last scream. With that, using the third painting as a projectile, I smash the fourth and final one. I don't even look at what the painting is, but as it collapses from the wall in a blast of ice, the wraith dissolves in its entirety.

"Alright, everyone." I turn toward the door. "You're good to come out now!"

The door cracks open slowly, and the three workers come out. They look around at the desolation, and the fisherman gives me a nod.

"Are you okay?"

"Okay enough." I nod at him. I look down at the blood staining the front of my shirt, and shrug. "It's not my color, I'll admit, but you know, it's growing on me."

The accountant just laughs, and I turn toward the wooden doors. Slowly I approach, though I'm stopped as the butcher bends down to look at the paintings.

"I wouldn't touch those, if I were you," I caution. "They were anchors for the wraith."

"What?" The butcher straightens back up. "What do you mean, anchors?"

I shrug. "I mean, I'm not exactly an expert on magic and things, but most of the time, it seems like undead creatures will have some sort of an anchor. A totem that they bind their life forces to, so that they remain alive as long as the item in question remains. This guy probably just thought that his paintings were so good that no one would ever touch them."

I shrug after a moment. "I guess pride always does go before a fall."

They all chuckle a bit, and the three of us slowly approach the doors. I hold my breath as I place my palms against them, and they shudder a bit under my touch.

"Alright, folks!" I flash a small smile at my audience. "First ice goblins, then an ice wraith. What do you think will be next?"

The chat fills with speculation, and, with that, I shove the doors wide open.

CHAPTER EIGHT

The doors *swish* across the ice as they fly fully open. I hold my breath and slowly step inside, taking a careful look around. The workers start to follow me, but I hold up my hand.

"I think it's still best that you stay back. I'll take care of the fighting; you can follow afterward."

They nod reluctantly. The fisherman in particular seems angsty; his hands are fidgeting like he wants a weapon. He turns around and walks back down into the dungeon, and I let him go. Everything that way is dead, so the worst he could do is stub his toe.

Anyway, I slowly walk into the next room, looking back and forth as I do. The room is massive, carved out of the ice just like the antechamber. It's at least a hundred feet wide and probably twice as long, with a massive domed ceiling covered with intricate carvings. There are even things that look like stained glass windows; slightly recessed areas in the walls are carved out, just like an ordinary stained glass window would be, and then layered with things like seaweed and colored sand. Behind those "windows" are some sort of flickering lights. Candles, maybe? It's hard to tell for certain.

In any case, the red carpet stretches from the double doors all the way across the room, up to where a series of steps lead to an icy throne. There's someone on the throne, and I can see a crown of frosty-white jewels, but I can't really tell more than that. I slowly walk forward, drawing out my Photonic Dagger and allowing it to expand into a sword. This just feels like a sword sort of scenario. I also snap my fingers, opening my pocket dimension.

"Burnie, I could use you right about now."

Burnie flashes out of the darkness and does a quick loop through the room, only to come land on my shoulder. Together, we approach the throne until we're less than fifty feet away. There, we stop. I can see the throne's occupant a lot better now and have little doubt that she'll be my next battle.

[RazorEdge: WHOA! She's pretty!]

[Moneybags: Do you think she'd be willing to come work for us?]

[ShadowDancer: This one's gonna be tough, Jason!]

[IceQueen: This isn't fair. *I'm* the only Ice Queen.]

The Ice Queen, for that's what she is, stirs. I honestly can't tell if she's made of flesh, or if she actually is carved out of ice. In any event, she wears long, thick royal robes and bears a scepter in her right hand, carved out of ice. The scepter is glowing from the top, a blueish light that feels cold even from such a distance. Slowly, she lets out a sigh, then rises, her perfect figure staring down at me as she takes on her full height.

"Why have you come here, killed my minions, and slain my porter?" Her voice is powerful, echoing throughout the room.

"In all fairness, they *did* all try to kill me first." I shrug. "I was just defending myself. For the most part."

"Ahh. The mantra of a predator." The Ice Queen chuckles softly. "Kill or be killed. Used as a justification for all their actions."

"Are you about to use it to try and kill *me?*" I take my stance and bring up my sword. "Because if that's the case, I'd rather skip the pleasantries and get on with the fighting."

"Have it your way." The queen yawns, as if bored, and waves the hand without the scepter. "Guards, take this insolent whelp away from here, please."

A steady *clank-clank* of heavy boots echoes through the air, and I look around to figure out where it's coming from. The Ice Queen sits back down on her throne, still with a rather bored look on her face . . . And, quite suddenly, two ice guards rise up out of the ice in front of her, one on either side of the red carpet.

They're dressed in full plate armor, built to kill and destroy. Both of them are equipped with swords, though it seems to me like they might be equipped with other weapons as well. The two of them stalk forward, swords at the ready, and I prepare to launch myself into battle.

"Burnie? Why don't you turn up the heat a little bit?"

Burnie gives an excited squawk, then flies up into the air, circles around once, and lets out a great gout of flame that pours across the two warriors. When it clears away, the two guards really seem none the worse for wear. Burnie circles around once more, and I take a deep breath and charge forward.

"I guess we'll just have to do this the old-fashioned way, then."

I leap forward, clearing the gap, and the first guard swings his sword at me. My own blade flashes through the air to meet him, and our swords come together with a mighty *crack.* Shards of ice flash through the air, and the guard's sword explodes beneath my own, leaving him with little more than a hilt.

I don't wait a moment longer, and simply lunge forward and smash my sword deep through the armor of the guard. The ice cracks and spiderwebs throughout his body, and with a creak, he topples over and explodes into snow against the ground. By now, though, the second guard is nearly upon me and lunges forward with his own sword flashing rapidly.

I block two quick strikes, falling backward a few steps, then catch a glimpse of Burnie circling for another attempt. I time my blocks, then step to the side as Burnie swoops down.

Fooooooom!

A great blast of flame erupts through the space where I was just standing, a fireball of some proportion. It hits the soldier dead in the chest, and this time, with a more focused blast, it does quite a bit more good. The ball of fire sinks into the ice and burns clean through, leaving the soldier standing there with a massive hole in the middle of his chest. He slowly staggers forward, only for the remaining bits of ice on either side of the hole to crack and break, snapping the guard in two. As he flops about on the floor, trying to figure out how to put himself back together, I lift my right foot and smash his head.

The monster goes still, and I turn my attention back to the Ice Queen.

"Oh, are you done now?" She seems to wake herself up from a nap. "Very well. I suppose I'll just have to try this again. Guards?"

The steady *clank-clank* begins to echo once more, and this time, four guards rise up from the ice. Two of them are equipped with swords; the other two are equipped with spears. They start to spread out, flanking me, and I glance up at Burnie.

"If you wouldn't mind thinning these guys out, I'd appreciate it."

Burnie swoops down and blasts one of the swordsmen with fire. The effect is similar to, if not a bit more powerful than, before. Cored clean through, the guard collapses and breaks into two pieces. The other three, perhaps sensing their danger and doom, quickly charge at me.

[LunarEclipse: QUICK! Burnie, you can do it! You're the MVP!!!]

[ViperQueen: YEAH!!! Go, Burnie, go!]

[FireStorm: Watch yourself, Jason!]

I give a nod to the chat as the warriors all hit. The remaining swordsman brings up his sword and slashes downward at me. I block it with relative ease, but that locks me in place as the two spear wielders lunge. I break my block and leap backward, then spin toward the first of the spear bearers. I lash out with my sword, smashing my blade into his neck. Ice cracks under the blow, and the guard staggers to the side somewhat. With that, I leap forward one more time, ready to bring an end to it, but I'm hit from the side by the *other* spear wielder.

The spearhead hits me in the hip and knocks me sideways. It presses down and cuts along the bone, not really doing any lasting harm—but *wow*, does it hurt. I stagger and miss my attack, and the swordsman lunges forward as well to run me through. I'm *just* able to slap his sword aside, giving me a bit of breathing room, and I spin away from the spear. Blood trickles down my leg, though the wound looks a whole lot worse than it actually is. I only hope I don't slip in the blood.

Suddenly, Burnie swoops down through the air once more, and lets out yet another blast. This one hits the spearman whose neck I had cracked. The fire strikes directly in his face, and when the fire has cleared away, the soldier is left quite headless. He slowly topples forward and crashes against the ice, and the Ice Queen sighs deeply.

"We'll just *have* to do something about that bird."

Horror shoots through me, and I look up at Burnie. "Quick, get inside!"

My portal opens, and Burnie dives for my pocket dimension. Before he can reach home, though, the Ice Queen raises her scepter. Light flares from the end, and a pale-blue beam of light shoots across the throne room and hits Burnie squarely. His feathers turn blue instead of golden-orange, and he falls to the ground with a squawk.

[RazorEdge: OH NO!!! BURNIE!!!]

[ChaosRider: Do you think he's okay?]

[ViperQueen: JASON! Watch out!!!]

I turn my attention away from Burnie as the swordsman attacks once more. I'm sick of these games now, and I grit my teeth and rise up to meet the strike. My sword smashes through his, and with that, I bring my sword back, swing around, and slash straight through his torso. Ice explodes under the blow, and the soldier falls backward, shattering to bits against the ground.

The single remaining spearman takes a step backward and draws back his spear as if to throw it. I don't give him the chance, as I spin around and throw my sword rather like a spear in its own right. The blade smashes through the chest of the monster, sinking in up to the hilt, sending spiderweb cracks throughout the rest of the icy body. Slowly, carefully, the guard tries to take a step forward, but at the first footfall, the entire leg explodes and falls apart. The guard topples to the side, smashing to bits as he lands, and I retrieve my sword and rush to Burnie's side.

He's gone cold, but he's not dead yet. "Rapid Heal," I breathe quickly. Healing energies flash across him, but I can't tell if they're doing any good. Quickly, I pick him up and stick him into the pocket dimension, then turn and face the Ice Queen. Bjorn steps out of the dimension to stand next to me, his fur bristling, and the queen slowly stands.

"Well. You've bested my guards. I could keep calling more, but I suspect that the result would only be the same, and I tire of this." She slowly walks down the steps, then reaches up and unclips her robes. They fall to the ground, leaving her standing in an icy-blue dress that, in my opinion, still seems quite unfit for combat, but to each their own. "Good day to you, interloper."

She raises the scepter, and a great torrent of freezing light, far more than was used on Burnie, comes flashing out. I'm hit almost instantly—I'm fast, but not faster than light—and let me tell you, it's *cold*. My skin frosts almost immediately; I feel like I'm standing in the Arctic without a scrap of clothing to my name. My lungs seem to stop working. I can't breathe. I . . .

I'm saved when Bjorn bounds forward, leaping toward the queen and placing himself in the path of the light. At first, I scream in horror . . . and then smile as I watch him standing there, almost *basking* in it. My body warms back up, and I take a deep breath and rush forward.

"Thanks, buddy!"

Bjorn says nothing but turns and leaps at the Ice Queen. He's fast, and he closes the distance in a mere instant. The queen, for her part, raises an eyebrow, then lifts a finger.

Wham!

A massive block of ice, probably five feet on every side, breaks away from the wall and slides across the room in the blink of an eye. It hits Bjorn squarely, sending him sliding across the room to smash into the far wall. I scowl and charge forward, feet pounding across the ice, and she gives another finger flick.

This time, ice explodes upward from underneath me. I'm tossed into the air and come down *hard* not far from her. When I land, though, I sink partway into the ice, making it impossible for me to continue to move. The Ice Queen chuckles, then bends down and puts her face not far from mine.

"When will you learn?" she hisses softly. Born bounds across the ice not far away, and she lifts her eyes and gives a simple wink. Another block of ice explodes from the wall and smashes into him, sweeping him across the floor to crash into a pillar. I can't see him, but he howls in anger, which makes me suspect that he's not too badly injured. "You can't beat me."

"And when will *you* learn," I grit my teeth and take a deep breath, "that I can smash through ice?"

With that, I use every ounce of my strength to smash my way upward. Ice crystals explode through the area, and I smash my fist into the Ice Queen's jaw. She's thrown backward onto her throne, down but not out, and I leap from the hole and race to her.

My sword flashes in my hand. As she starts to rise, I bring it crashing down, and she only just manages to block it with her scepter. The ice her scepter is made from is far harder than the rest of the ice, so I don't smash through it, but I certainly do seem to jar her. We lock eyes for a long moment, and I break contact only to strike at her head. For a few long moments we battle one-on-one. She's fast enough to block every single attack I can make, but she can't stand up or gain enough ground to use her ice ray. I have her pinned, at least somewhat, which is right where I want her.

Behind me, gray fur rushes through my vision, and I break contact with the Ice Queen and step back. She stands up, a wicked grin spreading across her face . . . only for Bjorn to spring on her with force. She's smashed back into the throne, where his jaws open wide and latch down around her face.

I can't really see what happens next, but there's a great deal of growling and snarling, followed by a sharp *smash*. When Bjorn steps back, the Ice Queen's body is missing its head. In its place is a simple pile of ice, which seems to confirm my question of whether or not the woman was actually made entirely of ice or not.

I turn around to find the three workers watching me intently. They're all now armed with goblin spears, which I imagine makes them feel a bit better in this dungeon. As long as it doesn't make them feel *too* much better, I don't think that it'll be too much of an issue.

"Alright." I sheath my sword and walk down from the throne. "Anyone see a way out of here?"

I do, Master.

I turn to look at Bjorn, who sniffs behind the throne. I turn and walk back up, where indeed, at the rear of the small area, there's a small door covered by a purple curtain. I walk up and pull the curtain aside, then twist the knob and push the door open.

We're working our way through the dungeon, bit by bit. The only question now is . . . what comes next?

CHAPTER NINE

I step through the door first, keeping my eyes peeled for any signs of danger. On the other side, I find myself in a small, narrow tunnel. It's tall, fit for a six-foot Ice Queen, but narrow—so much so that I have to turn my shoulders slightly sideways to fit. Thankfully, there seems to be no immediate sign of danger, which is a bonus. I go first, creeping along, the three workers come next, and Bjorn takes up the rear.

"When we get back, I'm putting in a sick day tomorrow." The accountant shudders, clutching his spear.

"I'm not even going to take a sick day." The butcher shakes his head. "I'm taking a week. I think that's fair."

[Moneybags: I don't think that's fair at all! I'm paying for you all to get back to work!]

[ShadowDancer: Oh, come on. Let them have a bit of time to recover.]

[ViperQueen: I'd like to see *you* get captured by ice goblins, held captive for several days in a row, and then go back to work the very next day.]

"I think ViperQueen has you there, Moneybags." I chuckle a bit. "You could hardly handle the prospect of your stockholders learning that there was a dungeon in your building. If you had actually been sucked inside one? You *can't* convince me that you wouldn't have taken a month off work at your vacation home in . . . I don't know. Anyone know where his vacation home is located?"

[ChaosRider: According to the internet, it's in Panama!]

"Alright, Panama." I laugh a bit. "What do you have to say?"

[Moneybags: Of course I wouldn't go there for a month! It has a giant dungeon in the basement too.]

The chat explodes with laughter, but I think Moneybags takes it all with good humor, for the most part. He has a lot of eyes on him, so even if he disagrees, I'm fairly certain that he'll agree to give the workers some time off, once I get this portal closed.

As long as I can get them back to the surface, of course.

The narrow tunnel continues to wind about, this way and that. We pass by several small doorways that seem to lead to treasure rooms, but I don't have time to worry about those right now. If it were just me, that would be one thing, but with three people I'm trying to keep alive, I can't afford the possibility of stumbling into a trap. Soon enough, though, we come to the end of the tunnel, where it simply opens up into what seems to be a far larger space.

I hold up my hand to stop the crowd, then slowly peer around the doorway. The space it opens into seems to be a tunnel in its own right, one sloping down through the ice. To my right, it tilts upward at a rather sharp angle, rising upward before curving away to the left. To my left, it ends in a large, sheer face of ice. There, a number of digging tools are left scattered around, mostly pickaxes and hammers, while a number of carts stand ready to haul the ice up to the surface. I'm not sure what the people here are digging toward, but I imagine that there is some sort of plan. In any case, once I confirm that there are no people lying in ambush, I step through and motion for the workers to follow.

They do so, with Bjorn following behind. Carefully, he places a paw on the smooth surface of the tunnel floor, crouches, and bounds up. His claws dig into the ice but can't prevent him from slowly sliding back down a few moments later.

Master, I may not be of much use to you here.

"Fair enough." I give him a nod. "Get back inside and take care of Burnie, then."

Bjorn bows to me, and the portal flickers and opens. He turns and bounds through, the portal closes, and I turn to take in the situation.

"Alright," I whisper softly, knowing how far a tunnel can bounce voices, "I'm going to start upward. You guys wait a bit, then follow behind. Make sure I can see you if anything happens, but also be far enough back in case you need to run."

"Do you think we'll *need* to run?" The accountant's voice quivers a bit.

"If we do, we'll be alright." The fisherman brandishes the spear.

"Just . . . Be careful," I caution him. "It may look easy to kill these things, but there's a big strength difference between someone with powers and someone without."

"We'll be alright."

I'm less confident than he seems, but I shrug and look around for the best way to climb up. Near the center of the tunnel are some stairs carved into the ice, and I take those as I start to climb steadily upward. My sword rests in my hand, though after a moment, I shrink it back into a dagger. I don't know why, but I have the distinct feeling that I'm going to need it in this form more.

The first bit of the climb is uneventful, almost too much so. Suddenly, though, I hear the faint chitter of voices, and I pause. I turn and hold up my hand to let the workers behind me know I detect something, then turn back and continue on up. The tunnel continues to curve . . . And there, I come into view of a work party.

A group of goblins is coming down, making their way along the same stairs that I'm descending. Most of them are carrying pickaxes, though several are armed with swords and spears and such things. When they see me, they immediately begin to chitter in that language of theirs and rush headlong down to meet me.

Dagger in hand, I rush up to return the favor. The first several raise their pickaxes, and I duck beneath the blows and stab them through their guts. They scream and fall forward, which in some ways is even worse than them simply attacking me, because now they're just *falling* on me. There's a reason why the high ground is important.

Anyway, I kick the corpses to the side as best I can. Another pickaxe flashes downward—thrown, I think, by one of the workers above. It clips me in the head and knocks me backward a few steps, and the goblins press the attack.

Another pickaxe flies down and hits me in the chest, while another slams into my shoulder. I'm not a great fan of this method of attack, and I grit my teeth and surge upward as hard as I can.

Yet another pickaxe flies down, and I reach up and snatch it out of the air with my free hand, rather by instinct. An idea flickers through my mind, and I race up and swing the pickaxe, using it as a hook of sorts. I whack the lead goblin on the torso, hook him firmly, and sling him backward out into space. He screams as he flashes down the tunnel, smacks into an ice wall, slides to the ground, and then slides further on down to the bottom of said tunnel. The goblins all pause, and a smile flickers across my face.

I quickly sheath my dagger and charge forward. The lead goblin tries to whack me with *his* pickaxe, but I simply reach up and grab hold of the handle just above his hand. We strain for custody of it for a moment, and I use the pickaxe in my left hand to hook his legs. With a sharp yank, he falls to the ground, and I suddenly have two of the weapons. I sling that particular goblin off into space, then charge forward.

The rest of the goblins quickly fall before me. Most of them I catch with the pickaxe and fling off into the distance. The others I either stab with the sharp end of the weapons, bludgeon with the duller ends, or they simply dive off the stairs and slide down to the bottom in terror. Either way, I clear out the path and turn around to motion for the workers to come and follow.

They do so quickly, and we return to forging upward just about as fast as we can move. I can hear more chittering coming from above, so I brandish my pickaxes and prepare to charge forward to meet the surge. Suddenly, though, I hear the workers cry out from below, and I glance over my shoulder.

"They're coming! They're coming!"

I frown for a moment, trying to process what I'm seeing, and then blink in understanding.

[ChaosRider: The goblins that survived are coming back up the stairs!]

[FireStorm: But Jason already has to fight the goblins coming *down* the stairs!]

[ViperQueen: How is he *possibly* going to keep the workers alive? I know how *I* would do it, but I'm not Jason.]

I'll admit, I don't rightly know the answer to that question. The workers, good people that they are, aren't exactly the best warriors on the block. I've seen the results of people who have tried to fight back against the monsters using conventional weaponry. Even guns and grenades don't do a whole lot against these things—though, admittedly, getting a large enough ordnance can do at least a little good.

In any event, these people are armed with goblin spears, and that just isn't going to cut it. Ahead of me, the next group of workers—which seems to be armed with a few more spears and swords this time—comes charging downward, with maybe a minute until contact, while the goblins below are coming along a bit more slowly, especially since the workers are now racing up the stairs just about as fast as they can go.

This is going to be close, but I think I can do it.

"Hang on, folks." I grit my teeth. "You're in for quite a ride."

I take a deep breath, then charge upward just as fast as I possibly can. It's a good thing I always liked doing stairs in high school gym. My legs burn, but my speed makes the goblins chitter in surprise. They all brandish their weapons and come down to meet me, and with that, we come crashing together.

I waste no time, but bowl through the goblins just as fast as my arms and my legs will take me. I don't worry too much about killing them, I just need them out of the way. A few of them *are* killed as I smash them against the walls and ceilings and things, but most I just knock to the side. As I near the end, two ice goblin leaders bar my way, each armed with a sword. I grit my teeth, and the first lunges forward.

"*Kra-kaw!*"

He brings the rusty weapon crashing down on me. I swing up a pickaxe and block it, knocking it to the side, but by then, the second goblin stabs down as well. I try to block that one, but I don't quite get it in time, and it scores a long gash down my right arm. I wince in pain as the blood flows, and the goblins chitter in delight. They both raise their weapons and strike at once, and I bring up both of my pickaxes to block.

This time I'm a bit more successful and stagger them. Seizing the opportunity, I attack the goblin on the left, smashing both of my weapons into him. He staggers but actually doesn't fall, which is somewhat annoying. Meanwhile, the goblin on the right recovers and leaps at me, stabbing at my torso. This time he lands a few more hits and pain floods my body.

"I am not . . . getting taken down . . . by a goblin!" I snarl, then hook my pickaxes around the back of the goblin's neck. With all my might, I bring his head smashing down into my knee, which seems to do the trick. Unconscious at the very least, he flops to the side and slides down the long track of ice, and I snarl and spin to the last one. This time, I don't have to hit him all that hard before he's knocked off, likely because I weakened him earlier. I don't really care what the reason is; I'm just glad that, as he slides off down the ice, he's gone. With that, I turn back toward the workers, who are pelting frantically up the stairs as the goblins behind them scream with delight and victory.

I don't say a word but race back down the stairs as quickly as I can. As I reach the workers—well, maybe five or ten stairs in advance—I jump up into the air and sail clean over their heads. The lead goblin has a moment to look surprised before my foot meets his face, blasting him back off the stairs. I come crashing back down to the stairs, breathing heavily, and face the last of them.

This time I'm not in a hurry, and I very slowly and methodically march down the stairs, picking off the last of the monsters. The ones with swords continue to charge up to challenge me, but several with pickaxes just jump off once more and go sliding back down to their work site. After a few moments have passed, I turn around and walk back up to meet the workers.

"Shouldn't you go pick off the stragglers?" the fisherman asks.

"No," I shake my head. "What happens if I go down there and another group of them decides to show up? I need to stay with you." I hear a distant chittering from above, and I give a nod. "I think we've got company. Stay close, and we'll see the surface here in just a few minutes."

CHAPTER TEN

The rest of the trip up the long tunnel is fairly easy. The workers stay closer to me, now that we know that there aren't really any ranged attacks to worry about. Plus, the further we get from the bottom, the longer it will take any surviving goblins to make it back up to us. I tear my way through three more groups of workers, and then . . . we come into the light of the sun once again.

[ChaosRider: Alright! Getting the workers out of the dungeon and back to the real world! You're the greatest!!!]

[ViperQueen: Yeah! Did you see the way he threw that one goblin up and over the heads of all the others? And his face was all . . .]

[ShadowDancer: Yeah! This is the best dungeon yet!]

I don't know about that, frankly; I've been in some pretty intense dungeons, for sure, and this one is certainly proving to be fun, at least in some respects. Anyway, the light looms ahead of me, almost blinding, and the four of us slowly stagger up and onto the surface.

As we walk out onto an immense plain of ice, I recognize some of it from the paintings below. In the distance is the very same mountain, huge and tall with gray slate peering out from beneath a cap of snow. There are some trees around its base too, but those are a long way off. Directly around the mouth of the cave are some rocky, rolling hills, all covered with snow. I walk to the top of one of them and turn around, where I see a glacier stretching out behind us. The mouth of the cave seems to have been carved into the edge of the glacier, while thick sheets of ice expand off toward the horizon.

"We're out!" The accountant beams. He points off across the glacier. "So, we need to go that way, right? We came through the portal under the ice, so if we go back that way, we can break through it and get free."

I frown in thought. The logic is sound, but dungeons are rarely that simple. I remember the thumping noises that I heard when I first came in, the strange shadows. I squint my eyes and hold my hand to my brow, peering over the wide expanse, and indeed, I glimpse a couple small, black dots slowly moving over the ice flow.

"I think there's something out there that will more or less prevent us from doing that." I shake my head. "I don't know what they are, and I'd probably be able to fight through them myself, but I don't really want to expose you guys to that danger."

"Danger, schmanger." The fisherman seems to be getting annoyed. "You keep using that line against us. I'll have you know that I once harpooned a great white shark that was trying to overturn our boat, and just a couple days ago, I fought off a kraken that was going after our catch. I might not be as fancy as you, but I'm not helpless."

"Yes, but could you fight a giant . . . I don't know, goblin-yak-dragon?" I hold up my hands. "Come on. There's a path here, leading through the hills. Our best chance is to follow it." I walk down the little hill and start following the path, which winds through the depressions between hills. "Stay close and watch for ambushes."

The workers grumble a bit, but they all fall in line, and I start forward once more. I draw out my sword and keep it at the ready, watching and waiting for whatever may come. I can glimpse dark forms moving around deeper in the hills, but it's impossible to know just how dangerous they might be, or if they're aware that we exist.

In any case, I soon catch a glimpse of small tendrils of smoke rising up in the distance. I'm also pretty certain I can hear the soft crash of ocean waves against a rocky shore. I hold my breath and creep forward a bit more slowly, more carefully, and I soon start to hear the idle chatter of goblin voices. The workers behind me freeze, and I creep forward to peer around the final hill.

The path slopes sharply downward, leading to a small cove on the edge of an immense ocean. Nestled in the cove is a little village, filled with dozens of hide-covered huts. Ice goblins mill about frantically, carrying long strings of fish and small animals. Meanwhile, several larger ships are anchored just off-shore, with rowboats carrying the residents of said ships up to the village.

As my eyes settle upon the newcomers, I frown in

confusion. At a glance, they seem to be orcs. Each one is a good six feet tall, with broad shoulders and powerful muscles. Their skin, though, is pale gray, almost white, a far cry from the greenish orcs I've seen in the past. They all have enormous weapons slung on their backs or hanging from their belts, and I hold my breath as I eye them warily.

"We're going to have to take a boat," I murmur. "That's the only thing that makes sense, but . . . Do I simply fight my way through the whole village?"

My question is answered for me a moment later as I hear the accountant scream. I spin around, only to find more ropes dropping over the people who have been charged to my care. Several of the ropes are flung toward me as well, but I cut them with my sword before they can land. Goblins, dozens of them, all rush down to pull the ropes tight. I snarl and rush forward, but before I can reach them, a massive hammer catches me from the side.

Wham!

I'm lifted off the ground and slammed into a nearby hillside. Dust and gravel and snow explode up from the impact, and I groan as I slowly sit up. One of the ice orcs snarls at me, holding a war hammer in his hands, and stalks toward me.

"I don't have time for this right now!" I rise up and lunge at him, preparing to duck underneath the blow and stab him through the gut. Quite unfortunately, he's a good bit faster than I expected and whirls his hammer around to catch me once again. I manage to spin myself at least slightly out of the way, so the blow isn't *quite* as bad, but I'm still tossed down the path away from the workers. The hapless workers, meanwhile, are all dragged away by the goblins, kicking and screaming while their captors laugh. The fisherman didn't even get a chance to use his spear.

I grit my teeth and charge toward them, but the ice orc steps in my path. His tusks glisten with drool, and he snarls and lifts the hammer high over his head to deliver a crushing blow. I quickly change the sword back into a dagger and throw it into his chest, where it slams in all the way up to the hilt. The orc staggers backward, and I rush up, yank it out, stab him several more times, then sweep his legs. He falls, dead before he hits the ground, and I charge off after the goblins.

The captives are taken down a small, winding path that I had missed earlier. Really, it looks like little more than a deer trail, nothing that would actually be an active warpath. Anyway, I glimpse them ahead and pound down the path as fast as I can go. Suddenly, as I turn the corner, something flickers through the air. I blink, but before I can figure out what it is, I run into a clothesline.

A very strong clothesline.

I've seen it before in the movies but never quite experienced it in real life. It's actually a bit low, so it doesn't hit me in the neck, but the thin strand of cable does catch my clavicle quite firmly. My feet leave the ground, and I fall flat on my back. I don't even have time to blink before half a dozen goblins are all swarming me, and another ice orc charges forward, lifts a hammer, and brings the massive iron head crashing down on *my* head.

I roll to the side in the nick of time, and the hammer smashes into the ground. Swords and spears slam down all around me, and several of them pierce my skin. It hurts like you wouldn't believe, but I don't have time to worry about pain.

I jump back to my feet, head swimming. The ice orc lumbers forward, slamming his chest into my body, knocking me back several more steps. The next swing of his hammer hits me again, and I'm again knocked to the ground. The goblins renew their attack, and I set my jaw.

"Bjorn, I need you. Goblins, *lay off.*"

One of the goblins stabs down at my face with a spear. I reach up and grab hold of the weapon and thrust it backward, smashing him in the face. I don't think I kill him, but that wasn't my intent anyway. He lets go, and I jump to my feet and throw the spear straight through the body of a second goblin. The spear goes all the way through and sticks in the snowy ground behind, holding the monster up. I don't bother thinking much about that, though, and turn to the next one in line.

This one has a sword. I snatch up my dagger, which had fallen from my hands at some point, and lunge past the goblin's defense—it's not a difficult task, as the goblin *is* still a goblin—and stab him through the chest. He lands a long mark across my shoulder in the process, but at this point, I can't bother worrying about pain. He falls, and I hear a grunt as the orc starts to swing again.

As I spin in his direction, another goblin leaps up to challenge me. The orc catches the ice goblin on the side and smashes him to the ground instead of me. His body, limp and crushed, lies on the ground trickling blood into the snow. The orc doesn't seem particularly concerned and brings back his hammer once more.

With a howl, Bjorn leaps into the mix, fangs flashing. He latches down on the orc's arm and drags him to the side, making the monster snarl with rage. The orc lets go of the hammer, dropping it with a *thump,* and turns to smash Bjorn in the face with his mighty fist. Bjorn is sent rolling across the ground with a whimper, and the orc turns back to me.

Another goblin leaps up at me, and I spin and catch him by the throat. With all my strength, I turn and throw the creature at the orc, where he slams into the orc's face in a jumble of arms and legs. Perhaps it's not the most conventional weapon—and in all reality, I don't really expect it to do any damage—but it distracts both of them. Quickly, I turn my dagger back into a sword, then rush forward.

The orc grabs the goblin and smashes him to the ground, killing him instantly. As a result, though, the orc doesn't have a moment to react before I slam my sword into his chest, running him clean through. The blade sticks out his back, and the orc gurgles for a few moments before slowly toppling over to the side. I pull the sword back out, then turn to face the last goblins of the ambush.

There are only two, and they turn to flee. I frankly don't care if they run off; I have bigger problems, but Bjorn seems to take issue with it. He leaps past me, even injured, and pounces on the two of them. Blood drips down from his fangs as he rips them apart, then steps back and glances at me.

Master, if you wish, I can track the captives for you.

"Please do." I give a nod. "We need to get to them before any lasting harm comes to them, and I don't know what the goblins have planned. They might just throw them in cages again, but they also might eat them or something."

Bjorn gives a nod, puts his nose to the ground, and starts sniffing. With that, he lets out a howl and charges forward, and I follow as best I can. He leads me along the path, then turns sharply into a rocky sort of ravine that I almost certainly would have missed. It gets narrower and narrower as we go along, until it suddenly drops sharply and comes out on the top of a small cliff overlooking a narrow inlet in the sea.

Down below, there's a small, wooden dock with a single boat. It looks sort of like a Viking boat, with the low profile and all the shields stuck up on the sides. Anyway, there are half a dozen orcs in it and several more that are loading the three workers onto it even as I watch. I crouch down for a moment, trying to plan my next move.

[ChaosRider: Go, Jason, go!!! Don't just stand there!]

[ShadowDancer: Shh! He's thinking!]

[IceQueen: If he thinks any longer, they're going to escape!]

I mostly ignore the chat. Down below, one of the orcs starts untying a rope holding the boat to the shore, which means that I likely have seconds before it launches. Quickly, I rise up, then jump off the cliff, sailing right past the group of goblins. When I hit the deck—and Bjorn lands right beside me—a dull *thump* rolls through the wooden planks, and all the orcs turn to face me.

"I dearly apologize, but I'm afraid I have need of those captives of yours." I give a small bow. "If you'd be so kind as to hand them over . . ."

Don't get me wrong, I know they're not going to agree. What I *don't* expect is for all the orcs on board to suddenly snatch up swords and cut the ropes. A wind springs to life, the sails catch, and the boat suddenly roars out to sea, sending up waves in its wake. The three remaining orcs on the dock all turn to me and snarl, and I drop into my stance, shrinking my sword back down into a dagger. I haven't lost the captives, not by a long shot—though now, I'm going to have to get a *bit* more creative with my approach.

CHAPTER ELEVEN

Of the three orcs, two of them are holding hammers, while the third is holding an *enormous* sword. The closest one to me raises his hammer, and I throw my dagger into his gut just as quickly as I can. He gasps and stumbles backward, and I leap up, yank out the dagger before he can fall into the water, stab him several more times for good measure, and then give him a kick. He tumbles into the freezing ocean with a *splash*, and his hammer falls to the deck with enough force to splinter the wood.

Bjorn rushes forward to take on the next orc, the one with the sword. He pauses to pounce, and manages to trick the orc into attacking early, thus missing him entirely. With that, he springs upon the beast and knocks him to the planks, and the last orc hefts his hammer high over his head, seemingly intent on delivering a devastating blow to my Frost Wolf.

I have no intention of allowing that to happen.

Quickly, I bend down and grab the heavy war hammer,

lifting it up with all my strength. It's heavy, though not quite as heavy as I feared, and I spin around once or twice to get momentum before letting go. The hammer flashes across the dock and slams into the monster's chest, blasting him backward and into the drink. That only leaves the orc with the sword, and Bjorn quickly rips out his throat.

"Alright, my faithful wolf." I pat Bjorn on the head. "Any injuries?"

Bjorn gives a shake of his head, and I nod. "Good. I saw some other boats back at the village. I guess we're going to have to fight our way through them after all."

Bjorn gives an excited howl, and we start back up the path. I open up my inventory and drink a Pumped!, which helps me recover some of my lost health as we trek back toward the village. I definitely hurry along—don't get me wrong—but I don't run too quickly, either. I need to save my energy for the upcoming battle. There are a *lot* of orcs and goblins to get through, and I don't know how much more time the workers have. Perhaps a lot. Perhaps they're already dead. It's impossible to know for certain, which means that I can't take any chances.

As I come up to the village, I find myself looking down at a proper battle line. The other goblins must have arrived and told everything that I was coming, and they've certainly turned out in number. There must be fifty goblins total, armed with everything from swords and spears to pitchforks and shovels. Behind them stand no fewer than ten orcs, all armed with far more formidable weapons. Behind all of that lies the ocean, and the two boats that I rather desperately need to get to.

"Well." I draw out both of my daggers. "I was originally

planning on leaving some of you alive, but it doesn't look like you're going to give me that option."

The goblins all snarl, and then on some unspoken command, they all charge forward. The orcs hold back, perhaps hoping that the goblins will soften me up.

I decide to disappoint them.

I start by throwing my Shadow Dagger into the midst of the goblins, killing one of the leaders. As his body falls, I expand my Photonic Dagger into a sword, rush forward, and leap into the air. My blade makes a keen whistling noise as it flashes, and I cut off three goblin heads in a single go. With that, I fly into their midst and change the weapon back into a dagger.

In such close-quarters combat, my blade flashes back and forth in a great flurry of light and energy. I carve through goblin necks, stab them through the chest, slash them across their bellies, and more. As they start to thin, several of them step backward and bounce on the balls of their feet, brandishing their weapons, and I change the dagger back into a sword, suitable for longer-range combat. They don't last long, especially as Bjorn enters the fray, bowling a number of them over and tearing them to pieces with his jaws. It only takes a few seconds for the last of them to fall down, and I turn in triumph to the row of orcs.

[ChaosRider: Go Jason! I think you might have set a new speed record for goblin killing!]

[IceQueen: Should I start a timer?]

[ShadowDancer: DO IT!!!]

"Works for me." I shrug. "Just sit back and watch the show."

With that, Bjorn and I charge forward to meet the orcs.

The leaders bring back their war hammers and prepare to strike, slamming down the massive weapons as hard as they can. I dodge to the side, and Bjorn does the same, but before I can land a strike against the monster, another one steps in with a sword to block. Steel meets steel, and I grit my teeth as several others come up from the side. I'm forced to disengage, but as I fall back, the orcs do the same. They seem to know that I struggle more against groups than one-on-one and are planning to use that to their advantage. Bjorn falls back as well, watching and waiting, and I let out a long, calculated breath.

"Alright, buddy." I glance at my Frost Wolf. "We're going to have to do this carefully, I think. When you see an opening, go for it, alright?"

Bjorn gives a simple dip of his frosty head. I take a deep breath, then stretch out my hand.

"Skill: Brief Acquisition."

Light flashes from my palm and strikes the center orc. I'm not certain if the skill will work—it's not a guarantee every time—but I frankly don't *need* it to work. All I need is a distraction. Thankfully it works, and one of the orcs with a sword spins around and cuts the attacking orc in half. Apparently, he's not taking any chances. With that, Bjorn springs forward, and I do the same. The death of the single orc opens up a small break in their line, which, while not much, is more than enough for me to take advantage of.

Bjorn and I leap over the corpse before it's even finished falling. I stab my sword through the orc who had done the slaying, and he falls as well. Meanwhile, Bjorn sinks his teeth into the gut of one of the war hammer orcs. That puts us right in the middle of their line, which is where I'd like to be.

Back-to-back, Bjorn and I stand tall against the orcs. My blade flashes through the air, sending bursts of light flickering across the dying village. I block the next orc in line several times, then slash *him* across the gut. He groans and falls back, though not quite dead, and I move on to the next orc in line. Once more I engage, and once more he falls.

I'm starting to learn the attack patterns of the orcs, which makes fighting them a *whole* lot easier. For that matter, I don't have any real issues until I come to the very last one in the line, which has a slightly different loincloth and a string of bones around his neck. He's holding something that looks more like a meat cleaver than a sword, and when I approach, he attacks like lightning, his cleaver able to adjust direction and attack again far faster and more efficiently than the swords are able to do. I pause and step back as I watch him, waiting for him to get tired or show an opening, or something. It doesn't seem to come; he just keeps pressing ever onward, and I grit my teeth.

"I guess this will have to be the hard way, then."

I haven't had time to retrieve my other dagger yet, which means I need to improvise. Quickly, I leap backward, then scoop up a large rock from the ground. The orc snarls and presses his attack, and I fling it at him with all my might. He swings and bats it aside with the cleaver, but that's all the opening I need. I jump up and bring my sword crashing down on his arm, cleaving straight through the bone. His right hand and forearm fall to the ground, and he snarls as he adjusts the cleaver in his left hand.

If I thought the fight was over, it certainly wasn't. He lunges back into motion—albeit a bit more slowly, more awkwardly, and tilted to one side. Once more, I watch him as he moves through his attacks, then lunge forward and feign an attack to the right. He overcompensates as he tries to adjust for missing a limb, and I spin back to the left. This time, I cut off his left hand at the wrist, and he snarls and staggers backward.

Orc blood drips down into the snow, and he bares his fangs before simply spreading his remaining arms and charging at me. I'm only *just* able to spin out of the way in time and land a long strike across his gut. He groans and staggers forward, and I lunge from behind and stab him through the back. The sword comes out right underneath his rib cage, and he lets out a roar of pain.

In one last act of defiance, he spins around and performs a flawless roundhouse kick that catches me in the side. I'm thrown backward into one of the huts, crushing it beneath my fall. As I climb back to my feet, the orc sways, then comes crashing down, dead as a doorknob. I let out a sigh of relief, and Bjorn pads over to me as I move to retrieve my weapons.

"Alright, my faithful followers." I glance upward. "How'd I do?"

[IceQueen: You took them all down in 1:15.]

[ShadowDancer: Not bad, not bad.]

[FireStorm: I bet I could have done it in a minute flat!]

I laugh a bit, then shake my head and turn toward the waterfront. "Well, I'm certainly glad that everyone had a good time watching me. We need to get after those workers. We've lost too much time already, I can tell."

Thankfully, nothing more jumps out at us as we make our way through the village. They're all gone—either fled to the hills or dead in a futile attempt to stop me. When I reach one of the rowboats, I carefully shove it off the beach into shallow waters, then hop inside, take up the oars, and glide off across the gentle waves.

It doesn't take me long to row to the larger boat, where I quickly scramble over the side and land on the wooden deck.

[RazorEdge: Jason? Quick question: do you know how to sail a boat?]

The question is repeated half a dozen times with minor variations, and I pause. "No. No, I do not know how to sail, but I can't imagine it would be *that* hard."

I stride up and down the deck, looking at the assorted rigging and sails and other such things. It makes very little sense to me until I reach the helm, where a number of instructions sit just next to the rudder.

"Pull this lever to go forward," I mutter softly, then reach out and take hold of it, "and pull this to turn . . ."

To me, it doesn't really look like something that would work in the real world, but then, there are a large number of things that work well enough in this dungeon-infested world that never would have been conceivable before. In any event, as I tug on the levers, wind fills the sails, and I set forth across the ocean. Bjorn slips back inside the portal to heal, and I set my sights on the water before me.

I don't know what I'm sailing into, but I know that there are innocents on the line at the end of it, not to mention the livelihood of an entire company. I stand tall, ready for anything . . .

Ready to win.

CHAPTER TWELVE

Thankfully, the trip across the waves isn't a long one. I've been sailing for little more than a couple minutes before I spy land on the horizon and turn my attention forward. At first, it's little more than a dark, rocky sort of smudge on the horizon, though it soon begins to grow into something larger and darker. Three or four minutes more and I'm staring at a massive, jet-black cliff face that seems to regard me with anger. Chunks of ice float about in the water, a testament to how deadly cold the ocean would be if I were to fall in. I grit my teeth and sail onward, looking for any hint of where to go.

I find it after a few more moments. Low in the cliff face, there's a small, semi-circular cave that extends back into the stone. I mean, it's probably a fully circular cave, but half of it is underwater, giving it the appearance of a simple arch. There are torches hanging on the walls, which I can see as I go forward, solidifying my resolve that this is where I need to be.

[Poll: Are the captives dead or alive?]

[A: Dead: 91%]

[B: Alive: 9%]

"Don't be so pessimistic," I chide my followers. "There's no telling what's happened to them. We thought they were dead once before, you know, and they came through it alright. We'll get them back, just you watch."

The chat seems optimistic as I forge onward, but inside, I don't know. The orcs are strong, and they're smart, far more so than the goblins. I could easily see them simply killing the captives right off the bat, to prevent them from being rescued or serving as a rallying point for anyone trying to save them. That said, at the end of the day, I don't have the faintest idea what will be coming next, so I just try to keep my spirits up and my blade ready.

As it happens, I wind up needing it quite a bit earlier than I originally thought.

I'm nearly to the cave when the ship suddenly shudders and stops. My first thought is that I've hit a rock, and I jump up from the helm and race to the prow. If the boat does start to sink, the water is almost certainly below freezing. I can't remember exactly, but I think the average length of time you're able to survive in something like that is just a few minutes, at least under usual circumstances, which means that I need to be ready to swim, and swim *fast*. Thankfully, though, after a few moments, I realize that it's not sinking after all, and I start to think. If I didn't hit a rock, then why . . .

I get my answer an instant later as a massive tentacle, two feet thick and impossibly long, erupts up out of the waves, showering me in water. I stumble back, and from the deep comes a resounding kraken call. The noise shakes the very boards beneath my feet, and I shudder. All around me, more and more tentacles emerge, and they all begin to wrap over top of the boat, preparing to smash it and bring it down.

"Not today." I race forward toward the closest tentacle, draw back my sword, and slash it clean through. Thankfully, krakens are mostly made of blubber and muscle, so my sword has few issues cutting the tentacle through. The massive blob of flesh comes crashing down to land on the deck of the ship, which makes it rock back and forth rather intensely, but I don't have time to focus on it. Instead, I rush forward along the deck, hacking away at all the tentacles rising up from the depth of the sea.

The first several tentacles I cut away aren't too difficult. They're easy to slice through, and aside from some kraken calls from the depths, nothing really tries to stop me. That all changes, though, as I reach the helm of the boat and turn around to come charging back up the opposite side. Tentacles now lay strewn across the deck, weighing down the boat so much that waves begin to lap over the edge. On top of that, smaller tentacles are starting to pop up—tentacles that are taking a much greater interest in me, as opposed to the boat itself.

Still, though, there's nothing I can do except charge forward toward the first of the great tentacles. It's arching over the boat and will soon come crashing down. I hack it through, only to hear a loud *splash*. Two smaller tentacles flash out of the water and wrap around my arms, one for each, and I grit my teeth and brace myself against the bulwarks as they start trying to pull me in.

With that, the larger tentacle hits the deck with a

resounding *boom*. By now, more water is starting to lap over, and I get the distinct feeling that I only have a few minutes before I'll be swimming in the bitter water with the monster. Now, getting dragged down to an underwater lair by ice goblins is one thing; getting sucked under by a kraken is something entirely different.

"I'm not going with you that easily." I grit my teeth, then pull with all my might. Slowly, I take a step back . . . then another. One of the large tentacles starts to come down across the boat, then a second one. I have seconds before this ship is smashed into bits.

Snap!

One of the tentacles snaps, the one on my right hand. I twirl my sword and cut through the tentacle holding the left hand, then explode into motion. I'm now faced with a distinct problem. If I cut through any more of the larger tentacles, I'll capsize, but if I don't, they'll just crush me and be done with it. My mind spins . . . And then a single idea pops into my head.

Quickly, I race along the length of the boat, stabbing—but not cutting—each of the larger tentacles. In pain, the kraken roars from beneath the waves, and the larger tentacles draw back slightly. It's not much, and they soon start to move again, but it gives me a bit of breathing room. Desperate, I throw myself to the rear of the craft and pull back on the lever to get the ship moving forward—and to my delight, it starts working! The larger tentacles start to close a bit faster, though, and I realize that I have a problem. Thinking fast, I let go of the lever, allowing the ship to glide to a halt, and bolt forward once again.

"Alright, kraken!" I hold out my left hand. "Come and get me!"

As I near one of the larger tentacles, another of the smaller ones explodes from the water and latches around my left wrist. My sword flashes through the air and cuts it off as close to the water as I can get, and with that, I spin around and bolt back to the helm once again. Here, the tentacle proves to work as a rather perfect rope. I tie one end around the lever, yank it back, and tie the other end to the railing behind. That done, I leap forward once more into battle against the monster.

[GoldenShield: Whoa! That's cold, Jason!]

[ViperQueen: And resourceful! I never would have thought about that!]

[DarkCynic: I might have. Hard to tell what you'll think of in any particular moment.]

I pay little attention to the chat as I battle desperately against the monster. I prick and stab, slash and cut, and slowly, bit by bit, the kraken tentacles are driven back. The ship continues to move forward, and, soon enough, we pass beyond the reach of the things. I can see something swirling beneath the waves, so I don't let the ship stop, but I do go loosen the tentacles while I work on cleaning the ship up. No sense in continuing full speed ahead, only to crash into the cliffs.

It takes me almost five minutes to toss the larger kraken tentacles overboard. With that, the ship rises a bit higher out of the water, which will give me a bit more leeway if anything else does happen. Satisfied, I cut the kraken rope, take my seat at the helm once more, and steer the ship onward toward the distant cave opening.

During the fight and subsequent cleanup, I drifted

off-course, and it takes me a moment to locate the entrance. Once I find it, I turn the ship and sail along the base of the cliffs, keeping a close eye out for sentries or traps. Thankfully, nothing appears, and I soon float up to the darkened cave. Carefully, slowly, I turn the ship and sail inside.

The noise of the sea fades as I sail underground. It's quiet . . . Almost eerily so. The cave isn't long, maybe a couple hundred feet, and is lit by flickering torches the whole way. At the far end, it opens up into a cavern, and as I sail inside, my jaw sets with determination.

The water from the ocean fills a basin that takes up probably a third of the room. There are a handful of orcish ships docked there, with quite a number of orcs marching about the room doing this or that. They all turn and look at me as I sail inside, and I realize that any chance of sneaking into their midst has gone utterly out the window. Thankfully, I only see one exit from the location, which ought to make it easy to figure out where the captives were taken. They're certainly nowhere around here.

"Hello!" I walk to the prow of the ship and draw my sword. "I come with a proposition! Lay down your weapons and take me to the people who were just brought here, and we can both be saved quite a lot of excess trouble and pain."

In response, a large arrow flashes past my ear and slams into the wooden floor of the ship. Splinters are blasted up into the air, and water begins to bubble up from the ocean, sinking the boat. Not quickly, I'll say, but a heap faster than I might have liked.

"Huh." I brace myself as I continue to sail toward the dock. "They have arrows now. That'll make life interesting."

All around me, the room seems to burst into motion as everyone prepares for battle. Soldiers grab swords and hammers and rush toward me, while archers take up their positions at a distance. More arrows flash by my head, and I gauge the distance between myself and the other boats. The moment I think I'm close enough, I back up a few steps and take a running leap, landing on one of the other craft, bolting toward the shore as fast as I can. This takes them off guard somewhat, as they were expecting me to land on one of the docks, but it doesn't seem to affect them *too* much. Bummer.

In any case, I launch myself onto land, sword blazing with light in my hand. The closest orc snarls and spins, lashing out with his sword as hard and fast as he can. I bend backwards, letting the blade pass within an inch of my chin, then stand back up and slash my sword upward, carving him from belly to neck. He staggers backward, dripping blood, and I spin as another orc leaps forward to deliver a crushing blow with his war hammer.

I jump to the side, but I mistime it slightly, and the shockwave catches my feet and sends me sprawling. With that, the orcs—smelling blood, so to speak—all come rushing forward, swarming the poor soldier who had fallen on the ground.

That turns out to be their mistake.

For starters, it conceals me from the archers, which I rather appreciate. I take a deep breath, time my attacks, and then roll and lash outward. My sword sweeps in a circle, cutting half a dozen orcish legs at once. I don't actually cut any of them clean off, which is a bummer, but I *do* succeed in knocking them down, which in turn knocks down more of them. I hear a grunt from behind me and stab backward without looking. The grunt turns into a squeal, and an orc carrying a war hammer falls past me, dead, and flattens another soldier as he lands with a flop.

With that, I spin and leap into battle, sword blazing, carving through everything that comes my way. Two orcs, both with swords, join their attacks together and start to drive me backward onto one of the boats. They coordinate well, each attacking during the brief recovery moment that it takes after the other strikes. I grit my teeth as I try to find a break in their pattern, and my feet hit the deck of the ship. Suddenly, an idea springs through my mind, and I leap backward, then charge up onto the prow.

Now, Viking ships from Earth—at least in the movies—all had large serpent carvings on the prow. These don't have any carvings, but they certainly do have large, upturned shafts of wood that are carved into rather elegant swirls. I jump up onto one of these, then throw myself into the air, sailing over the heads of the two orcs. I time myself carefully, then lash out as I land. The heads of both orcs hit the ground an instant after I do, and their bodies follow an instant later.

"*GRAAAAAAAAW!*"

A particularly large orc with a cleaver charges at me, fury in his eyes. I brace myself, only to see one of the archers taking aim behind. Quickly, I jump to the side, and the archer adjusts his aim and lets fly. There's a sharp *snap* and a gurgle, and the orc falls to the ground, dead by the hand of his comrade.

Now, the archer doesn't seem particularly broken up about this fact and has another arrow notched before the next swordsman reaches me. Now that there are fewer and fewer soldiers about, I have to start watching the arrows a bit more. I take a deep breath, then dive forward, dodge-rolling underneath a sweeping attack from the swordsman. An arrow flashes over my head, and as I come up, I turn my sword into a dagger and stab him in the gut. The orc groans and collapses, and I snatch up the orcish sword from the ground.

Without really aiming, I spin and throw the sword at the nearest bowman. It carves through the air, whistling sharply, and hits the archer through the chest. He's knocked backward off his perch, and I give a satisfied nod.

Snick!

Pain flares through my right leg, and I look down to see an arrow protruding from my flesh. I gasp and drop to one knee, then snarl as an orc with a war hammer charges forward. He brings the weapon up over his head, and I quickly throw my dagger at him. It hits him in the belly, and while it doesn't actually *kill* him, it does make him double over and come crashing to the ground. I grit my teeth. A sense of danger flashes through my mind, and I dive to the side. Another arrow passes through the area where my chest had just been. This isn't good, and it's only getting worse.

I need to get the last few archers, and I need to do it quickly. Glancing around, I see two of them. Without many options, I pull out my Shadow Dagger and throw it at the closest one. It's a hit, though I can't see to what extent. The archer falls, in any case, and that's the important bit. Now, though, I'm down both my main weapons. I have a few others stored in my inventory, but I don't really have time to get to them, so . . . I reach down and take hold of the arrow sticking out of my leg.

Don't get any ideas; I don't rip it clean out of me—yet—but

I do break off the arrowhead and a few inches of the shaft. Equipped with that dart, I spin and throw it with all my might. This time my aim is spot on, and I see it slam into the chest of the orc. He gurgles and falls, letting loose a drawn arrow. *That* arrow flashes across the cavern and hits another orc starting to charge me, downing him as well.

I grit my teeth and force myself to my feet, looking back and forth. There are a few downed orcs that aren't quite dead yet, but otherwise, all the others seem to have either died or left. Good.

I hobble around the field of battle and retrieve my weapons, then sit down on a post on the docks and open my inventory. I pull out some bandages and other minor healing items, then grab hold of the arrow, grit my teeth, and pull it out. Blood gushes down my leg, and I slap the bandage across it just as quickly as I can. The blood flow stops after a moment, and as I wait, the pain subsides as well.

"Perfect." I let out a sigh of relief and stand up, then grab a Pumped! Lemon-Lime and crack it open. I don't chug it, but despite being actually quite thirsty, I take a few moments to savor it. "And now, I think we're ready to move on."

[LunarEclipse: Yeah! You can do it!!!]

[ChaosRider: Do you think he's almost to the end of the dungeon?]

[ViperQueen: Totally! I bet there's only one last chamber, and the captives are there with the boss right at this very moment.]

"If that's true, ViperQueen, it means that we don't have a moment to spare." I start walking toward the gaping tunnel, a dagger in each hand. "Let's bring this fish-packing saga to an end!"

CHAPTER THIRTEEN

The tunnel isn't a long one, and as I stride down it, I definitely get the impression that we're walking toward the boss room. Don't get me wrong, I'm more than ready to be done with this dungeon, but I'm also apprehensive about it. Captives being held by the boss is never a good sign. There are dozens of things that they could be used for, and very few of them would make for pleasant dinner conversation. Still, though, I forge onward. There's nothing to be done about it except to save them, so onward I push.

The torches lining the walls are ominous and don't seem to cast a lot of light. Soon, I arrive at a large set of iron doors. They're marked with orcish writing, though as I don't read orcish, I can't translate what's being said. Instead, after a quick glance at my health, I stride forward, place my hands against the doors, and shove them open.

They fly open with a resounding *crash*, and I find myself walking into a room not unlike the throne room that the Ice

Queen had built for herself. It's all carved from stone instead of ice, and the stained glass windows are real windows, but other than that, there aren't any real differences until you get to the throne itself.

There, though, things certainly take a turn.

Instead of a throne, at the top of the short flight of stairs sits an altar. One of the workers—I think it's the fisherman—is bound with ropes and laid out on top of the altar, while an orcish priest dressed in long ceremonial robes the color of blood chants in a strange, orcish language. Behind the altar is the throne, and upon the throne, the Ice King.

He's no idol, that's for sure. His flesh is just the same as the Ice Queen, and his robes are quite similar. The orcish priest glances over his shoulder at me, and the Ice King's scepter flares in warning. Sufficiently chastised, the priest goes back to his sacrifice, and the Ice King rises.

"Where are the others?" I demand. "The other two?"

The Ice King doesn't say a word but points his scepter off to my left. I glance in that direction, where I find the accountant and the butcher bound and placed on a smaller table. They're both thrashing as they try to escape, but it largely looks like a futile gesture to me.

"Alright, then." I lift my daggers. "Why don't you come down here and fight me?"

The Ice King smiles, though it doesn't reach his eyes. Snow and ice whirl up around him, and he vanishes, only to appear before me in a similar swirl. His scepter flashes up and touches my chin, and my whole body seems to freeze. He pushes it upward a bit more, tilting my head back to look upon him, and for a moment, our eyes lock.

It's hard to say what passes between us in that moment. He's obviously ancient and incredibly powerful and is likely sustained by the sacrifices that the orcs offer to him. He regards me for a long moment, then lowers his scepter and takes a step back.

"You are powerful." His voice sounds like icicles grating against one another. "More powerful than any other human I've seen or heard of. You would make a good sacrifice. Alone, your power would sustain me for a thousand years."

I chuckle softly. "There's a whole village of dead goblins and a cave full of dead orcs that say your priests won't be able to take me."

The Ice King's mouth twitches upward, amused. "You would make an even better ally."

"An ally?" I raise an eyebrow.

"Indeed." The king inclines his head. "You know, I once came from a physical world, like yourself. I raged against the Rifts, against the dungeons, for a time, until I realized that their power could be harnessed." His hand closes into a fist. "Taken. You feel it too. In all my time, many warriors have faced me, and none could match your strength. If you joined by my side, we could rise to the top, leave this paltry dungeon behind, become the masters of a Rift! A-Ranked, maybe even S, in time."

"It's an interesting proposition." I frown, as if in thought, though I keep my eye turned toward the orcish priest. He's just finished chanting, and I can see him drawing a long, ceremonial blade. I have a distinct feeling that the king is stalling until the sacrifice can be completed, and a fresh, new surge of power can flow through him. "Do you mind if I ask your associate what you're like to work with?"

I turn toward the orc, and the king does as well. As such, he doesn't see me throw my dagger until it's too late. The weapon slams into the orc at the back of the neck, and he staggers backward and tumbles down the stairs. The ceremonial blade clatters to the ground, and the king hisses and spins to me.

By that time, my other dagger has already slammed deep into his chest. Ice cracks and fractures, and he snarls and teleports away in another burst of snow. He howls in rage, a deep and inhuman cry, and another orcish priest bursts through a door and races toward the altar.

"Do we really have to do this again?" I throw my second dagger, hitting this orc in the side. It's not a perfect shot, but it's good enough, and he collapses to the ground, sliding across the stone for a few moments. I start walking toward the king, feeling a great deal of confidence flowing through me. "End this, and end it now, and we can call everything square."

"Never!" the king shrieks. He's losing focus now, losing the battle, and we both know it. With that, he leaps over the altar and snatches up the ceremonial blade himself. With the weapon in one hand and the scepter in the other, he charges toward me, robes fluttering in the wind behind him.

"Bjorn? An appearance right now sure wouldn't go amiss."

There's a flicker of dark energy, and Bjorn explodes from the portal and slams into the king, driving him to the ground. The king snarls, and it's at this point that I truly realize how strong he actually is. He sucker punches Bjorn in the face, and the mighty wolf is thrown up into the air and comes crashing down not far from the altar. He seems to struggle to rise, and I grit my teeth.

[GoldenShield: NO!!! Not Bjorn! We can't have another Garg!]

"He's alright, guys." I charge forward at the king and spring upon him. "I do need to teach this guy a les—"

The king's scepter flares with light, and a blast of energy hits me in the chest. Like the queen's scepter, the ray is impossibly cold, but this one has the added effect of flinging me up to smash into the ceiling. I groan as stone cracks around me, then come crashing down in the midst of a torrent of rubble. A particularly large rock cracks me on the head, which isn't terribly pleasant.

"You will teach me no lesson." The king rises. Without looking, he fires another ray at Bjorn, blasting the wolf up the stairs to land next to the altar. "You will fall, and I will drink your life energies for millennia."

"Maybe." I shrug, then bend down and pick up the very stone that had just beaned me. "Maybe, though . . ."

I throw the rock with all my might, but the king is faster. His scepter blazes with light, and he blasts away the stone. I fling both of my daggers next, but he simply blasts them away as well. As the Shadow Dagger is being tossed off into a corner, I scoop up another rock and throw it, then charge forward. To my dismay, when he blasts *this* rock away, he sends it straight backward, hitting me in the chest. I'm shot across the room, where I slam into a pillar, sending cracks all the way up to the ceiling. The Ice King teleports himself over to me and grabs hold of my neck, lifting me off the ground.

"You're weak," he hisses softly.

"And here I thought you were going on and on about how

strong I was." I raise an eyebrow. "Start in about how weak I am, and you're liable to hurt my ego."

"Funny too." The king squeezes a bit harder. "You're no match for me, and that's the important part. You. Will. Die."

"The odds *are* in favor of me dying at some point, but you're under the same general arrangement." I shrug. "Now . . . I do want to make something clear. If we were to continue fighting, I'm quite certain I could beat you."

To prove my point, I lift my hands up above his arm, lock them together, and bring them smashing down. Ice shatters, and I fall back to the ground as his arm breaks. I then reach up and yank his hand free from my neck and throw it into his face, blasting him backward across the floor. When he recovers, he stares at me with hatred.

"What's your point?" he snarls. "You think we're about to *stop* fighting?"

I shrug. "More or less, yeah."

I give no other answers. Behind him, the fisherman—who had been freed by Bjorn—throws the ceremonial dagger from the second priest up to Bjorn. Bjorn snatches it out of the air with his jaws, turns, and stabs the altar itself. Light and energy explode from the crack, and a resounding *boom* shakes the room.

The Ice King screams, and streams of energy seem to pour off of him. I take the opportunity to lunge forward and smash a fist into his face, blasting him backward once more. Bjorn bounds down from the altar and grabs hold of his torso, shakes him about quite violently, and throws him into a pillar. I scoop up another rock from the ground, take aim, and let fly.

BOOM!!!

Stone and ice explode outward from the point of impact. When it's faded away, there's nothing left but the king's scepter on the ground and a large chunk of the column missing. I slowly walk over and pick up the weapon, feeling its weight in my hand.

[Weapon Acquired: Scepter of the Ice King.]

[Level: C]

[Details: May be used to generate a thermal and kinetic ray, scaled based on the power of the wielder.]

[You have leveled up!]

[Congratulations! You are now Level 21!]

I blink in surprise. It's been so long since I leveled up that I had honestly forgotten all about it. I stick the scepter into my inventory, then gather up my two daggers while the fisherman frees his two friends. Bjorn pads over, dips his head, and re-enters the pocket dimension. Meanwhile, I regard the three captives and hold out my hand.

"Are the three of you alright?"

They look at each other and give a few shaky nods of their heads.

[DarkCynic: Yeah, Jason! You got them all out!]

[ViperQueen: You're the best!]

[Moneybags: I have to give it to you; your reputation wasn't exaggerated. Good work!]

Congratulations continue to circle through the chat, and I turn toward the center of the room. Dark energy pulses and flickers, and a portal opens up. I place my hand on the shoulder of the accountant, and motion for him to walk forward.

"Come on." I give a smile and a nod. "Let's get you three back home."

CHAPTER FOURTEEN

When the four of us come flying out the other end of the interdimensional straw, we find ourselves standing back in the midst of the packing line. The portal flares with energy, then slowly starts to fade and collapse on itself. A few moments later, it's gone, and I let out a sigh of relief. Mr. Cunningham comes racing down the stairs, a wide smile on his face, and we all turn toward him.

"Welcome back!" He holds out his sweaty hands and shakes the hand of each of the returned workers. "It's a joy to see you here again, I'll have you know that. If you'll head up to the main office, I've put together the paperwork to give you each a week of paid time off in gratitude for remaining loyal to our company through this time of adversity."

The workers all smile and nod, though I have a feeling that they're simply happy to be back on Earth's soil. I wave as they're led away and slowly start to walk toward the stairs myself. Before I even get out of the room, crates of fish are being rolled down the lines once again as the packing plant rolls once more into full production. It's an odd, and frankly strange, sort of thing, but I suppose that's just life these days. I give a final wave, though no one returns it, and make my way back through the packing plant to the front.

As I step outside, I take a deep breath and look about. Traffic on the streets is increasing once more. Several goblins walk down the sidewalk on the opposite side, seemingly just as confused about events as everyone else. They don't seem to be threatening anyone, in any case, so I decide not to worry about it. A few streets down, I catch sight of a fellow warrior carefully riding some sort of giant, wooly creature down the road amidst the taxi cabs and other such things. The sun is just starting to set, casting long shadows across the landscape, along with fiery hues along the skyscrapers that stick up high enough to still catch the rays of the sun's light.

Suddenly, I hear chopper blades from overhead, and I glance up to see a helicopter slowly descending. Traffic on the street stops, and with a *thump*, the chopper lands just in front of me. The door slides open, and Mr. Wang leans out, a broad smile across his face.

"Come, Jason! You've earned it!"

I smile and jog forward, climbing up into the seat. The door slams shut, and the helicopter lifts off, sailing up into the sky. Soon, we're up over the peaks of the skyscrapers, flashing off above the heights of the city.

"Thanks for the lift." I give Mr. Wang a nod. "How'd you know I was out?"

"I've been following you on my phone, the same as everyone else." Mr. Wang pulls out his cell phone and opens the

RiftWatch app. He turns it toward me, where I suddenly find an exact image of what I can see myself. Of course, since I'm looking at a phone, I can see the image of a phone inside the phone . . . and inside that, another phone, and inside that . . .

It starts to hurt my head, and I look away. Mr. Wang laughs, and he leans back in the seat, spreading his arms wide.

"This is the life, Jason Lee, and I hope you know that. We're living high on the hog, to borrow an expression. Soon we'll be at your penthouse, where we can discuss matters in further depth."

I blink in surprise. "*My* penthouse?"

Sure enough, a few minutes later we land on a helipad on one of the fanciest skyscrapers I've ever seen. We both climb down and walk through a set of glass doors, where I find myself in something that looks to have come off the set of a movie. I mean, this house has an indoor waterfall, couches that look more expensive than most cars, a bedroom with a massive, king-sized bed and blankets that seem to be made out of bear skins, and a wide assortment of other things. There are also *loads* of empty weapon racks, as well as wall mounts for the stuffed heads of things I defeat in the dungeons.

"You may consider this as your base of operations for the time being." Mr. Wang spreads his arms, then flops onto one of my couches. "Mmm, this feels good! Genuine leather, I'm told, taken from the hides of dire bears harvested from Alaska."

"In three days?"

"Almost four. Or is it a week?" Mr. Wang shrugs. "Time in this world. Never seems to stop." He turns to look at the window of the living room, which incidentally takes up the entire wall. Outside, I can see the immense skyline of New

York, brimming with light and life. "If you'll look right over there . . . That skyscraper with the red, blue, and orange lights on top? That's *my* penthouse. Just bought it while you were in the dungeon. It's actually a bit smaller than this one, if I'm being honest, but I just couldn't resist getting this for you."

"You do realize that I'm hardly ever going to be here, right?" I raise a questioning eyebrow.

"But of course!" Mr. Wang laughs and stands up. "Think of this as a player home. It's a good place to kick back between dungeons, have a drink, store all your loot that you don't want to sell, and it's a good place to find you if I ever have need of you. If you have any friends, they can meet you here. I've already sent John the address, by the way. I do hope that's okay, but you two seem tight, so I imagine that it'll be fine."

"That's perfectly fine, yes." I laugh softly, then shake my head. "This is too much."

"Not half!" Mr. Wang shakes his head. "Last month, the top dogs of this world were the politicians, the business-men, the people with family ties stretching back for centu-ries. Today? Not so. Today, while still powerful, they all take a back seat to people like you and me." Mr. Wang sighs deeply, then rises. "In any case, enjoy yourself. Night is coming, and I imagine that you'll need sleep before tomorrow's dungeon."

"And what's tomorrow's dungeon?" I ask with a laugh as Mr. Wang stands up to leave.

"That, my dear boy, is still to be decided." He shrugs and pulls out his phone. "I'll leave the bidding running until . . . What time do you wake up?"

"I dunno. We'll say six?"

"Then I'll let it run until seven. That'll give you time to

catch a good breakfast, I'd say." Mr. Wang chuckles. "Right now, bidding is at fifty million and rising rapidly. You're going to be making more money per day than most people make in a lifetime. Enjoy this life, Jason Lee!"

With that, Mr. Wang walks back out of the room. He vanishes through the glass doors, and a few moments later, the helicopter flies right past my window. I have to admit I'm amazed; it's only a few feet away, and I can't hear it through the thick glass. I take a look around, then slowly and carefully sit down on one of the couches.

[ChaosRider: Enjoy yourself, Jason! You've earned this!]

[ShadowDancer: Yeah, Jason! Do it for us!]

[DarkCynic: Please, Jason, show us around!]

I just laugh and shake my head. I don't really understand, not yet. "If I've earned this, what about all the other people down on the street who are fighting in dungeons too?"

[RazorEdge: If they were better, *they'd* have earned it, not you!]

I can't really argue with that logic, but I also still feel uncomfortable. Each room in this penthouse is larger than my entire apartment, and everything looks to be tremendously expensive. Carefully, trying not to touch anything, I stand up and start to take a tour of the place.

The kitchen, as I browse through it, is mostly empty. It has a handful of baking and cooking supplies, for if I want to cook something myself, but the main feature is a computer screen that can be used to order a chef to come up and do the cooking for me. The fridge is stocked with Pumped!, which is a bonus. I load up my inventory with as much as it can hold, then keep moving through the apartment.

The bathroom and shower are more elegant than any I've seen before, all made of black marble and other such things. The bed feels like a giant marshmallow, a far cry from some of the rooftops and dungeons that I've slept in since this apocalypse started. I could go on and on, but the point is that the place was simply extraordinary. Finally, I wind up sitting down on one of the couches again and open up my portal.

"Well, in any case, I do need to check over my pets before I do much more. Come forth, everyone!"

There's a pause. Bjorn emerges first, strong and powerful as always. He looks around, then hops up onto the couch next to me. A great deal of his fur immediately starts to shed, and it's *thick*, burly stuff. I chuckle a bit, then turn my attention to the others. Ratatoskr is next. He looks around, and his little eyes seem to light up. He flashes off without a word, and I have little doubt that he'll soon steal just about everything that the home has to offer. After him comes my White Mare, whose hooves clop daintily across the marble floor. She looks around in confusion, then takes a bite of some flowers in a vase. Krak is next, now standing about a foot and a half tall. He looks around the room, eyes wide, and rushes over to stare out the window. I don't know *what's* going through his head, but Bjorn shifts himself to watch the former dungeon boss.

That only leaves Burnie, who refuses to emerge. I frown in confusion, then rise and walk toward the portal. None of the monsters stop me, and I quickly step through into the pocket dimension. Now, to be fair, I've never actually looked inside this place since I acquired the skill, so I don't really know what to expect. I'm sort of afraid it'll just be a black void, but instead I find myself stepping into a little flower garden. The sun is shining, while brilliant colors of poppies and orchids and daisies and more all look out at me, beaming with joy. On the edges of the garden, ivy-covered arches lead to what seem to be small realms, of sorts, tailored for each pet. Through one arch, I see a wide, sweeping plain, and through another, I see a snowy wasteland. I spend a moment looking around, until I find one that's filled with a raging fire. Quickly, I step through that archway and find myself looking up at a burning tree.

Burnie is in a nest in the tree, his feathers a cold blue. He's awake, but he looks to be weary, his head hanging limply over the edge of the nest. The crackling flames don't seem to touch him, and I hold out my arm. I can't enter the area due to the flames—my heat resistance just isn't that high—but I get as close as I can. He wearily rises up, then flaps his wings and rather awkwardly flies down to land on my arm. He's weak, terribly so, and I turn and carry him back out.

When I emerge into the penthouse once more, the other animals rush to my side. I sit down on my couch with Burnie flopping wearily across my lap. Carefully, I stroke the back of his neck.

Master . . . I feel cold.

"Don't worry." I give a small smile. "We'll get you feeling better. Skill: Rapid Heal."

There's a flash of light, and Burnie's head lifts a little bit, but not much.

I'm fully healed, Master. There's just something . . . wrong.

I stroke my chin and sit back, desperately wishing that there were something I could do. "Does anyone in the chat happen to know anything about monster physiology?"

[RazorEdge: I don't, but I do know that there's a warrior

living down in Central Park who specializes in seeing all sorts of weird stuff inside of monsters. Weak spots, veins, hearts, that sort of thing.]

"Huh." I cross my arms. That's interesting and not something I've ever heard of before. "Can you get him here?"

[FireStorm: Her! Not him. Is Mr. Wang watching this chat?]

[FXR: He certainly is! Hang in there, Jason. It'll just be a few minutes.]

"You hear that?" I smile and stroke the back of the bird's neck. "Well, you probably can't, actually. Just a few more minutes, and we'll get you feeling better, alright?"

Burnie gives a weak sort of squawk, and I lean back on the couch to wait. As it happens, I really only have to wait about five minutes before a helicopter roars past my window and lands on the helipad. I place Burnie carefully on the couch, then rise and make my way to the glass doors. There, I step outside and hold the door open as a woman sweeps inside, awe written on her face.

How to describe her? She's not terribly tall, maybe coming up to my shoulder, and wears long, elven-like robes. She has her hair drawn back in a ponytail, which doesn't exactly match the elvish attire, but I imagine that it's a good bit easier for her to use in combat. She has a quiver of arrows hanging across her back, filled with an assortment of arrows that look to be quite varied. Ratatoskr in particular yelps and scampers back away from her, but she simply smiles and holds out her hand.

"My name is Ali." She beams, and I shake her hand firmly. "You're Jason Lee? *The* Jason Lee?"

"That's what people say." I shrug and chuckle softly. "Truth be told, I don't always know what that means, but it seems to carry a lot of weight."

"Of course it does!" She laughs. "I'm still pretty low in the rankings, myself. Not that we really have *official* rankings, but I think I have like twenty followers or something, and a hundred more who might tune in every now and again. Not nearly like you."

I shrug. "Who knows, you might get up there someday!"

"If I do, it'll just be because of you. I already have like ten thousand people watching me right now, and the number keeps going up." She sighs, then claps her hands. "Anyway, I'm told that I'm coming to help heal something?"

"Yes." I nod and lead her down to the couch. Burnie looks up at her wearily, and she drops down to her knees next to the impromptu veterinary table. "He seems to be at full health— I've healed him and everything—but something's just not quite right."

Ali gives a nod. "I can see his health bar, and it's at full. He's not listing any conditions, temporary or permanent, which leads me to suspect that there's something affecting him physically. If we were in a game, I'd call it a glitch. Happens quite a bit with monsters, actually, but you'd never know it unless you were looking for it." She slowly holds up her hands, which start to glow with an odd energy. "Skill: Scan Monster."

Burnie flickers with an odd blue light, and she leans forward and frowns. "I can see everything inside of him. Overall, he looks good. Except . . . Hang on . . . There's something here . . ." She frowns, then takes out a small knife. "Sorry, Burnie. This may hurt a bit."

She reaches forward and pricks his leg. A tiny drop of blood leaks out, and she nods once more.

"Skill: Enhanced Scan." She glances over at me and winces. "Sorry. I have to actually injure a monster for that one to work. Let's see here . . ." She turns back to Burnie, then nods. "And there we go. He's got something lodged in his heart. Looks like a piece of ice crystal to me."

"How do we get it out?" I smile as a thought hits me. "Act of true love?"

"Unfortunately, no. We're in a video game, not a fairy tale, though I'll admit it would be nice." Ali laughs at my joke, then re-focuses. "It looks like something was shot into him, and then he healed around it." She reaches out and touches Burnie's feathers, making him wince.

"Can you get it out?"

"Maybe," she murmurs. "This is going to take some time, though. I was planning on taking tomorrow off, anyway. Why don't you go get some rest, and I'll take care of him through the night. When you wake up in the morning, you'll have a fresh and active Phoenix once again."

I don't love the idea, but I nod. "Thanks, I appreciate it. If you need anything, just come get me; you know where to find me. You're welcome to anything you can find in the house, though I'll admit that I cleaned out all the Pumped! in the fridge."

"I'm not a fan of the stuff, anyway. Too much sugar, and there are plenty of other healing items that work just as well." Ali shrugs. "Now, from what I gather, you're going to have a big day tomorrow regardless of what happens, so like I said, go get some sleep. I'll take care of Burnie. No need to worry."

I nod, then reluctantly withdraw to the bedroom. As I flop down under the expensive covers, a great many thoughts all swirl through my head, like speculation about the dungeon I'll be facing the next day and worry about Burnie.

[ShadowDancer: Hey, Jason, don't you have to accept your rewards for leveling up?]

[RazorEdge: YEAH!!! Show us what cool stuff you have for us!]

I sigh and shake my head. "I'll do it in the morning. I can't right now, not with Burnie on the operating table." The chat seems to agree with me after a moment, but I don't really care. In any case, as I close my eyes and sleep starts to come, the chat disconnects, and I fall into that great void of slumber and rest.

CHAPTER FIFTEEN

When I wake up the following morning, the sun is just beginning to peek over the horizon. I rise, stretch, and make my way into the living room. There, as the windows face to the west, I find myself looking at a skyline that seems to be on fire as the fresh morning light shines off a hundred thousand windows and beams.

"Good morning!" Ali stands up from her place next to the couch. For someone who's stayed awake all night, she certainly seems perky. "I think you'll find that Burnie is all fit and ready to go!"

I smile and step around the couch, where Burnie is indeed standing on his own two feet, preening himself. He looks up and tilts his head sideways at me and seems to smile. I rush forward and stroke his neck, and my chat explodes.

[FireStorm: BURNIE!!! YOU'RE ALIVE!!!]

[ShadowDancer: Hooray! Glad to see you up and moving once more!]

[IceQueen: The dream team is reborn!]

I smile at the enthusiastic chat, then glance over at Ali. "How'd you do it?"

"It was really rather simple." She shrugs, blushing slightly. "There's a battlefield skill I have called Fuse. It's essentially used for fusing bones and things together or attaching monsters to rocks and things like that. It's really quite useful, though it has its limitations. I used the skill to melt and fuse the ice crystal into Burnie's heart, so that it was working *with* his heart, instead of against it."

"Wonderful!" I beam. "How long did that take?"

"About an hour after you went to bed. One of my viewers suggested it. I gave it a try, and it worked, and I was able to get a good night's sleep." She nods toward the helipad. "Shall we go give it a whirl?"

"I wouldn't have it any other way."

On our way out, I briefly stop by the computer and ask a chef to make us some breakfast, and then Ali, all my monsters, and I go out onto the rooftop. Burnie flexes his wings and shoots up into the air, where he begins to circle.

"Alright!" I glance around and notice some pterosaurs flying not far away. "See if you can take those down!"

Burnie folds his wings and drops, then launches three fireballs on his final approach. The flames blast the flying reptiles from the sky, and he zooms around and flies back up to swoop above my head.

"Perfect!" I grin with delight. "Come on down, and we'll—"

"He's not done yet." Ali holds up a hand. She draws her bow out of her inventory, then grabs an arrow from her quiver. "Burnie, get this next! Just like we practiced!"

She fires the arrow off into the distance. A split second after it leaves the bow—maybe after going fifty or a hundred feet—wings unfurl, and the thing transforms into some sort of monster; I can't tell exactly what kind. Before it can get very far, though, Burnie flashes down upon it, letting loose a blast of ice that encases the monster and sends it tumbling from the sky.

"Don't worry, I'll get that too." Ali steps up to the edge of the rooftop and notches another arrow, which she fires at the falling debris. The second arrow intercepts the first about halfway down, and a mighty explosion destroys the falling object before it can smash to the streets below and destroy . . . well . . . whatever might be there to hit.

"So he can do fire *and* ice now?" My jaw hangs open. The chat explodes, but I don't pay it much attention as Burnie swoops down to land on my shoulder. I can see now that the edges of his feathers are tinged with blue, which I think accents the red and gold rather well.

"Yep!" Ali beams, then holds up a finger. "With a caveat. He *does* just have a single ice crystal, and that ice crystal is part of his heart now. If he tries to use ice power too much, it'll put a pretty severe strain on him and may even kill him. His primary ability is fire, and you'll do well to stick with that."

"Well, I've got another ice monster, so that shouldn't be too much of an issue." I scratch Bjorn behind the ears, then shrug. "How can I ever repay you?"

"I saw you order some breakfast; I'd say that would be a good start. And then maybe a couple zillion in vet fees?" She grins. "I'd say you can afford it."

I smile, then frown. "You know, I don't know if *I've* actually been paid for any of my jobs yet. Mr. Wang has bought everything I could need, but I don't know that I've actually seen the money. In any case, I'll have him send you sizable compensation, whatever you think would be necessary."

Ali grimaces. "Honestly, what would be best is some sort of housing. A lot of us lower-tier warriors, who don't dungeon surf like you, are getting kicked out of our apartments left and right. We don't have a way to earn real income, and even if we did, we're a liability beyond belief. The only ones I know who have kept their homes are doing it by refusing to take on the livestream, and even that only helps a little bit."

"Well, I'm sure Mr. Wang can work a deal with you."

"Indeed I can!"

The voice blares from a megaphone, and a helicopter roars into view. My animals all move back out of the way, as do Ali and I, and it lands with a flourish. Mr. Wang is already leaning out of the door, and he hops down and makes his way over to the two of us. Ali seems speechless, and he holds out his hand.

"Let me drop off Jason at his next assignment, and then I'll fly you right back over to Central Park, and we'll discuss the nature of the housing you'd like." Mr. Wang smiles from ear to ear. "I have a distinct feeling that we'll need you again for your particular skills, and I like to keep my business associates happy."

Ali's jaw hangs wide open, and she nods mutely. Behind me, the doors swing open to allow a butler to come rushing out, and Mr. Wang waves us both to the helicopter. I open up my pocket dimension to allow all my pets to scramble back inside. A moment later, we've boarded and are eating a rather lovely . . . Well, truth be told, I know it's some sort of egg-based dish, but I'm not familiar enough with rich-people language to know precisely what it happens to be. It's tasty, though, and they made quite a lot of it—which, as I'm burning through an enormous number of calories per day now, I rather appreciate.

"Jason!" Mr. Wang smiles as we roar through the sky. "Would you like to hear who you'll be helping next?"

"Hit me with it," I say around a mouthful of egg. "What do we have? Industrial car factory?"

"Not even close!"

"Uhh . . ." I frown in thought. "Cheese-making factory?"

"You're thinking too small! The world has more than factories, you know." Mr. Wang beams. "Today, you'll be headed for the Southern Bank of North-Western Manhattan, East Branch."

"That's quite the name." I snort.

"Yes, well, with so many millions of people all crammed into a single city, you *do* have to have a place to store all that money." Mr. Wang shrugs. "Now, get yourself ready! Prepare for battle! You don't seem to have any pre-dungeon things that you do to warm up, but if you do, now's your chance!"

I laugh a bit at that. Soon, the helicopter comes roaring down in front of the face of a massive bank. It has large pillars styled like those of the Greeks—everything that you might expect from a massive bank in central New York. Once more, cars come to a screeching stop as Mr. Wang lands in the middle of the street, and I jump out.

"I'll see you around, Ali!" I call out to her as the helicopter starts to roar away. She waves, and I think I hear her calling back, but I can't quite make out the words. In any event, horns honk quite loudly in my ears, and I turn and leap off the street just about as quickly as I can. As I stumble onto the sidewalk, I bump into a handful of elegantly dressed rich folks, most of whom sniff at me rather disdainfully before marching away in disgust. I watch them go, rather confused, then make my way up the stairs and into the bank.

I'm met at the door by a rather pudgy-looking banker. He's far more composed than Mr. Cunningham, though as I shake his hand, I can feel that he's quite sweaty too. He certainly has even more stockholders watching over his shoulder than Mr. Cunningham, and I decide that I rather like being able to go into dungeons and punch the things that are trying to eat me alive.

"Jason Lee," I introduce myself.

"Mr. O'Donald." The man smiles cheerfully, if somewhat worriedly. "Thank you for coming. Are you aware of the sum of money that we paid for your services? From what my livestream-watchers tell me, this morning was enough of a blur for you that it wasn't disclosed, and I firmly believe in open transactions."

I give a nod. "Your livestream-watchers are sharp."

"They look for the things I tell them to, and they do it well." O'Donald turns and leads me into the bank. "In answer, I'm currently paying you one hundred million dollars and some change. We added ten thousand or so at the last moment to secure our place; you understand how that goes."

I whistle softly. "Sounds like more than change to me, but I'll take your word for it. Where are we headed?"

"Downstairs." Mr. O'Donald leads me to a large staircase, one with a number of guards stationed on either side, trying to look inconspicuous. We start down the stairs, and the air grows cooler as we make our way underground. "We have all our vaults down here, the really big ones, you understand."

"Ahh." I smile as I do begin to understand. "Is the dungeon inside one of your vaults?"

"Yes." Mr. O'Donald flashes a small, thin smile at me. "Which, thankfully, means that nothing *inside* the dungeon can come out, as it'll be stopped by seventeen inches of reinforced steel. However, it's also blocking access to the lockboxes of some of our wealthiest clientele. You understand what's stored inside: priceless family heirlooms, original paintings that are hundreds of years old, that sort of thing. I cannot understate the monetary value of what's inside that vault. If you need *anything*, I'm more than willing to pay for it, up to a great deal more than I've already paid."

"In that case, I'll need . . . Oh . . . Let's start with a billion dollar processing fee." I chuckle, making a joke.

"Done," Mr. O'Donald answers without blinking. "I'll have my—"

"No, no!" I laugh and shake my head. "Not that I'd turn down a billion dollars, but I didn't think you'd actually take me seriously."

"Boy, I take nothing more seriously than money."

"Apparently so." I puff out my cheeks and shake my head. "Alright, well . . . Lead me to the vault."

Mr. O'Donald nods. We soon reach the bottom of the stairs, where we come out into a long hallway lined with vaults on either side. Several guards stand by idly, keeping a sharp eye out for any unusual activity. They look at me and tip their hats, but otherwise don't really respond as Mr. O'Donald leads me to a large vault near the end of the hall.

"And here we are." The banker nods and walks up to an electric pad beside the massive door. "If there's anything else you need to do, now's your chance. Once I open this door, I'll have to ask that you get inside and get through the portal just as quickly as you can."

"Of course." I pause, then snap my fingers. "That's right! I haven't leveled up yet!"

Mr. O'Donald bows and takes a step back, and I quickly open up my interface.

[Accept Reward?]

"Yes," I nod.

[Please accept from the following rewards:]

[Level D Weapon]

[Level D Monster]

[Monster Trainer Skill]

I pause for a moment, then smile and glance at the chat. "I usually let you guys help me decide. What should I go for?"

Almost immediately, the chat explodes into a flurry of activity.

[ShadowDancer: Go for the creature! Burnie could have a friend!!!]

[ViperQueen: Are you kidding? He literally has a dungeon boss! Go for the weapon. You're always throwing your daggers and then having to find other things to use.]

[ChaosRider: Nah, go for the skill! You've got some good ones, but *those* are how you always manage to come back from things!]

I nod slowly. Truth be told, I *am* rather conflicted. I agree with ViperQueen: I don't need another pet at the moment. That said, another weapon would be useful. Of course, if I got a bad weapon, it would just take up space, like my bow and arrows that I don't think I've ever really used. On the other hand, skills are almost always useful. Some I might use less than others, but some have proved to be invaluable.

"I'll take the skill," I nod after a moment.

[Skill Acquired!]

[Mirror Image: A tamed monster will temporarily generate an illusory image. This duplicate will not deal damage, nor can it be harmed. Illusion is controlled by target creature.]

"Huh." I frown. "That's . . . interesting. Might be useful, might not be. I guess we'll see!"

I give Mr. O'Donald a nod, and he turns to the electric pad. A number of lights flicker across it, and I see him typing several things, pressing his palm to a reader, and more. Finally, the door clicks and rumbles open, and I'm left facing a massive, swirling portal. Dark energy crackles and flickers inside, and I take a deep breath.

With that, I rush forward, leap into the air, and enter the portal. Once more, I'm sucked across dimensional lines . . . ever onward to my next battle.

CHAPTER SIXTEEN

Dark energy pours around me for a long and painful moment. Then, with a loud *pop*, I come out the other side, landing firmly on the ground. I quickly look around, trying to take in the situation. Opening chambers are often filled with monsters ready to attack the moment you appear, so I have to be on my guard.

"Puny human!"

The voice is loud and powerful, and something moves off to my right. I see that I'm in some sort of a forest clearing, but that's all I have time to process as I dive forward. Something swishes through the air behind me and slams into the ground. A shock wave rolls outward from the point of impact, and I quickly come back to my feet and spin around.

I have only a few seconds, but now, I'm able to take a bit more time to look around. Sure enough, I'm in a forest clearing, with the trees around the edge growing so closely together that I wouldn't have the faintest hope of squeezing through, no matter how hard I tried. There are a handful of flowers and rocks and things scattered throughout the clearing—normal environmental stuff . . . And, of course, the troll.

This thing is huge, relatively speaking at least. It stands probably ten feet tall, has boogers dripping out its oversized nose, and carries a club the size of my entire body. It seems confused that I managed to dodge out of the way, but that confusion vanishes as its beady eyes turn and find me.

"Human live? Human die!"

"I can see you performed *excellently* in your high school speech classes." I take a step back as the creature lumbers forward and brings its club crashing down. It misses me again, and I frown. The thing isn't all that fast or accurate, which means that it's likely to be a *tank*. "Question: is there *any* chance we could just decide to be friends and go about our business? If everyone else is like you, this dungeon is going to take a while."

The troll seems to brighten. "Friends?"

[RazorEdge: Wait . . . Is that actually going to work?]

[ShadowDancer: Could he tame a monster just by asking? Is that just how *epic* our Jason is?]

[DarkCynic: Or is that just how stupid trolls are?]

"Friends!" The troll seems to be seizing upon the idea, and he raises his voice. "Friends! Come!"

A loud thumping noise echoes through the woods, and I glance over my shoulder. With a mighty crash, another troll smashes his way through the trees and stomps into the clearing as well, followed by a third troll. On the bright side, they've now given me my way out. On the slightly less bright side . . .

"Kill human!" they all bellow at once, and the three trolls

slowly begin to converge on me. All their clubs are raised aloft, and I get the distinct feeling that even if they have slow attacks, three of them swinging at the same time is going to be difficult to dodge. I backpedal a bit and draw out my two daggers. Quickly, I fling my Shadow Dagger with all my might. It sails into the belly of the first troll and sticks fast in his rolls of fat.

He doesn't even flinch.

"Huh." I frown and stroke my chin. "Good to know. Guess we have to do this the hard way. Burnie! Krak! I need you!"

I transform my Photonic Dagger into a sword and rush forward. The blade twines through the air, and I leap at the closest troll. He brings his club crashing down, which I dodge and land a long slash across his belly. The blade cuts deep, and troll blood leaks out—a thick, oily sort of stuff.

The troll frowns, then belly-bumps my face. I'm blasted backward across the clearing like I got hit by a mountain. The other two trolls both lunge forward, swinging their clubs in close succession, and I roll out of the way as fast as I can.

Thump-thump!

They both impact where I had been, and I rush forward. Suddenly, with a distinct burst of speed, one of the trolls whirls and catches me with the club.

Wham!

I'm lifted clean off my feet and flung across the clearing. As I come down, the original troll lumbers forward and swings his club horizontally, seemingly looking to smear my brains across the ground. I narrowly duck, only to hear the distinct *whoosh* of another club heading my way. I glance up just in time to see another troll upon me, and I grit my teeth.

Foooooooom!

Burnie flashes overhead, firing a blast of raging flame into the face of the second troll. He stumbles back, momentarily off guard, and I seize my chance and rush upon him. I jump into the air, blade flashing brilliantly, and drive the sword deep into his belly. With all my might, I cut upward until the blade flashes back out of his flesh higher up his chest. He staggers backward, health reduced to nearly half, and I give a satisfied nod.

Behind you!

I don't bother to look, but simply dive to the side. The first troll lunges forward, lashing out with his club. It cleaves through the place where I had just been, shaking the ground as it impacts it. Burnie whirls overhead once more, and I leap at that first troll, ready to make an end of this. While he's still recovering, I duck around behind him and land half a dozen long strikes on his back and legs. This makes him stumble forward, and I follow, attacking with all the energy and speed that I can manage. I'm doing well, near as I can tell, but he's *so* big and has so much health. I need to find a way to end this quicker.

Master! Krak scampers along through the grass and climbs up onto my shoulder. *Master, I can help! Get me up onto them!*

I shrug. "Alright. I called you out here to see what you could do. Let's give it a whirl."

I rush forward once more, and the troll turns to look at me. He raises his club, and I dodge to the side and rush past him. Krak scampers down my arm, and I raise my hand as high as I can. As Krak reaches my palm, he jumps into space, landing on the shoulder of the creature.

"*Kr-kaw!*" Krak whirls as he lands, slamming the troll's head with his tail. The troll staggers a bit, and Krak draws out a small sword—little more than a table knife, really—and stabs the monster in the neck. Troll blood begins to rush down a bit more freely, and I grimace. Still, the monster does seem affected, and I turn my attention elsewhere.

The other two trolls are coming along, thumping across the ground to meet me. I grit my teeth, then rush forward to meet them instead. The one troll still has a long gash from my sword, and I intend to take him down first. "Burnie! On me!"

Burnie swoops down as I make my attack. He fires a minor fireball into the troll's face—just enough to confuse him and make it harder for him to track us—and with that, we attack in tandem. My Phoenix launches a *massive* fireball that hits the troll in the chest, burning away the thick layers of skin and fat there, and I jump up and plunge in my sword. Together, we knock the troll backward several feet, and the monster stumbles and comes crashing down with a mighty *thud*. I jump off him just as the third troll brings his club smashing down, making a loud, rather sickening *thwack* noise as he pummels his dead friend.

Another troll scream echoes through the clearing as well, and I spin around to see Krak still sawing away at the neck of the first troll. After a moment, the giant monster sways and collapses, shaking the ground. That only leaves one, and there are three of us to face him.

"I'll take the left." I give a nod. "Krak, you take the right. Burnie, you go right down the middle."

My pets both give calls of acknowledgement, and with that, we charge forward. The troll stares at us, a bit uncertain of who to attack. He finally lifts his club and turns toward me, but by then it's too late.

FOOOOOM!

Burnie fires a *massive* fireball into the face of the troll, nearly burning off his entire head, it seems like. The troll howls, and I duck underneath the club and drive my sword deep into its side, searching for the heart. When I don't find it, I sigh, then transform my sword into a dagger and proceed to simply stab it as many times as I can. On the other side of the beast, Krak leaps up onto the creature's leg and climbs up to the head, where he again pulls out his sword and begins hacking away.

"Kill . . . human!" the monster bellows. "Monsters . . . no . . . work . . . humans . . ."

Burnie responds to this by encasing the troll's head in ice. I laugh a bit as the troll staggers, and I slowly step back.

"Everyone! Pull back!"

Krak leaps off the troll's shoulder and lands on the ground, and Burnie swoops down to land on my shoulder. The three of us retreat a few feet as the troll begins to flail about wildly, swinging his club madly as he searches for us. He doesn't think to smash the ice off his face, though. When almost thirty seconds have passed, quite unable to breathe, the troll falls headlong across the ground. I race up and cut off the monster's head, just to be on the safe side, and the three of us look around the clearing.

I don't see any further monsters, which is a positive sign. Truth be told, I don't really see much of anything, except what I've already described. The exit looks dark and foreboding, and I slowly walk to look down what seems to be a long path through the forest.

[ChaosRider: That was epic, you guys! What a great team-up there at the end!]

[ViperQueen: YEAH! Krak for the win, totally!]

[ShadowDancer: Really, though! I don't know how you would have done that without him!]

I can't disagree with that, and I turn and nod at Krak. "Good work out there. I suppose I should probably ask: what *can* you do?"

Krak scampers up to me and bows.

My capabilities are far lower than they used to be, Master, but I do still have some skills. I have my sword, which you've seen, and my Tail Whip skill. It won't do damage to anything with a higher power level than myself, but if I use it strategically, I can still make things trip or stumble. I also have a Shock Wave skill, and a Venom skill.

"Nice!" I nod down at him with a smile. "Can you show me the Shock Wave?"

Krak doesn't answer but gives a bow. A moment later, he lifts up his right foot and stomps down as hard as he can. The tiniest little ripple of a shock wave rumbles out from his foot. I feel the ground quake a little bit under my toes, but if I'm being honest, the footfalls of the trolls were quite a bit more powerful.

"I see." I nod. "And the Venom?"

You might appreciate it if I don't *demonstrate on present company.* Krak seems to laugh a bit at his joke. *That said, I can explain it. It deals . . . one point of damage per minute, for ten minutes.*

I blink in surprise. "So . . . you can deal ten damage with it?"

In fairness, I can bite more than once and make it cumulative!

Krak stamps his foot, making another of the tiny shock waves. *You did cut off my head and force me to regenerate as a hatchling. You're lucky I even have these skills!*

"That's a fair enough point, I suppose." I chuckle softly and shake my head. "In that case, let's be off. This forest looks like it's going to hold quite a few jump scares, and I'd rather just get them over with."

Master?

I turn to look down at Krak once more. "What is it?"

One of the ways I might be the most helpful, at least for the time being, is to help you navigate the dungeons. As a former dungeon boss, I do happen to know quite a few things about dungeons—tricks and tips that most people might not know.

I nod slowly. That could be *incredibly* useful. "Is there something here that you'd like to show me? A secret pathway, or something?"

Not a secret pathway, Master, but a secret! Krak seems to be quite excited and starts to run in circles while he talks. He certainly seems to have all the energy of a hatchling, that's for sure. *Nearly every single opening chamber, in every dungeon you come across, is going to have a secret room. Sometimes it'll just be a little cubbyhole; sometimes it could almost be a full dungeon in and of itself. There will always be a mini-boss—sometimes a micro-boss, in the case of the cubbyholes—and some sort of valuable loot.*

"Really?" I blink in surprise.

Yep! The mini-boss . . . You might call him a boss in training. After the main boss is defeated, the dungeon closes, right? What do you think happens to that dungeon?

I hazard a guess, "It . . . floats about in an interdimensional void for all of eternity?"

Nope! The mini-boss moves out of its hiding place and takes up custody of the dungeon! Now, if you can take out the mini-boss, then things get a bit more complicated, but we can discuss that at a later date.

"Alright, then!" I chuckle and shake my head. "I assume you're about to show me where the secret entrance is located, then?"

Yes, Master! Ordinarily, I probably wouldn't be able to just find it right off the bat. My perception is terrible, you know; however, I happened to notice something about this group of flowers when one of the trolls stepped on it.

Krak races over to a small cluster of red flowers, drops to all fours, and vanishes into their midst. There's a pause, and with a rumble, the whole group of flowers suddenly lifts up. There's a trap door, covered with the plants, and a dark hole beneath.

Just go on down, and you'll find riches galore! If nothing else, probably a new weapon or something to display in your house.

"Fair enough." I take a deep breath, then slowly ease myself into the hole. It's a long shaft straight down, with rungs of a ladder leading down into the darkness. Slowly, carefully, I begin my descent . . . uncertain of what I'll find at the bottom.

CHAPTER SEVENTEEN

The shaft is long and narrow, so tight that I can barely squeeze through in some places. It's been very roughly hewn out of the soil and stone, like someone did it with little more than a pickaxe and shovel. Krak climbs down the rungs of the ladder just above me, happy enough with the arrangement, but Burnie goes back into the pocket dimension. He doesn't seem too fond of tight places, and being a bird, I can't really blame him.

In any case, I soon start to see flickers of light from below and feel my heart thumping in my chest. "Alright, everyone! I'm starting a poll. Give me your guesses on what we'll find here!"

[RazorEdge: I bet it's loads of gold and gems, and a fire-breathing dragon!]

[IceQueen: No, silly. This is a forest dungeon. It's going to be a walking tree, or something like that, and the treasure will be some magic sap or something along those lines!]

[DarkCynic: My guess is that it's another elemental, like that porter you fought!]

I frankly don't know what to guess. My mind swirls with questions. Does the type of dungeon affect the boss, or the other way around? Is there really that much coordination between the dungeons, some level of organization about how they're all put together? I don't have the faintest idea, really, and I'm not sure I want to ask Krak for the answer. He'd be able to tell me, certainly, but is that really something I *want* to know?

In any case, the light grows steadily brighter, and I soon find myself climbing down out of the ceiling of a large cave. It's probably fifty feet long, twenty wide, and seems to entirely consist of a single room. There doesn't seem to be any heaps of treasure, or even a treasure chest, that I can see.

"Krak?" I ask as I hop off the ladder. "Is there any chance that these things are ever empty?"

Krak jumps down from the ladder and lands on my head. For a long moment, he just looks around.

I've never heard of an empty one before. My guess is that it's a trap. If you start walking forward . . . just a bit . . .

I follow his instructions, slowly inching my way across the room. The chat cheers me on, and I'm not sure if I'm grateful or not for their support of me walking into a trap. The cave is rocky and doesn't seem to have any stalactites or stalagmites. That, to me, means that it's been built more recently. Which . . .

The ground rumbles, and suddenly, part of the floor in front of me heaves upward. I step back as I glimpse two large pincers and a great many legs, and as I reach the ladder, a massive, ten-foot-long scorpion emerges and snarls at me. Its barbed tail flicks up over top of its head, waving and bobbing, and I draw my sword and take a stance.

Yup! It was a trap. You're welcome, Master!

Krak jumps off my shoulders and scampers up the ladder. I can't say I blame him; he's unlikely to be of much help against the monster, but . . . still. I let out a long breath, then give a nod and rush at the thing.

The scorpion is like lightning. Its tail carves through the air, almost faster than I can see, angling straight for my chest. I bring up my sword and narrowly bat it out of the way, but it lunges with its pincers next. One of them latches around my right leg, and I stumble as I try to evade it. I wind up falling on my back, staring up at the ceiling, and it lunges with its stinger once more.

This time, I can only barely swat it out of the way, and the sharpened point slams into the stone just next to my head. I grimace as I feel the bristles from the stinger on my face, and it pulls back and starts to drag me back down into its lair. I know if I wind up going down there, I'll be dead within seconds.

Desperate, I sit up, turn my sword back into a dagger, and hack down at the pincer holding my leg. For a long moment, nothing really seems to happen, but when I target the small gap in the chitin between the larger part of the pincer and the arm, I'm just able to stick the blade in.

"Come on . . . And . . . There we go!" I give the blade a sharp twist, and the pincer is snapped off the scorpion's limb. It hisses angrily and slithers back, and I climb to my feet—notably with a scorpion pincer still clamped down on my leg. "Come at me now!"

The scorpion backs down into its lair, then jumps forward. I spin out of the way, and it passes by me. With that, I lash out, slashing down at the base of its tail. My blade connects but simply bounces off its armor there. The thing spins, and I once more find myself in the firing line of the monster.

Without much other choice, I jump forward, up and over the thing, and grab hold of the tail. It's strong as it begins to fight against me, but I hang on, nonetheless. An idea strikes me, and I look down at the back of the monster, looking for any gaps in its armor. I find one particular seam, right behind the head, and give a nod.

"That'll have to do."

[ChaosRider: Wait . . . Is Jason really going to do that?]

[IceQueen: This will be the best!!!]

I grit my teeth and pull with all my might, forcing the tail head steadily downward. "Come on!"

The scorpion, seemingly sensing my plan, fights against me and tries to skitter away, but I hang on tightly and fight even harder. Slowly, slowly, I force the head of the tail down. The barb glistens with venom, and I let out a long breath, seeming to relax slightly. The scorpion relaxes as well, and with that, I throw every last ounce of my strength into it.

The tail head is forced down firmly, and the stinger stabs neatly between the gaps in the armor. There's a loud screech, and it starts to thrash about for a few moments, then goes still. I hold the stinger in place for a few long seconds, counting to ten in my head, then let go. The body of the scorpion remains still, which I appreciate. It's dead and won't be bothering me any longer.

"You can come down now, Krak!" I call up to the lizard,

then walk over to the hidden entrance of the trap. Having closed when the scorpion last came out, it's rather hard to find, but my fingers eventually locate the small crack in the ground. I heave with all my might, and the door slowly slides up and out of the way, revealing the pit where the scorpion apparently lived. It's not large, maybe three feet deep and half a dozen long, which I suppose it could probably fold up into if it wanted. I kneel down and start to crawl inside, looking for anything that looks like loot.

Master? You're not going to find anything in there! Krak almost sounds like he's laughing. *Here!*

I frown, then crawl back out and watch my lizard. He rushes to the rear of the cave, where he feels around on the stone wall for a moment. Suddenly, there's a scraping sort of noise, and he pulls aside a small door revealing a tiny little cubby behind. I walk over and reach inside, and my hand closes on the hilt of a sword. I pull it out slowly, finding a blade made from greenish-silver metal.

[Weapon Acquired: Blade of the Scorpion]

[Level: E]

[Details: Deal 15 points of venom damage over the course of ten seconds with each successful attack.]

"An E-Ranked sword?" I blink in surprise. "That tough of a battle, and I get an E-Ranked sword?"

You'd be surprised how effective such a weapon can be in battle. That effect is really quite powerful. The E-ranking likely only pertains to the base damage, which would be sufficiently offset by the venom. Krak pauses to think. *Actually, as you get higher up, monsters—particularly bosses—will scale their attacks based on the ranking of the weapons and armor coming against them.*

Something like this, ranked lower but with a favorable effect, would actually benefit you quite nicely.

"Interesting," I murmur, then tuck the sword into my inventory. "Well, I'll keep it around. If nothing else, I have a new wall hanging! At best, it'll come in handy sometime." With that, I start back toward the ladder and climb up once more. "Thanks for the tip, Krak."

Always a pleasure to be at your service.

When I reach the surface, I pause and take a look around. The troll bodies have despawned, though they don't look to be spawning again anytime soon. The exit is still in place, and I start walking toward the darkened corridor.

"Burnie? I could sure use you right about now."

Burnie flies out of the portal obediently and lands on my shoulder. Krak climbs up onto my other shoulder, and together, the three of us approach the forest entrance.

Now, I know I've been building it up, but I really can't say just how creepy this forest seems. I can't explain exactly *why*, just that it gives me the shivers even looking at it. The pathway isn't wide, maybe ten feet or so, and is filled with tall, swishing grass that comes up to my waist. On either side, the trees grow so thickly together that there isn't a hope of passing between them. The tree canopies, despite having leaves, seem to be a snarl of branches and death and grow to cover the top of the pathway. I let out a long breath, then slowly start down the path.

My sword of light is held firmly in my hand, and helps to light the way, while Burnie casts a bit more light. Ahead, I can see two particularly large trees that seem extra twisted, almost like something you'd see in a swamp. Between them, I can see fog and darkness, but that's about it. I hold my breath as we continue to creep forward, waiting for whatever comes next.

You shall not enter the Forest of Gloom.

The voice echoes through my head, and I blink in surprise. There aren't many monsters who will communicate with humans voluntarily, especially those that don't possess vocal cords. I hold my sword a bit higher and issue my own statement.

"Forest of Gloom? That's the worst name I've heard for a forest . . . pretty much ever."

In response, something seems to move in those dark trees. The branches twist together and move down the trunk . . . No. No, those aren't branches. A moment later, a giant spider climbs down onto the path, barring my way. It must have a legspan of twenty feet at least. The red hourglass across its abdomen gives me little doubt that this thing is deadly and that I need to watch myself *very* carefully.

I am the guardian of this path. I will stop you from entering.

"You'll try." I shrug. "Burnie? Let's give this widow a little welcoming present."

Burnie lets out a loud squawk, then launches a massive fireball at the spider. It hits firmly, knocking the beast backward slightly. With that, though, the widow flashes forward, legs snarling across the ground as she streaks toward us.

She doesn't issue any more challenges, but I think I understand her well enough. I race to meet her, my sword flashing through the air as we come together. She springs at me, venom flickering on her fangs, and I lash out to block. My sword meets her face, which I find out is surprisingly sturdy for a spider.

Blade meets chitin, and I'm driven backward several feet

as the spider strains to knock me down once more. One fang glistens on either side of the blade, snapping and snarling as she tries to eat me. Or, at least, to bite and poison me. My muscles strain as I fight to keep the beast from doing just that. Eight large eyes, four on either side of the sword, are locked dead with mine.

"You . . . will . . . die," she hisses—this time quite audibly.

"Come . . . up . . . with," I grit my teeth, "a . . . new . . . line!"

With that, I draw out my Shadow Dagger and stab the monster in one of her many eyes. The move knocks me backward slightly, as I have to take one hand away from its firm grip on the sword—but all in all, it seems to be a net gain. The spider shrieks and falls backward in a heap of legs, and I spring forward.

Quickly, I drive my blade into her belly—which, as everyone knows, is the softest part of the spider. It sinks in up to the hilt, and the spider screams and wails in pain. Suddenly, though, I see her abdomen twist around to point at me, and before I know what's happening, a great blob of silk erupts through the air and splats onto my left arm.

For a moment, I'm mostly just surprised, but the move had its intended effect. In that moment, I jerk backward, and that gives her the room that she needs. Legs slam into my chest, knocking me away from her, and a flurry of spider silk comes fast and heavy. Dozens of the projectiles slam into me, gluing me to the ground in half a second. I fall backward to land flat on my back, and sure enough, I'm good and stuck. I grit my teeth and strain against the restraints with all my might, but it's not enough.

The spider slowly rolls back onto her belly, then rises

upward. Blood and spider guts drip down onto the ground, but still, she holds herself together and staggers toward me. I have a feeling that I've mortally wounded her; the only question is whether or not she'll die before she *also* mortally wounds me.

Thankfully, I don't have to find out the hard way, as Burnie swoops overhead and cuts loose with a great blast of flame. It doesn't kill the monster either, but it knocks her backward into some trees. As she rises once more, Burnie comes down and starts burning away the restraints around my arms and legs. He's only just finished with my left side when the spider, smoking and wobbling, pushes herself back upright once more and again staggers over to me.

Burnie is forced to flash up into the air to avoid being bitten, and within an instant, the spider stands over me. Her legs are shaky—she can barely stand up—but there she is.

"You," her voice wavers, "will . . . die."

I respond by kicking the hilt of my sword, which is still lodged in her abdomen, with my left leg. It's driven into her even more and twists and slices through a good bit more of her internal organs. The spider's seven remaining eyes become glazed, and she falls on me with a loud *thud*. Thankfully, her fangs curl up and don't pierce me, which is a bonus. I groan and shove the thing off me—at least, as best I can—and Burnie flies down to continue burning away the spider silk to help me stand up.

The fight didn't go as well as I'd hoped, but I think I'm getting a feel for this dungeon. Trolls, spiders, venom . . . It's a place where taking a single hit is going to have dire consequences; a place where I'll have to tread extremely carefully.

And it's a place that I'm going to defeat.

CHAPTER EIGHTEEN

When I'm fully freed from the entanglements of the spider, I rise up and slowly walk up to peer through the gap in the trees. Through it, I can see nothing but mist—mist and water.

Well, I suppose that's not entirely true. There's a thin strip of land marked here and there by some fading signs, surrounded on all sides by a wide expanse of murky liquid. I can hear things rustling through the thick tree branches overhead, along with the quiet croak of frogs off in the distance. Something ripples through the water not far from me, but it's gone before I can see what it is.

You know, I spent a great deal of time as an intermediate boss in one of these swamps, Krak comments as I slowly step down onto the stretch of land. The soil is soft beneath my feet, but it holds up well enough. *It was a whole lot less terrifying when I was the one who could eat anything that annoyed me, instead of the other way around.*

"Well, you've got me with you." I shrug as I slowly start forward. The ground seems laden with traps. I don't know that for sure, but it just *feels* like any misstep would suck me down into a pit of quicksand or something. "We'll make it through alright."

I'm not concerned that we won't. I'm simply saying that it's a bit frightening, and I now understand why a number of my lesser minions were always complaining about it.

I have to laugh at that and try to continue the casual banter as the two of us move forward—well, three after a moment, when Burnie swoops down to land on my shoulder. He launches a few gouts of flame to try and clear the fog, and it does work *slightly*, but the fog only rolls back after a couple of seconds every time, and he never clears more than a few feet.

"So, you had minions." I nod at Krak. "How many? And how long did it take you to make it all the way up to a dungeon boss?"

I've had lots of minions! Probably a few thousand over the years, Krak answers, shrugging. *Let me see . . . I started out as a hatchling. Never knew my parents; they were both killed by warriors who attacked the dungeon and cleared it out. You know how that goes. Anyway, I lived in that cleared dungeon until I was a full lizardman and then moved out to join with a group of other lizardmen living in a volcano dungeon.*

"Do tell." I reach a small fork in the path. One of them looks clearly like a trap, and I bend down and pick up a stone. When I toss it in that direction, a large swamp plant explodes up out of the water and gobbles it up. That much determined, I turn the other direction.

Yup! I lived with them for probably thirty or forty years, or so. Hard to tell. We had a few small battles, but nothing major until this really powerful group of warriors came through. Our leader was killed, and I came up with this plan to lure the warriors into a magma trap. It killed them all, and I was promoted to leader. Had maybe forty people under my command at that point. Eventually, when the dungeon boss was slain and the mini-boss moved up, I was promoted to a micro-boss and sent to the swamp, as I mentioned. I was there for a while, then got promoted to the hidden mini-boss of the dungeon where you eventually found me. After that, it was only a matter of time before I got promoted all the way to boss.

"Fascinating!" I shake my head, and my curiosity gets the better of me. "What is there, then? Some sort of governing body that makes all these decisions? A dungeon king, who rules over all the dungeons, or . . ."

Not king. Queen.

I'm really not sure what to make of that, and I decide not to ask any more questions for a while. Thankfully, I'm spared from it as I spy what seems to be a clearing just ahead. The fog draws back as I approach, revealing a large, flat circle of land almost a hundred feet wide. There's a single large stone at the center, maybe twenty feet tall, which tapers to a point like a pyramid. This is a battle arena—of that, I'm absolutely certain.

"Alright, Krak." I nod, and the lizardman hops down to the ground. "You get up on top of that rock there and keep an eye out for things. You're going to be my spotter. Burnie, get ready to . . . burn."

I shall do my best, Master. Burnie swoops down and flashes around my head for a moment before rising up into the sky once again. *Do keep in mind that this is a swamp, which means water. I may not be as much use as I sometimes am.*

A loud croak echoes across the waters, and things begin to splash at the edge of the battle. Squelching noises join the splashing, the sound of very large feet being pulled through mud.

And then, the first one appears.

Another troll lumbers from the swamp, a tried and true swamp troll. He has great strands of aquatic plants hanging from his shoulders and neck and head. He seems fatter than the other trolls, as if he's been engorged with water. I don't see any club, but at the end of the day, that doesn't mean a whole lot. Trolls are massive and they're strong, so if one decides to come after me, I have little doubt that he'll be able to do some damage.

"Kill . . . human!"

The troll's voice sounds rather like someone gargling a drink. He lumbers forward, opens his mouth, and vomits a great deal of muddy water at me. I dive backward as the slimy stuff explodes across the terrain, and with that, he thumps forward, picking up speed on the land. More such noises begin to echo on the other side of the clearing, and I have the distinct feeling that I'm going to have my hands full *very* quickly.

Master! You have two more . . . No, three!

Burnie flashes overhead and launches a fireball into the face of the troll, but as he had predicted, it does absolutely nothing. The troll snarls and thumps after me, and I rush forward to engage.

The monster makes a fist and throws it at me. He's fast, much faster than the others, and I only narrowly duck underneath. My sword blazes in my hand, and I land a long cut across his belly. As I do, a great deal of water bursts out, mixed with troll blood, and pours over me. I gasp and stagger backward, and the troll thumps his chest and advances.

He doesn't seem to have been affected by the cut at all, save to grow slightly thinner as water continues to pour out. I reach the stone, then brace myself against it and shove off, blasting across the clearing as fast as I can go. The troll throws another punch, but I drop to the ground and land on the slimy water, sliding straight past. As I come up on the other side, I slash the troll through the side, then slam my sword into the back of his right knee. The monster howls and falls to that knee, and I quickly turn my sword back into a dagger.

Drawing out my second dagger, I rush forward and stab the troll a dozen times in rapid succession. Water bursts out, soaking me to the bone, but I pay it little attention. As the troll struggles to rise, I hear a *thump* behind me, and a great hand latches down onto my back.

Before I know what's happening, the monster grunts and flings me up into the sky. I fly up over the height of the trees, flip over, and come down. I see that second troll making a fist, likely to punch me on my way back down. *That's* going to hurt, no two ways about it. I also see half a dozen other trolls all approaching, and quite rapidly, but I don't have time to figure out what to do with them.

Quickly, I expand my Photonic Dagger into a sword, fling the Shadow Dagger at another troll, and draw the sword of light back over my head. As the troll throws his punch, I slash down with all my might. My aim is true, and I cut the wrist clean through on my downward approach. I land on the severed hand an instant later—which hurts a great deal, but it hurts a great deal less than the impact of the punch would have. Blood and water gush down from the stump of the troll's wrist, and he snarls and howls with pain.

I leap back to my feet and turn as yet another troll lumbers forward. Steel flashes in my hands as I land a cut from his belly all the way up his chest, and with that, I leap out of the way and move onward. There are loads of the creatures now, all thumping about, punching, and kicking, and I fight with every last ounce of energy I have.

About this time, I realize that Bjorn would be helpful, but I don't have the time or space to call him. Instead, I race toward the stone and jump upward, planting my feet against the sheer rock face, allowing me to subsequently launch myself backward, performing a perfect backflip over one of the trolls. I cut his head clean off, and the blubbery body comes crashing down to the ground, giving me an instant of breathing room.

"Burnie! I need your ice, whatever you can give me!"

Burnie flashes down, carving through the air with a fury. His feathers flicker blue, and he launches a spear of ice that hits a troll right behind me. The troll's whole body grows a coat of frost, and with a stagger, he stumbles and falls headlong across the ground. If he's not dead, he's certainly injured and down for the count, which is exactly what I need.

"Just like that! I don't know how much you can do, but give me more if at all possible!"

I charge forward into the midst of the trolls, my blade carving them like Thanksgiving turkeys. Bits of flesh fall to the ground, along with a great deal of the disgusting swamp juice that they all seem basted in. Burnie swoops down just overhead, blasting every troll that he can, though I can tell that it's starting to have an effect on him. His feathers are turning more and more blue, but . . . well . . . His attacks are *fantastically* effective.

"Don't strain yourself!" I call as yet another troll falls. There are only two left, near as I can tell. "I've got this! You go rest!"

Burnie doesn't argue but flies over to land next to Krak. With that, I race full speed at the first of the two, who already sports a number of cuts and slices. As I approach, he balls his hand into a fist and launches a massive punch, but I step back, dodging it, and slam my sword deep into his belly. Quickly, I pull it sideways, wrapping under his arm and all the way around to his back, where I whip it out with a flourish. The troll stumbles and falls, and I turn to the final one.

That last troll seems not to understand that every single other troll who has challenged me has fallen. He thumps his chest and starts forward, and I take a deep breath and charge at him. By now my arms and legs are aching, but I know I can take him.

Just like the other trolls, he starts with a punch, but unlike the others—maybe just because he's the last one—he follows it with a second and then a third. I'm taken slightly aback, as there's ordinarily a brief pause where I can attack, but this one gives me no quarter. My feet slip in the swamp water as I stagger backward, watching and waiting for an opening.

"Come on." I grit my teeth. "I know you're going to give me something."

The troll doesn't say a word, but indeed, after a brief moment, he does let off the attack and staggers back. I grin and leap forward, only to see the troll throwing himself forward as well.

Now . . . I'm strong. However, I weigh around two hundred pounds. This troll has to top out at something more like four thousand, at the very least. If you know how the laws of the conservation of momentum work, well . . . Let's just say that I don't affect the troll's motion all that much.

WHAM!

Getting blasted back into that stone *hurts*, I can assure you of that. As I slide to the ground, the troll lunges forward, bringing up his fist to drive home one final strike. A great many things flash before my eyes, but I'm not yet ready to die. Quickly, I drive my sword upward into the thing's belly, which pauses him for a brief moment. It's not much, but it's enough, and I stand up and pull the sword with all my might, cutting through the thing as hard as I can.

That makes the troll stagger backward, dripping slime, and I sense victory. Before I can do anything, though, a blast of ice flashes down from the top of the rock, hitting the troll dead in the center of the chest. He moans, then collapses in a heap, dead.

[You have leveled up!]

[Congratulations! You are now Level 22!]

I look upward, and Burnie slowly staggers and falls off the stone. He drifts down through the air, and I catch him. His feathers are blue, and his body is cold. He seems to be shivering, and I clutch him close to me.

[LunarEclipse: NOOOO! Not again!!!]

[ViperQueen: Jason had him! Why'd you do that???]

[ShadowDancer: Heal him, Jason!!!]

Master . . . Burnie's eyes flicker open for a moment. *I . . . I . . . I was . . .*

With that, they close once more, and his whole body turns to ice. Suddenly, I'm holding what essentially amounts to a carved statue of a Phoenix instead of my good friend, and I fall to my knees.

The world swirls around me, and I grit my teeth. After a moment, though, I shake my head.

Ali healed him once; she'll be able to do it again. All I have to do is get him back to her. My thoughts swirl around, then solidify with determination. I have a plan.

I just have to get to the end of the dungeon.

CHAPTER NINETEEN

B jorn." I stand up slowly. The statue is going to start melting soon. "Bjorn, I need you now!"

The portal flickers, and Bjorn steps out. His eyes set upon Burnie, and he leaps forward.

"Take him into your domain. Make sure he stays cold."

Right away, Master.

With that, Bjorn is gone, and the portal flickers closed. Krak jumps down from the top of the rock and lands on my shoulders, and I glance up at him.

"Did . . . Did it look worse from up there than down here?" I ask softly. "I mean . . . The fight was going alright, you know? I had the troll. Why'd he do that?"

Krak simply holds up his little, scaly hands. *I'm afraid I don't know. It certainly looked to me like you had it under control, but I'm not a Phoenix. Fire creatures are generally more prone to outbursts of emotion.*

"Fair enough, I suppose." I let out a long breath, then

shrug. "Well, on the somewhat brighter side, I just leveled up again. What about you?"

I'm afraid that I level up slightly differently than you. I am, however, benefiting from your experience points, you may rest assured of that. Krak gives me a nod. *Why don't you do all the folks watching us a favor, and go ahead and choose your reward?*

[DarkCynic: Yeah, Jason!!! Let's see what you've got!]

[ViperQueen: It's the best way to honor Burnie, really. He'd want you to keep fighting.]

[LunarEclipse: Pretty please???]

[Originalgoth: Good riddance! I'm glad that bird is gone.]

"Alright, alright!" I hold up my hand. I want to tell off Originalgoth, but I decide that I just don't feel like it right at that moment. "I'll check my rewards. Let's see here . . ."

I choose the option from my interface, and a moment later, the standard options appear.

[Please accept from the following rewards:]

[Level D Weapon]

[Level D Monster]

[Monster Trainer Skill]

The chat immediately explodes with all sorts of suggestions. This time, though, I mostly ignore them. My resolve solidifies, and I choose the weapon.

[GrendleH8tr: That seems out of character.]

[IceQueen: If it works, don't challenge him!]

[DarkCynic: Yeah! Let Jason have his fun!]

A loot box appears in my hands. It feels heavy, and I quickly flip the latches and open it up. There's a flash of light, and in my hands appears a dagger. I smile as my hand closes around the blade, and I hold it up to take a look at it.

[Weapon Acquired: Diamond Dagger]

[Level: D]

[Details: Ignores up to 50 points of damage resistance.]

"That will come in handy when fighting more bugs." I slip the dagger into my inventory along with my Shadow Dagger. "Now, all I need is a belt to hold all these daggers, so I'm not always having to yank them out of my inventory!"

It's mostly a joke, but the chat immediately explodes with suggestions about how to obtain that very thing. I chuckle at it, then turn away.

Truth be told, there's a reason I chose the weapon. Sure, a new skill would be useful, but all my skills pertain to my creatures, and those very creatures are suffering from a rather high mortality rate at the moment. That's really why I didn't choose a new creature too. With Burnie's not death, I hope, but severe injury, I need to figure out how to protect them better.

I need to become stronger. Yes, they're there to help me, but I'm also there to help them. A full-sized dungeon boss, like what Krak will grow up to be, wouldn't be able to protect a person who wasn't able to fight for themselves.

"Alright, Krak." I glance over my shoulder. Part of me wants to send him back into the portal as well, but with his knowledge of dungeons, I somehow feel like he's better equipped to survive out here. "Help me figure out where to go from here."

Krak scampers over to me, and we walk to the narrow path that led us to the battle area. From that point, we start walking to the right, looking for anything else that might branch away. Unfortunately, we don't seem to find anything. There's nothing but swamp water on any and all sides, and we soon come back around to that initial entry point.

"Any ideas, Krak?" I glance down at the lizard.

Well . . . It's not likely, but it's possible that you have to wade out through the water. Maybe even swim.

"Are you *trying* to get me killed?" I chuckle a bit at Krak. "In what situation have you ever seen a swamp where the water wouldn't just insta-kill you?"

That's fair, I suppose. Krak shrugs. *Still, I don't see any other way out. Do you?*

I shake my head, then turn and look at the stone. There's something about it . . . After all, why would it be here in the first place? Remembering the other hidden doors I've come across recently, I make my way over to it, carefully stepping over troll bodies and puddles of slime. As I reach the stone, I place my hands against it, then draw out my new Diamond Dagger. I hold the hilt backward and begin tapping the rock with the pommel.

You think you'll hear something?

"That's my hope." I nod as I slowly walk around the thing, tapping constantly. "If I don't, there's no harm, but if I do . . ."

The taps, which are sharp and high-pitched, suddenly drop. I smile, then press my ear to the stone and tap some more. The sound echoes inside a hollow chasm, and I grin and step back.

"Right here, Krak." I start feeling around the area, looking for any hint of a crack. Suddenly, I find something. It's so small I can't really even see it, but I can feel it underneath my fingertips. Carefully, I flip the dagger around and start trying to use the blade to pry it open. "Just have to find the catch."

Krak nods and rushes over, then starts to climb up. As he leaps onto a small outcropping, it suddenly slides downward, and I hear gears and things turning within. There's a loud *thump-thump-thump*, and with that, the door swings outward, taking Krak along with it. He jumps free, and we look down inside.

The hole drops straight down and doesn't have so much as a handhold. I frown, then slowly dangle my legs over the edge. Krak rushes up, then trips and falls against me. I lose my balance and slip over the edge, plunging into the darkness.

Sorry, Master!

I gasp as the world grows almost impossibly dark . . . Then, with a loud *thump*, I land on a patch of mossy ground lit by the soft glow of a number of mushrooms.

I'm in a wide tunnel now that curves gently out of sight after about fifty feet or so. Large mushrooms—red and blue, mostly—grow out of the walls and ceiling. Their light isn't much, but it's something. All around me, the air is damp and moist and filled with the smell of natural decay. Well . . . It really just smells like a swamp, you know? We might be under-ground—and we might be quite a distance underground— but at the end of the day, we're in a swamp.

There's a sharp scream from beside me, and Krak hits the ground with a *thump*. He climbs back to his feet and gives his body a shake, then slowly looks around.

I think we figured out where we need to go.

"It seems so." I keep my Diamond Dagger in my hand as I start forward, looking left and right for any signs of activity. There are no clear signs of an ambush that I can see, but that also doesn't mean a whole lot. I half expect the mushrooms to turn into monsters and try to eat me, but they stay on the walls, which is exactly where they should be.

As the tunnel bends, it seems to slope upward, which I judge as a positive sign. It's hard to tell exactly how much we turn, but I get the feeling that we've wrapped around to face exactly opposite of the initial direction when we come to a larger cave.

It's just about as swampy of a cave as you might imagine. Defying all physics, the walls, ceiling, and floor are all made of moist dirt, which should have meant that the thing would just collapse. Tree roots snarl down from the ceiling and across the walls, harboring a number of creepy-looking eyes. Water drips down from some parts of the ceiling, filling up shallow, stagnant pools here and there.

[ShadowDancer: This is gross!]

[IceQueen: Yeah! Kill whatever's in here and get out!]

[ChaosRider: You'll do great, Jason!]

I turn slowly about, looking for the monster in question. So far, the creatures in this swamp have *not* been apt to make an appearance right at the start. There's a low rumble, and suddenly, the pools of stagnant water begin to ripple.

Something pokes up out of one of them. It looks like a small tendril or a sprout. It grows taller and broader, and similar things begin to emerge from the others. As they grow, the stems take on form, broadening and spreading out to take on human-like shapes. They're misshapen, rather like mandrake roots, but . . . there they are. With leaves for hair, gnarled and knobby roots for legs, and long, grasping limbs for arms . . . well . . . they're fantastically grotesque.

And they're all looking right at me.

"Well, don't stand around on my account." I throw my Diamond Dagger into the heart of the closest one. It staggers and falls, and I draw out my Shadow Dagger as well. It sails into the heart of the next, and it falls as well. "There we go! An easy one."

As the things land, roots grow down out of their bodies, and more sprouts pop out of their backs, growing into new warriors.

"Oh. So this is one of *those* sorts of monsters?" I sigh, then draw out my sword of light. "Well, nothing to be done about it. Let's see if there's a limit to the number of times they can regenerate."

Krak responds by climbing up the walls to hide in the snarls of roots, and I rush forward, my sword blazing with light. I cut through the newly formed warriors before they can fully animate, then spring upon the rest. They lumber forward, lashing out at me, whipping and stinging my skin with the speed of their attacks. My sword flashes faster, though, cutting off their arms and legs. One particularly large one splashes through a puddle and raises both arms, and I raise my sword and bring it down on its head. The thing is bisected top to bottom, and the two halves fall apart with dull *splats*. With that, I spin and cut off the head of the next one in line, then move onward through the chaos and turmoil.

They aren't hard to kill, that much is for sure, but the more of them I cut down, the faster they regrow. It's like trying to maintain a lawn in a nice neighborhood, where everyone has crazy high expectations of how things should look. My arms soon begin to ache as I frantically hack them down.

"Krak!" I shout out. "Any input would be useful!"

There's a long pause before he answers.

Well . . . My guess is that you're going to have to kill them in a way that they can't respawn.

"Great. That's very . . . helpful?"

I spy, toward the back of the cave, a small platform of stone sitting just in front of a darkened doorway. I can't see much, but I can see that there isn't water or soil, and I nod.

"Thanks, Krak!"

With that, I reach out and grab the closest of the plant monsters by the throat, turn, and sling it at the doorway with all my might. It slams against the door hard enough to splinter the wood and slides to the ground, dead. For a moment, it does attempt to sprout roots, but they simply flail about on the stone for a moment before withering.

Good. So that's what I'll do. I take a deep breath, then rush forward, cutting my way through the mass of tangled limbs until I arrive at that platform. When I feel the stone under my feet, I turn around and simply let them all come to me.

By now there must be close to a hundred of them, which, of course, is almost entirely my fault. As they charge at me, I simply cut them apart, throw them onto the stone—or just let them fall there naturally—and move on. Bodies pile up around me; though thankfully, they start to despawn after a few minutes. My arms grow even more weary, and I start to notice just how deadly this room could be if you didn't figure out the trick quickly enough. Once there were two or three hundred of the things, it wouldn't really matter how fast you were; you'd be overwhelmed simply by sheer numbers.

Thankfully, I don't have that problem. All things considered, it really doesn't take that long before I've hacked them all down and dumped the carcasses where they can't regenerate. Well, mostly. One of them manages to sneak a root off the edge and raises up a warrior right behind me, but I'm able to cut *that* one down with ease. And I'm a whole lot more careful with where I put *it*, so it doesn't happen again.

With that, Krak scampers back down to the floor, and I let out a long breath as I look around the room.

"What do you think?" I glance down at him. "Are we getting close to the dungeon boss yet?"

Close, but not there yet. Krak shakes his head. *Through that door will probably be a mini-boss, then there will be another group of minions, and then the dungeon boss. Provided, of course, that it follows a standard pattern.*

"That's what I was thinking too." I sheath my sword, then slowly approach the doors. As I lay my hands upon them, they unlock with a loud *thunk* and start to swing inward. "Let's go see what sort of creature passes for a mini-boss in this swamp."

CHAPTER TWENTY

The doors open slowly, revealing a dark chamber behind. A dank, musty sort of smell drifts out, one that I've always associated with basements. A soft lantern flickers to life as the doors fully open, and Krak and I step inside. It's no surprise to me when the door slams back shut, and I slowly take a look around.

The basement isn't large; it's hardly big enough to even fight a duel if someone were to appear. There are shelves wrapping around three sides, all of which are filled with canning jars. Inside the jars are a wide assortment of things, all of which look rather gross. Frogs. Fish. An assortment of body parts. I shudder as I look over it all over, and my chat just about explodes.

[DarkCynic: Who could have done all this?]

[IceQueen: Are these for display, or food, or . . .]

[GoldenShield: AHH! I see an eyeball!!!]

Krak scampers over to a small ladder that leads to a trap

door in the middle of the room. He tilts his head back, then climbs up the ladder to the top and presses his ear to the wood.

I can hear something moving around up there. Can't quite tell what it is, though. Maybe cloth drifting across a wooden floor, or something.

"So, it's hovering, floating. A wraith or something along those lines."

I grit my teeth as I slowly start walking around the edges of the room, looking at the assortment of pickled items. My chat seems drawn to it all with a morbid curiosity, but I have a slightly different reason. I want to see if there's any indication of what the weakness of the creature above might be. There are frog parts and fish parts, and I think I can recognize some birds and salamanders and other such things. In any case, my mind is drawn back to the other wraiths and such things that I've fought over the last few days. There's always been some sort of physical object that they've been attached to. Hidden in the midst of these shelves would be a far better place to put something along those lines than, say, a painting on the wall.

Still, though, I don't find anything, which is somewhat frustrating. The only pattern I see is that most of the body parts are taken from smaller creatures as opposed to larger ones, but that's the only correlation I can see between any of them. Satisfied enough that the room is little more than an aesthetic entry point, I join Krak at the ladder and take hold of the first rung.

Whooooooooooosh!

The trap door suddenly flies open, and a powerful gale shrieks through the room. Before I know what's happening,

I'm picked up and sucked into the room above and flung down onto the floor with a powerful *slam*. The trap door clicks shut behind me, and I struggle to rise as I look upon my attacker.

A woman stands before me, old and twisted, with warts on her nose and a sinister smile upon her face. Her feet are drifting a few inches above the ground, while her tattered, old cloak drifts idly against the wooden floor. She has her hands outstretched and cackles wildly.

"So good of you to come by!" She smiles with sick glee. "Would you care to stay for some dinner?"

I glance around the room wildly. I'm in a shack—quite a large one, actually. There are a number of doors branching off into other rooms, while a rickety back door seems to open into a yard of some sort. There's a table not far away, set with a single plate and a rather large silver platter. A carving fork and knife sit just beside it, and I get the feeling that I'm intended to serve as the main course.

"You know what? I actually just had breakfast, so I think I'll pass." I draw out my Diamond Dagger and give it a twirl around my palm. "I don't suppose you'd be kind enough to show me the way out of here? I'm quite busy, and I'd love to get moving again."

The witch simply cackles once more. "You should know better than that! I'm going to eat you, whether you agree to it or not!"

"There isn't a chance in the world that I'm going to agree to it, so . . ." I shrug. "Hit me with your best shot."

The witch smiles again, then begins to wiggle her fingers. It looks like she's trying to tickle the air, and the sight of it

makes me pause. I suppose that's why I don't hear the jar flying off the counter to smash against my head.

Crash!

Glass and a pickling brine explode around my head as the
jar hits and knocks me forward. I land on the ground, gasping
in pain, and the witch swoops forward. Krak, as usual, scampers out of the way, and I grit my teeth.

"Alright, then." As she comes upon me, I rise up and grab
hold of her throat. She's surprisingly light, and she screams as
I clamp down on her neck. "Maybe I'll take your second-best
shot. Anyhow—"

I pull my arm back, winding up, and throw her into a cabinet. Wood explodes around her, and herbs and dried feet and
gizzards and other such things come crashing down around
her. She snarls as she rises back up once more, and with that,
the fight is on.

I spring at the witch, preparing to throw my dagger. Before
I can reach her, she snaps her fingers, and I hear the sharp
snick of things coming through the air. I quickly throw myself
to the side, dodging a large number of knives and forks. They
slam into the wall instead, imbedding themselves quite deeply.
I snarl, then dive toward the hearth, where a pot bubbles merrily over a roaring fire.

"Don't you go over there!" the witch shrieks. I hear her clap
her hands, and a cabinet nearby explodes open. A great number of jars fly out, all of which slam into me with immense
force. I'm driven backward under the force of them, slipping
on the brine that leaks down across my clothes even as the
glass cuts my skin. One last jar lags a bit behind the others—a
jar holding what looks like a turkey leg—and I reach up and

catch it before it hits me. It takes all my strength, but I spin and throw the jar straight into her face. There's a great blast of glass and brine, and she's smashed into a closet.

A broom closet.

The closet door fractures and comes crashing down, revealing a large number of cleaning supplies. She turns to dig through the rubble, and I take a moment to leap upon the crackling hearth. There, I reach inside and grab hold of the handle of the pot, ignoring the pain. Flame crackles and blazes around me, but I do my best to bear it, yanking the pot free. I turn and throw it with all my might, sending a raging, boiling vat of brownish soup crashing over the witch.

There are few words that can properly describe the noise that the witch makes. She has a broom in her hand, and as the liquid pours across her, she falls backward, shrieking and crying and writhing as if she had been plunged into the very pits of hell. Which . . . I mean, it *is* boiling soup, and if I remember high school chemistry, there's something or other about the boiling point of water elevating when more things are added into it . . . I don't know. Anyway, she's momentarily knocked backward, and I take the opportunity to throw my Diamond Dagger at her.

"If you won't go like the Wicked Witch of the West, I suppose we'll just have to do things a bit more manually."

The weapon carves through the air, and her eyes seize upon it. She twitches a single finger, and the blade draws to a halt just in front of her burned, puffy nose.

[ChaosRider: Really, Jason? You *threw* something at a witch you knew had telekinetic power?]

[RazorEdge: Even I would have known not to do that.]

[ViperQueen: Better duck!]

"You know what? I don't need your criticisms right now." I dive to the side as the knife flashes past me, right where my head had just been, and hits the chimney hard enough to slam all the way up to the hilt, right into the stone. "The pot worked! Guess I'll just have to keep doing this the hard way."

I charge at the witch, my feet pounding across the wooden floor of the shack. As I reach her, she finally seems to recover a bit more of her bodily control and points the shaft of the broom at my chest.

Kra-Boooooooooom!!!

A great blast of white energy erupts from the broom and hits me firmly. I'm thrown backward with extreme force, smashing against the back door of the home hard enough to crack the thing. The witch smiles and points the broom at me once more, and I reach behind me, grab hold of the door, and rip it off its hinges. With that, I bring it up in front of me and charge at the woman, using what remains of the door as a shield.

Kra-Boooooom!

A second blast of energy hits the door, blasting it into splinters. I avoid the attack, though, and charge at the monster. She has a moment to look surprised before I reach her, grab the broom, and rip it from her hands. Magic flares down the shaft of the weapon, discharged just before I took it from her, and I smile.

With all my might, I grab hold of the bristly part of the broom and swing it like a baseball bat. The shaft of the weapon hits her in the head right as the flash of magic reaches the end.

The explosion is powerful enough to slam me back against

the floor of the home, but that's alright by me. The wall behind her is torn to shreds, and the witch is shot out into the yard. I quickly rise up and follow, leaping through the rubble and debris and into the muddy area.

The shack sits in a large clearing, I'd guess about two hundred feet across, surrounded by swamp trees and swamp water on all sides. There's a small pig pen, a chicken coop, and a few other farmyard odds and ends. A thick fog hangs overhead, shrouding the whole thing in shadow. The witch picks herself up from the ground, snarling and cackling.

"You think you've won, but I haven't given up! Not at all! In fact, I'm more powerful than ever!" The witch raises her hands. "Now come! Come and destroy, my friends!"

I hear a snort, and three massive pigs race out of their small shelter and crash into the gate. There's a sickening crunch of bone, and they all stand up, taking on more humanoid forms. With that, they tear through the gate, leaving it in shambles, and charge at me, snorting and squealing and snarling. Boar tusks glisten in the faint light, and I brace myself.

"Time to bring home the bacon!" I draw out my Photonic Dagger and expand it into a sword. "Well . . . Check that. I'm not bringing this bacon anywhere, but . . . I . . ."

[RazorEdge: We get what you're trying to say!]

[ShadowDancer: Get this pork!]

[IceQueen: This seems like a "pig" problem!]

I snort a bit at the chat, then step forward as the first of the pigs reaches me. He grunts and squeals, and I chop off his head. The body of the farmyard monster falls headlong into a puddle, and the other two throw themselves upon me, chomping and squealing and biting. I have to take a step back to avoid their initial attacks, then stab the next one through the gut. The monster squeals and collapses, and with that, I spin to the last one.

"I've heard that pigs are almost identical to humans, inside." I give my sword a twirl. "Shall we test that out?"

The monster squeals and charges forward, and I give my sword one final swing. I won't describe what follows, but . . . well . . . I'm no doctor, but the insides of a pig do indeed look quite like the insides of people.

Anyway, with that last swine down, I spin around to find the witch. By now, though, she's gone, and I grit my teeth as I spin to look around the clearing. The pigs weren't meant to try and defeat me—she certainly knew I wouldn't be taken down by such low-level monsters—but they served as a distraction . . . Which is exactly the same tactic I'm always trying to use against monsters.

I'll have to be more careful next time.

Suddenly, I catch sight of the witch shooting up into the sky. She's riding a pitchfork instead of a broom and comes to a halt just above the chimney. Slowly, she turns around to look down at me, and lightning begins to crackle in her hands.

"Say goodbye, boy! Your time is up!"

A flash of lighting comes down a moment later, and I narrowly dodge out of the way. It scorches along the ground, sending up a loud hiss of steam as it burns the damp earth.

"Krak!" I glance back at the ruins of the house. "If you have any ideas, now might be a good time!"

I have one idea!

Krak's head pops up out of the basement, and he emerges a moment later. He's dragging something, though I can't quite see what. I dive to the side, dodging another blast of lightning, and the witch cackles. I know I can't throw anything at her—she'll simply dodge it—and she's too high to reach. Suddenly, though, Krak reaches my side, and he groans and lifts up a small jar.

Threaten to destroy this!

I frown, but I nod and hold up the jar. Inside, floating in the water, seem to be some sort of reptile eggs, though I can't tell what sort exactly. "Hey, witch! Come down here and let me defeat you, or I'm destroying this!"

The witch's eyes grow wide. "You can't! You . . . Ahhhhhh!"

She lets out a loud shriek and comes racing down from the sky, flashing along on her pitchfork like a bolt of lightning. The jar twitches in my grasp as she tries to pull it from me telekinetically, but I resist and brace my feet. A moment later, she's upon me, and I flash into motion.

The sword is still in my hand, and as she stretches out a lightning-wrapped hand and reaches for the jar, I bring up the weapon and attack her with all my might. The sword smashes through the shaft of the pitchfork and cleaves through her misty body. She screams, and the whole apparatus collapses to the ground. Her cloak flutters around whatever is left of her, and she rises up into the air once more.

"Here. Catch." I toss the jar up into the air over my head. She immediately stretches out a hand to reach it, and it turns and flashes through the air to her hand. At the same time, though, I turn my sword back into a dagger and throw it into her face.

There's a loud scream, and the witch bursts into green smoke. A moment later, the jar hits the ground and shatters, leaking brine across the ground. The eggs inside bounce and roll and are set upon by large crows that flash down from the trees overhead to start gobbling them up.

"That was easy." I chuckle after a moment and sheath the sword. Slowly, I walk back into the house to pull the Diamond Dagger out of the chimney, expecting some sort of retribution any moment. "What were those, Krak?"

Some sort of giant lizard eggs! Maybe dragon, maybe basilisk, or could be wyrms or wyverns, or any other such thing. I figure she probably meant to use them to create a monster, so they'd be valuable to her.

"Enough to charge at me and risk death." I grab gold of my dagger and give it a few yanks. It's stuck tight, so it takes a moment before it comes free. "In any case, I'm glad you knew what they were. Much appreciated."

Anything for you! Now, we should move on. Some of these mini-bosses have respawn sequences, if you stick around too long.

"Good to know." I smile and walk back out of the house, ready to finish up the dungeon. "After you."

CHAPTER TWENTY-ONE

Unfortunately, it takes us a few minutes before we're able to figure out how to move on. The trap door to the basement is locked, likely upon the witch's death, which points us forward. Based on my limited directional processing, as well as the natural ambience, I think we're back in the same swamp that I more or less started the dungeon in, but it's hard to know for sure.

In any case, knowing that we have to move onward from the hut, we circle the perimeter of the clearing three times before Krak points out a narrow trail winding through the weeds. I walk up to it and peer out, nodding as I discern the path. It vanishes off into the swamp, a narrow strip of land hardly two inches wide. Water laps up on either side of it, and I take a deep breath.

"This is going to be tricky." I slowly step out and plant my right foot on the path, if it can even be called by such a name. My foot sinks a bit, and water splashes up on either side of my shoe. Water swirls just a few feet away, and I see a set of eyeballs surrounded by thick scales rise up to watch me. It doesn't attack, not yet, but I know I'm being watched. "Easy now. Let's get this started."

Krak nods at me from behind, then backs up and runs forward. His flying leap brings him to my leg, where his little claws dig into my calf muscles. I yelp in pain, but he simply scampers to my shoulders, where he plops down to stare out through the mist.

Be careful where you step! One wrong foot, and we'll be food!

"Trust me, I think I've figured that out." I ease my way along, the *squelch-squelch* of my feet echoing rather like a gong in the still air. "Just keep an eye out, and tell me if you see anything that wants us dead."

I can see many such things!

"Anything you think might actively attack us."

Right. Will do!

Krak seems to be growing cheery in the gloom, and I chuckle. Suddenly, off to my right, I catch a glimpse of something through the fog. I can't be sure, but it looks like one of the old paths that I followed when I first entered the bog. That means that we *are* in the same swamp. I don't know exactly what that means, other than the fact that we're likely to see the same sorts of creatures around here. Trolls . . . Giant spiders . . .

The trees above me suddenly shake rather ominously, and I see something dark rumble through the canopy. I can't see much, but it makes the tree limbs themselves look as though they're shifting and moving about, and I give a nod.

"Spiders it is, then." I grimace and draw out my sword,

holding it forward to shine a bit of light into the gloom ahead. "Alright, Krak. You're a lizard. You like eating bugs?"

Indeed! I've actually rather enjoyed being a hatchling again for that very fact. Full-grown lizardmen have to spend a decent amount of time hunting either for catches of smaller insects or for the really big spiders and things. As a full dungeon boss, I pretty much had to forget about it. Anything that grew that big was going to be a henchman at the very least, and it makes the other dungeon bosses angry when you eat their foot soldiers.

"I'll take your word for it." I chuckle. "On the bright side, we ought to have more than enough for you to eat here in just a few minutes."

Wonderful! I think I sense a clearing up ahead.

I hold my sword a bit tighter, and sure enough, after only a few moments the fog begins to clear a bit. My footsteps become a bit surer, and soon, I come stumbling up gratefully onto a patch of land that's . . . a *bit* firmer.

Really, it's actually several patches of land. I think I can see three islands, all connected to each other by the most rotten bridges I've ever seen. The wooden planks are twisted and decayed, and the ropes look like they'll snap if the breeze blows too hard. I slowly turn my head back and forth, looking for anything that might come jumping out at me.

Hissssssssssssssss.

The water ripples, and I glimpse the head of a serpent slide up from the swamp and into the narrow channels of water that run between the three islands. It seems to pause at the place where all three channels meet, and I see it poke its head just *barely* above the water, watching.

I stare back at it, not wanting it to think me afraid.

Suddenly, though, a soft rustle runs through the surrounding tree branches. I turn my back on the snake, keeping an eye on it, while dark shadows start to jump down from the trees.

Three said shadows leap onto my island, coming close enough to resolve into the giant spiders I suspected them to be. One seems to be a tarantula. One is a brown recluse. The third is black and looks rather like a jumping spider. I bring up my sword, and the three spiders slowly come to a stop.

None of them speak, and I don't say a word to them. Krak jumps off my shoulder and scampers away, and with that, the battle is launched into motion. The jumping spider springs at me, sailing high into the air, preparing to deal a crushing blow on the way down.

I dodge roll out of the way . . . At least I try. The brown recluse fires a blob of webbing at my feet, and its aim is directly on target. I'm sealed in place by the blob of silk, unable to move as the massive bulk of the jumping spider comes straight down. Desperately, I point the sword upward, and stab at the thing with all my might.

There's a loud scream as it hits, and I honestly can't tell whether it comes from myself or the spider. I'm blasted into the ground with extraordinary force, but I keep my sword held firmly, and as the jumping spider staggers backward, I can see goop dripping down from a large wound onto the ground. It's going to take a moment for the thing to heal from that attack, I'm sure of it. I decide to not give it the time, and I quickly lash downward, cutting away the last of the spider thread.

My foot free, I race at the jumping spider. The brown recluse starts firing a great deal more thread my way, while the tarantula hisses and simply charges. My sword blazes with light as I deflect the attacks and smack them into the ground, desperately fighting to reach the jumping spider.

As I come upon it, I raise my sword, but the thing simply leaps up into the air, sailing high over my head. I scowl, then gasp as the tarantula hits me from behind. A massive, hairy leg smashes me into the ground, and I groan as the dirt below me takes on a rather good imprint of my face.

[DarkCynic: That has to hurt!]

[ViperQueen: Yeah, but he'll get right back up! Won't you, Jason?]

[FireStorm: Tell us you're alright!]

"Just . . . peachy." I take a deep breath. The tarantula starts to lower itself to bite me, and I flip around the sword in my grasp and stab upward as best I can. It's not particularly easy, but I manage to wound the thing, and it shrieks and stumbles backward. With that, I jump back to my feet, lunge upon it, and drive the sword down at its face.

Crack!

My sword rings out as it slams into the hard head of the tarantula. Despite not having any visible armor, it stops my sword firmly, and I grit my teeth as we strain against one another. The thing has recovered from my stab wound, it seems like. Off to one side, I see the brown recluse slowly approaching, and know that I only have a few moments before it hits me too. Its abdomen twists as it lines itself up for a good shot.

"Alright, then." I take a deep breath. "I guess I'll take a cue from," I have to pause for another breath, "your brother!"

With that, I jump up into the air, landing on the back of

the tarantula. It whirls around, trying to buck me off, and I quickly drive my sword deep into its back, holding on for dear life. It spins faster and faster, but with my perch and hand-hold, I stay rather firmly in place. My muscles strain as I try to keep myself positioned, and carefully, I open up my inventory and pull out my Shadow Dagger.

With that, I begin to stab the monster as fast as I can. My knife blazes through the air as I inflict a dozen long stab wounds across the thing, then keep going. Goop drips down onto the ground, making the sides of the monster slick, but still it's not dying.

"Come . . . on!" I grunt. The brown recluse is starting to get closer, watching for an opportunity. Suddenly, an idea pops through my head, and I swing around the sword until I'm on the front side of the spider. It snarls and prepares to throw me, and after a moment, I transform the sword back into a dagger and pull it out.

Rather like I've been shot from a slingshot, I'm flung down the front of the monster toward its head. I place the daggers together, forming an X, and as I reach the head, I slash downward at the joint where it meets the body. My blades flash through that gap, carving it clean off, and the tarantula head falls to the ground.

I don't stop moving, though. My feet hit the top of its head as it strikes the earth, and I launch myself up into the air once more. The main body of the tarantula is still wobbling and twitching as I come down hard on top of the brown recluse. My sword blazes with light, and I do the same maneuver, except with the sword. Its head drops to the ground as well, and both spider bodies tip to the side and land with loud *thumps*.

[ChaosRider: That's the way to do it, Jason!!!]

[DarkCynic: Practically a two-for-one deal, I'd say!]

[ViperQueen: Jason sure keeps the excitement high, that's for sure!]

I chuckle, then turn toward the jumping spider. Somehow, I'm unsurprised to find that it's jumped across one of the channels and is watching me from one of the other islands. The snake rises out of the water with a bit more interest, and I sigh.

"Alright, well . . ." I take a deep breath and crouch down, taking my stance. "This ought to be interesting. It's times like this that I sort of wish I had taken a more distance-based class."

[DarkCynic: And just cheesed everything? That's not our Jason.]

[IceQueen: Yeah! That's why none of the archers have any good following. Except Ali. She's actually getting up there now!]

I chuckle at that, then launch myself from my stance and bolt forward. As I reach the water, I leap up into the air even as the snake bolts forward. At this moment, several things happen all at once. The snake rises out of the water, mouth open, ready to intercept me. At the same time, the jumping spider springs up into the air, sailing off for the next island.

I really, *really* don't want it doing that.

My sword blazes with light, and I slash it through the air at the snake. Steel meets scales, and the head of the snake flies past me as I cut it clean off. With that, I transform it back into a dagger, and before I even hit the ground, I fling it through the air at the jumping spider.

The great monster squeals as it strikes home, and yelps

again as the second blade, my Shadow Dagger, plunges deep into its abdomen as well. It lands, then spins and faces me. I land as well, spin, and launch my Diamond Dagger with all my might. My aim is perfect, and it hits the spider dead between the eyes.

The spider's eyes glaze over—all eight of them—and the beast slowly topples to the side, dead. Ooze drips across the ground, and Krak races over to retrieve my three daggers. With that, I let out a long breath and glance around the area, looking for the next section of path.

Good show, Master! You had me worried for a moment!

"I'm glad it was only for a moment." I give the lizard a nod as Krak rushes back over to my side and hands my weapons to me. "I don't suppose you see the way out of here?"

Actually, I do! This way!

Krak races across the damp ground to some fronds on the side of the area and pulls them back to reveal another narrow path. This one has a distinct *gloom* about it, as if the very light were being sucked from the air . . . as if we were heading into the heart of the swamp itself.

"Well, alright, then." I take hold of my sword and slowly start walking forward. "If you're right, and I think you are, this will be the boss of the dungeon." A smile spreads across my face. "Let's go take him down."

CHAPTER TWENTY-TWO

The path is long and dark, of that there's no question. The air around me seems to leech the light out of the air, and when I draw my sword and hold it out for illumination, it only seems to glow with a faded dullness. Everything feels heavy. The tree trunks around me are laden with moss and mold, and the long, beard-like moss that hangs from the branches seems to sink lower than usual. All around, the feeling of gloom hangs heavy over the place.

[ChaosRider: Wow . . . I don't know if Jason's going to come out of this alive!]

[DarkCynic: Yeah! Anything that can create an effect like this is going to be *powerful*.]

[GrendleH8tr: Like usual, just keep your head about you. This is nothing but smoke and mirrors. You can push through it.]

I give a nod to the chat. Thankfully, I'm not really affected by the gloom; I just wish I could see the path better. In fact, in some ways I'm actually sort of excited by all this darkness and dreariness. This is going to make for *quite* the battle, which frankly just sounds exciting to me.

As Krak and I stumble along, I glimpse the faintest little ray of light up ahead. My chat explodes with excitement, but I hold back. Things like that are often a trap. Sure enough, as I approach, I find a little purple flower gleaming with a single beam of sun shining down through the canopy. A small butterfly flitters through the air and lands on it, and with a loud *whump*, a much larger purple flower erupts out of the darkness and swallows it. It pulls back after a second, and I continue onward.

Now, this is the sort of place I used to live in! I would hide in a pool just next to the path and jump people without any warning! Ahh, that was the—

I quit listening as I pick up something else through the gloom. A small patch of darkness that seems even darker than everywhere else. The path leads right into it, and I give a nod. Slowly, I take my stance, then bolt forward.

As I come crashing through the darkness, I feel a great deal of vines and moss snagging at my face. Quickly, I whirl around, carving through it all, and come stumbling out into a bright—if still unpleasant—little castle courtyard. The walls are crumbling, and the little tower at the middle is probably only about ten feet across and hardly looks to be of any real use. Still, I can see books and tools stacked on a windowsill high up the side, which means that someone does live there. The fog here seems to have parted, which tells me that the source of the gloom and darkness stems from this place.

"Krak, go poke around in that tower," I order.

With pleasure!

Krak jumps off my shoulders and scampers to the tower. He looks up, scratches his head, then starts climbing up via a number of cracks and chips. I take a deep breath, then cup my hands around my mouth.

"Hello! Is the proprietor of this establishment at home?"

There's a long pause. Krak reaches the windowsill and dives inside, his tail vanishing with a little flick. A few more moments pass until smoke suddenly billows up from a point just a few feet in front of me. When it's gone away, I find myself looking at a sorcerer in a long, red robe. He looks just as ancient as the witch and floats just a few inches off the ground as well.

"Welcome." He spreads his arms slightly. "Welcome to my home. My name is Magus. Simon Magus. You may have heard of me."

"The name rings a bell." I take my stance and point the tip of the sword at his belly. "Now, are you the one who's going to try and kill me?"

The sorcerer chuckles a bit and floats a few feet farther back. "That hardly seems like a fitting label. I welcome all who come into my home! What you do here depends on you, not on me."

"And how exactly do you welcome people?" I ask, raising an eyebrow. Krak's face appears in the window, and he gives a shake of his head before vanishing once more.

"Food! How else?" Simon snaps his fingers, and a long table appears in the courtyard, laden with cheese, bread, sausages, turkey, quail, and dozens of other such foods. "What would you like? Speak it, and I'll make it for you."

"How stupid do you think I am?" I raise an eyebrow. "Eating your food is the quickest way I could wind up as one of your little puppets."

"Yes, well . . ." Simon shrugs. "You do have to admit, getting people to eat my food is the quickest way I'm able to *get* said puppets. It gets more people than you'd think, really." He stretches. "It gets terribly tedious trying to beat everyone up in order to enslave them or drain their life forces. Someone as old as me has to conserve energy where they can, you know."

"Right." I shrug. "Well, I know it's improper to hit first, but . . ."

I lunge forward, slashing at the sorcerer. Simon simply vanishes in a puff of smoke, reappears on the walls, and then raises his hands.

"Goodbye, Jason Lee! I do wish you all the best in the next life, whatever that may be for you."

With a loud *crash*, the wall behind me explodes into slivers. I spin as a stone golem, twenty feet tall at least, stomps into the courtyard. The broken debris begins to roll across the ground toward him, absorbing into his body even as he stands there. Another crash signals the arrival of a second golem, on the opposite side of the courtyard.

"When we've siphoned your life force, I hope you'll find it some sort of consolation to know that you'll be creating a more powerful weapon for me than I've ever been able to build before." Simon smiles and bows politely. "Your sacrifice is most helpful."

"Not today, I don't think." I charge at the first golem. He balls his hand into a fist and swings at me, over a ton of stone throwing its power behind a single fist. I dodge that first strike and slash upward, trying to cut his hand from his arm.

Whack!

The sword meets stone—and fails to do a thing. It doesn't exactly surprise me, but it *is* somewhat annoying. I spin out of the way as he lifts a foot and tries to stomp on me and quickly shrink the sword back into a dagger to try and stab him. There's no real effect, and I scowl. My Shadow Dagger is the same, and while my Diamond Dagger does chip the stone, there's still not a lot that happens. I get the distinct feeling that piercing and slashing weapons aren't going to be super helpful here.

The question is, what weapons *will* be useful? Also, is it even worth trying to defeat the golems, or should I just focus my energy on Simon? I imagine he'll just teleport away, but it's always possible that there's some sort of a trick I can exploit.

Unfortunately, I'm given no time to figure it out as the golem spins around. His massive fist flies once more, and I duck. The monster takes the opportunity to unleash a rapid-fire series of strikes, punches, kicks, and other such attacks that leave me with little time to think. I'm thrown into pure survival mode, dodging and leaping and ducking.

Master!

I glance up at Krak, who's back on the windowsill.

I found something! It's a diagram of how he makes the golems! There's a totem at the exact center that you have to destroy, which will break his command over the stone!

"And how do I get to the center?" I scowl.

Here! This used to be down in the courtyard, but it looks like he moved it! Can't say as I blame him. I'd have done the same.

Krak ducks back inside, and I hear a muffled grunt in my

head. I have to dodge another strike, and he appears in the window again.

It's too heavy for me to lift! Can I drink a growth potion? Won't affect me too much, and I think it's temporary.

"Go for it!"

There's a long pause. A moment passes, and a large war hammer suddenly flies down out from the window. Simon lets out an angry scream, and I dive forward, rolling between the legs of the golem, and raise my hand. The handle *thwacks* firmly into my palm, and with that, I spin and smash it into the leg of the golem.

Now, I'm no strength build, but I've got a good bit of muscle on me. Stone cracks and explodes under my strike, and the whole leg fractures and falls off. I grin as the golem falls to the ground and jump forward, bringing the war hammer up over my head.

Wham!

I bring it crashing down onto the golem's head, splitting it from top to bottom. He groans and falls apart slightly, and a light shines from within. Quickly, I thrust my left hand into the crack, stretching for that totem. My hand closes down on something . . . And with that, the stone shifts and slams back shut.

"YOW!"

I don't cry out in pain much—at least I try not to—but this *hurts*. Stone grinds against stone, trying to grind my very bones to dust along with it. I grit my teeth and pull, but nothing happens. Desperately, I start trying to whack the golem with the hammer, but I cannot stress how terrible my leverage is at this moment, and I'm unable to do anything more than chip a few bits of rubble off the thing.

Simon laughs, his voice cutting through the air. "You've trapped yourself! This is even better than I could have hoped! Now all we have to do is crush you!"

The golem holding me turns to face the other golem, and they start stomping toward each other. I have seconds before I'm crushed, so I do the only thing I can think of.

I start squeezing the totem.

Almost instantly, fire explodes outward from the totem, resisting my pull. I can feel my flesh charring, roasting, but I have no other option. I pull and squeeze harder, and it fights back harder. The golems break into a run, preparing to belly bump and crush me into smithereens.

And I give one last yank.

The totem suddenly breaks free, and the golem simply crumbles. I find myself amidst a great avalanche of rubble, sliding out at the feet of the second golem. He looks down at me, confused, and I throw the hammer upward with all my might.

Bong!

The hammer clips the head of the monster and snaps his head back, and he staggers backward for a brief moment. I glance down at the totem in my hand, finding it charred to dust, and let the ashes fall. My hand aches as I open my fingers, but I know I have to do it. Quickly, I stretch both hands skyward, reaching for the now falling hammer.

When the handle falls *smack* into my hands, the pain is worse than almost anything I've ever felt before. The golem, recovering from the hit, roars and thunders forward.

And so, with one last oomph of energy, I fling the hammer straight into his chest.

Stone explodes around the impact of the weapon, blasting

a great deal of rubble about. I don't see the hammer hit the totem, necessarily, but the whole thing crumbles to dust an instant later, and I let out a sigh of relief as I now turn and face Simon Magus.

"You . . . You fool!" he screeches. "You'll pay for this! Face the wrath of Simon Magus!"

He rises off the wall, hovering, and then dives. For dramatic effect, his cloak grows longer and longer, like a cape or the tail of a bird, and he spirals around the tower. I take a deep breath and draw out two of my daggers—I don't even look at which ones—and shove down the pain in my hands as he comes to stop just in front of the tower.

"Feel my—"

Wham!

A large stone lands smack on his head, smashing him into the ground. He groans as he slowly rises up, pushing the stone to the side.

"It'll take more than—"

Crash!

The peaked roof of the tower, admittedly somewhat rotted and crumbling, lands on the sorcerer next. There's a large blast of dust and rubble that rises up into the air, and Simon vanishes from sight. I blink in surprise, then look up as the rubble starts to shift and move.

SMASH!!!

An enormous, thirty-foot-tall lizardman lands on the rubble next, grinding pretty much all of it into gravel. Krak looks down at me and bows.

The growth formula seems to have worked a bit better than I thought. I hope that was the right move?

"I'd say so." I give a nod and smile. Krak starts to shrink, and a few moments later, has reverted to the size of a hatchling.

[You have leveled up!]

[Congratulations! You are now Level 23!]

I smile at the message, then hold out my hand. Krak races over and jumps up onto me, and I take a deep breath. With a rumble, another wall collapses, revealing a short path back to the original clearing where we came in. Without another word, I start striding forward, ready to get out of the dungeon.

It was a fun battle, in many ways, but . . . Well, a good meal and a bit of rest sounds rather nice. Not to mention the matter of getting paid and getting ready for the next fight. I quickly stride toward the portal, ready to be free . . . Ready to meet another satisfied customer.

CHAPTER TWENTY-THREE

The portal crackles and surges around me, and with that ordinary interdimensional straw-slurping action, I'm ejected back into the bank. I smile and look around and find Mr. O'Donald standing just in front of the vault, flanked by two security guards. I turn around to look back into the vault, and the portal flickers and closes a moment later. Inside, now, all I can see are a great many lockboxes, several of which have been pried open.

"Quickly, shut that!" Mr. O'Donald waves at the guards, and they slam the door closed so fast that the skin nearly gets taken off my nose. "I don't mean to be rude, but until we can do a proper inventory, I wouldn't want speculation to run rampant about what we may or may not have lost."

I can help with that, I think! Krak jumps down from my shoulder and starts to approach the banker. Both security guards immediately raise their guns, and he pauses.

"Wait." I hold up a hand, realizing that since they aren't

watching the live stream, they can't hear his voice. "He's not trying to attack. He says he can help with something."

The guards look at each other and, at a nod from Mr. O'Donald, lower their weapons. Krak dips his head, thankful, and opens up his own inventory. A few moments later, with a flicker of light, a large pile of paintings, jewelry boxes, documents, and other such items appears with a flash in front of the banker.

I found them in Simon's tower!

[DarkCynic: That's super cool!!!!]

[ShadowDancer: Krak for the win!!! What a good little lizard!]

[FireStorm: Is that the Mona Lisa??????]

[LunarEclipse: Nah, that's Starry Ni . . . Huh.]

"Apparently these were being hoarded by the final boss of the dungeon." I shrug. "I can't guarantee that they're all there, of course, but I do trust Krak with my life."

Mr. O'Donald's jaw drops open, and he bends down to hold out his hand. Krak shakes it gravely, and he slowly rises and gives me a nod.

"You truly were worth every penny. You can rest assured that I'll be giving you a full endorsement, both on the news when they come to interview me and in person to my other banker friends. We'll make sure that any other issues like this are referred to you, and you alone."

I give a bow in thanks, and one of the guards motions with his hand to head toward the front of the bank. I follow as he leads me up and out of the bank, practically seeing dollar signs dancing before my eyes.

[Private Message: FXR: Just saw you got through! Great

job, kid! You'll see the money in your bank account before you get back to the apartment. Speaking of which, I'm afraid I'm a bit busy at the moment. Tied up in some national security negotiations with the White House. You know how all that goes, I'm sure. Anyhow, it's almost lunchtime. If you want to get something to eat, I can have another assignment for you this afternoon. Cheers!]

I chuckle at the message and soon find myself on the street. The guard smiles and walks back inside, and I open up my pocket dimension.

"Alright, Krak. Probably best you went inside. Lightfax! I need you!"

Krak grumbles but goes back into the pocket dimension obediently. With a flash, Lightfax slowly steps out onto the street, her mane streaming behind her in the wind. I smile and climb up onto her back, and people around me all turn to stare.

"That's a good girl." I pat her neck. "Why don't you take me to Central Park?"

Lightfax dips her head, turns, and dashes through the streets. She stays on the sidewalk for a short time but detours into the road itself as we enter areas that are more and more packed with pedestrians. In the street, though, she's forced to contend with cars, none of which seem terribly delighted to be sharing the street with a horse. Nevertheless, she forges onward, and we soon come racing up to Central Park.

Now *this* place has changed. Once, it served as a refuge for the survivors of the initial wave of battles. Now, it's sort of just reverting back into a park. Nothing too ordinary about that, you know? The walls are still up, and there's a larger-than-normal number of homeless people camping about inside, but most people seem to have packed up and gone back into the city. As I canter through the entrance, I look about and catch sight of a familiar face.

The face I had hoped to see.

"Ali!" I smile as I trot over to her. She's sitting at a park bench with some other warriors, all women. As I approach, they all stand up and walk away, smiling and waving at Ali. I dismount and sit down across from her, and she smiles and gives a nod of her head.

"What can I do for you?" She beams. "I was hoping I'd get a chance to see you again, but I wasn't sure after I managed to heal Burnie, you know?"

"I've actually got a bit of a problem with Burnie again. Not necessarily why I came to see you, but . . ." I open up my inventory and pull out the still-frozen Burnie. Ali winces, then grimaces.

"I wish I could help you, but . . . he's not even reading as a creature anymore. He's *just* a block of ice." She sighs. "I wouldn't give up hope if I were you; I've seen crazier things in this world, but . . ."

I grimace, then slide Burnie back into my inventory. "I'll have him placed in a freezer until I have time to think about it more. Maybe this evening."

"Pass him to me." Ali holds out a hand. "I can go get him put away as soon as we're done talking. There's a veterinarian, an *actual* real-life veterinarian, who might have some ideas. In the meantime, you look hungry. Want some lunch?"

"I'd love some, but . . ." I flash an embarrassed sort of smile and stretch out my left hand. The blackened fingers are still quite charred, with bits of red flesh peeking out between the blackened skin. "I was hoping you might be able to help me heal this."

"Yow! I heard on the chat that you'd been injured, but I was hoping it was an exaggeration." Ali reaches over and takes my hand. "You do realize that I mainly work with animals, right? Not people And I'm not even technically a healer. I just know how to put them down."

I shrug. "Wars have always produced great advancements in medicine as people strive to learn to kill each other more effectively."

"Have you tried any healing items?" she asks, not really looking away from the hand.

"Not yet." I shake my hand. "The whole arm got beat up pretty bad. I want to make sure everything's set in place before I heal it, so I don't wind up healing something into the wrong shape."

"Not a bad idea," Ali murmurs softly. Quite suddenly, she reaches out and jabs me with a pin that appears in her hand, and I wince in pain. That seems to give her the information she needs, and she nods slowly and thoughtfully.

"Pretty much everything looks good. You've got a minor break in your . . . Well, one of the curvy bones in your arm. Your hand bones largely look good, though they're a little battered. No bone bruises, near as I can tell, and everything *seems* set in place." She pulls out a small spray bottle and applies some salve to the flesh. It starts to heal even in front of my eyes, and she gives a nod. "There! Good as new. Or at least it will be."

The hand starts to lighten up, and I smile in relief. A few

minutes later, Burnie has been carefully placed in Ali's inventory, and I've ordered some burgers from a nearby stand. We sigh and relax as we start eating, and I give her a nod.

"Who were those people earlier? Friends of yours?"

"That coalition I mentioned. Warriors who need housing," Ali shrugs, "at least some of the women. Mr. Wang told me to start spreading the word. He's willing to help, though he doesn't exactly know how, just yet, so . . . that's what I'm doing. A lot of people are interested. We're being kicked to the streets left and right."

"I'm really sorry to hear that." I sigh. "You know, you're always welcome to use the penthouse any time you want."

"Believe me when I say that I appreciate the offer, and I'll probably take you up on it at some point, but I don't want to abuse the privilege too much." She shrugs. "I go over there too much, and people will start to talk."

"Fair enough." I munch away on the last of my burger, then sigh in contentment. "Well, what do you have planned for the rest of the day?"

"There's a minor Rift forming a few blocks from here." Ali shrugs. "F-Ranked, nothing nearly as intense as what you went through, but a Rift nonetheless. I think it's set to open in a couple hours, so we're going to go take that on. You're welcome to come with us, if you want."

"That'll depend on what Mr. Wang has for me." I shrug. "I'm allowed to skip any assignment I want, but some of these dungeons *are* rather life-threatening. The bank dungeon was pretty harmless, but the one in the fish packing plant was a bit more deadly. Several workers had already walked inside, but I suppose you know that story."

"I've heard it, yeah." Ali crosses her arms, then pauses. "Do you mind if I ask you a question?"

"Go for it." I nod. I think I hear helicopter blades in the distance, which likely means that Mr. Wang's next arrival is imminent, but I ignore it for a moment.

"What are you going to do with all of this?" Ali holds up her hands. "Just keep fighting?"

"I don't know!" I laugh a bit. "This world only appeared a week ago or so. It could all vanish tomorrow, or this could be our permanent reality! Impossible to know for sure, you know? I don't have the faintest idea. I'm just . . . I don't know. Trying to make the world a better place, at least for the time being. I was chosen as a warrior, so that's what I'm going to do. Fight. If and when the necessity for fighting goes away . . . we'll see. And if it never does, I can always reevaluate my life in a month or so. Right now, though, this is what I enjoy doing, and I have a steady gig, so that's what I'm going to keep doing."

"Fair enough." Ali finishes the last of her burger, then rises. "Well, go have fun! I hope everything works out the way you're hoping it does. And I really will have my friend take a look at Burnie. I can't promise anything, but we'll sure try our best."

I give a nod and rise as well. The whir of copter blades grows louder and louder, and the vehicle comes down with a loud *whir* just a few dozen feet away. People finally seem to notice me and turn and pull out their phones to take pictures.

"Jason Lee!" Mr. Wang hops down from the helicopter and strides over to the two of us. "Ali Gordon! It's a pleasure to see the both of you alive and well."

"Thanks, I think." I hold out my hand, which he shakes. "I thought you were busy discussing—"

"Let's not discuss private chats in a place where everything you see and hear is broadcast to the public, eh?" Mr. Wang raises an eyebrow. "Now, if you please, I put up another bid, and I've got another job for you."

"I'll take it." I stretch a bit. "I can get the kinks from the last dungeon worked out on the way to the next one. What's the target?"

"Your client is the Empire State Building." Mr. Wang gives me a smile. "The payment is being handled by the general organization that oversees the building's tenants, but in truth, nearly five hundred of the businesses that operate out of the building voted on hiring you and provided funds to do so."

"Really?" I raise an eyebrow. "And what's the payment?"

"One billion, even." My jaw drops, and Mr. Wang turns slightly to Ali. "And if you come along with him, that goes up to a billion and a half. I happened to mention your housing woes to the right people, and since everyone loves a good sob story, if you're willing to venture inside, you'll receive the entire extra five hundred million. That's actually a higher amount than Jason himself will be getting."

My jaw drops even further. "And just what percentage of these deals are you taking?"

"Enough to live on, Jason, and giving you more than the same," Mr. Wang says to dismiss my concern. "Now, Ali, what do you say? I can't guarantee that this opportunity will crop up again. In fact, if you deny it now . . ."

Ali's face twitches. I know she'd rather be in the Rift with her friends, but I also know how desperately she wants to provide for people. "How strong is the dungeon?"

"I believe that it's a Rank C. The same as the Rift Jason took down at the Statue of Liberty."

My mind suddenly flashes back to the first dungeon I tackled for Mr. Wang, the fish packing plant. In that dungeon, I had to keep other people alive, and it was almost impossible. Here, Ali would actually want to fight. In a lot of ways, she *needed* to fight to show the people funding her new project—as well as the warriors themselves—that she was ready and willing to fight for them. That will make it even harder to keep her alive, I'm sure of that fact. That said, I know what her answer *has* to be. If she turns this down, she'll never get another chance like this.

"I accept." She gives a nod. "Jason will take care of me, I'm sure, but I'm also not half bad in a fight. I'll make it through alright."

[ChaosRider: THIS WILL BE THE MOST EPIC TEAM-UP EVER!!!]

[GoldenShield: John's worked with other warriors before, you know. Remember John?]

[ViperQueen: Yeah, but John's a melee type warrior too. She's ranged. Two different fighting styles, all working together!]

"Wonderful!" Mr. Wang claps his hands. "In that case, why don't you hop in the chopper? We'll have you over there in a jiffy!"

Ali wordlessly walks forward, and I can see the nervousness written all over her face. I don't know what her level is, but I do know it's quite a bit lower than my own. I'm going to have to take extra care, both to give her opportunities to shine as well as to keep her safe no matter the cost.

It's easily going to be the hardest dungeon I've yet entered—of that, I'm positive.

Of course, if it were easy, anyone would do it. Challenges are what keep me going nowadays. I enjoy what I do, and I'm ready to fight.

If it's hard, well . . . that will only make the joy of taking it all down that much sweeter.

CHAPTER TWENTY-FOUR

It only takes a few minutes for us to arrive at the Empire State Building. As we drift down through the sky to land in front of the structure, I sigh deeply. I know it's not the largest building in the world anymore, far from it, but it's just so iconic. Honestly, I sort of hope a giant monkey emerges from a dungeon at some point, simply because it would look so cool. Still, taking on a dungeon inside the building is nothing to sniff at, so I'm not complaining.

Traffic grinds to a stop as we come down for a landing. A long line of tourists wraps out the front door and around the building, and they all pull out their phones as Mr. Wang pulls the helicopter doors open, and the two of us hop out.

"You're going to do great!" Mr. Wang calls out over the roar of the helicopter blades. "I've got some more business to take care of, but I'll be watching you two, and I'll make sure I have a helicopter here when you guys come out! Go kick some monster butt!"

Mr. Wang makes a few excited fist pumps, then leaps back into the helicopter. He roars away in a blast of energy, and I chuckle and turn toward the entrance. The crowds part as we slowly walk inside, finding ourselves in the tall, broad entry area. The granite stone walls seem impeccable, utterly untouched by the chaos outside. An elevator nearby dings, and I see a man in a tattered suit stagger off, chased by a female aide who looks equally tattered. They stagger through the lobby, and Ali glances at me.

"How long have you known Mr. Wang, anyway?"

"As of right now," I check my watch, "twenty-four hours? Maybe twenty-six?"

Ali laughs. "He's certainly an energetic one, I gather."

"You can say that again." I nod and grin. "He's . . . I like him."

"I do too. Sometimes I wonder what will happen to him if this all ends." Ali smiles softly. "Will he just keep his spoils and retire? Will he find a way to leverage himself for another purpose? Will he do something else entirely?"

"Believe me when I say that I don't have the faintest idea." I laugh at the thought of Mr. Wang running around in a non-apocalyptic world. In any case, just a moment later, the man and woman reach us, and I hold out my hand.

"I presume you're the ones who will be guiding us to the dungeon?"

"Yes, indeed." The man gasps and wipes his forehead with a handkerchief. "Please excuse our appearance. I'm afraid things have been a *bit* wild. A giant eagle of some sort collided with the upper floors, and then a giant mole tunneled into the basement, and we got some giant rats in the offices of . . . some tech company. I'm afraid I can't remember which one."

"And don't forget the actual giant." The woman gives a nod and hands him a clipboard. "Here. I can take them the rest of the way. I got a text on the way down that there's an infestation of giant fleas in the offices of DogsN'Us, fiftieth floor."

"Those have been there since *long* before all this, but I'll go." The man gives a nod, then turns and rushes off. As he vanishes, the woman nods at the elevator.

"This way, please."

Ali and I follow her into the elevator. The bellboy there steps out, and she proceeds to type a code into the button panel, pressing the second floor, then the tenth, then the hundredth, and then a number of others. When she finishes, the elevator gives a lurch and starts rumbling downward, and she turns to face us.

"It sounds like you've had quite the morning." I try to sound energetic and upbeat.

The woman takes a deep breath, then nods. "Indeed. My name is Ms. Ferguson. I currently serve on the governing board for the entire tower. Since this all went down, I'm afraid that all of us have been working overtime to satisfy the needs of everyone who . . . well . . . really just everyone. The tower seems to be falling apart at the seams, near as I can tell."

"Well, hopefully this will help." I nod at the panel of buttons. "Are we heading to a secret basement?"

"Sub-basement ten, yes." Ms. Ferguson nods. "Not really secret, but highly classified. We'll be there in just . . . Here we go."

There's a ding, and the doors slide open. Ali and I step out and look around, and my eyes grow slightly wide. The basement is large, with a ceiling probably twenty feet high or so.

There are pipes and furnaces and air ducts and fuse boxes and all manner of other utility-type things scattered throughout the area. Of course, the primary focal point is the massive Rift sitting about fifty feet in front of us. It's broad, at least thirty feet, and the top of it seems to extend into the floor above.

"It…" Ms. Ferguson shrugs. "It actually extends two floors below and three floors above, but due to floor layouts, this is the easiest access point."

"We were told this was a dungeon." I glance over at Ali, whose eyes have gone wide. "This is a Rift."

"Is there a difference?" Ms. Ferguson blinks a few times and brushes some hair back out of her eyes. "It's a portal. You go through it and kill things, and so on."

I rub my jaw. Dungeons will sometimes spit out monsters when they first form, but after that, they typically just stay put and get in the way of things. Rifts, on the other hand, are much larger and have a tendency to spit things out.

"Well, it explains all the pest issues you're having," I answer after a moment.

"Do we need to increase our bid?" Ms. Ferguson sounds desperate. "I can go ask for more money. A few businesses were on the brink of donating to the fund, and I can probably squeeze a bit more out of some of the others."

"See what you can do. I'm sure Ali and the others could use it." I give her a nod. "In the meantime, I think we'll head in. This could take a while, so it'd be best if we can get a good start on it."

"As you wish."

Ms. Ferguson bows to us, then turns and walks out of the room. As she enters the elevator, the doors slide shut, and the car rumbles upward. I let out a long breath, then square my shoulders and face the Rift.

"Don't worry about a thing." I clap my hand down on Ali's shoulder. "We'll make it through. Just let me level up real quick, and we'll get on it."

"You haven't leveled up?" Ali turns to me.

I shrug. "Life's been a bit crazy since I exited the last dungeon. Let's see here . . ."

[Please accept from the following rewards:]

[Level D Weapon]

[Level D Monster]

[Monster Trainer Skill]

My chat immediately explodes with suggestions, but I glance at Ali. "Last time, I took a weapon. What should I take this time?"

"I don't know." Ali shakes her head. "I don't know that I should be . . . Well . . ." She shrugs. "I'm not really the one to make that sort of decision for you."

"Just give it a try!" I answer. "We're going to be in this together. What should I get?"

"Uhh . . ." She shrugs. "New . . . skill."

"You got it!" I nod. "Skill!"

[Skill Acquired!]

[Miniaturize: Shrink a target-tamed creature down to a fraction of its size.]

"What use is *that?*" I blink in surprise.

"Stealth?" Ali suggests. "I mean . . . maybe?"

"Just seems to me like it would make the target almost completely ineffective." I shrug. "Anyway, I suppose there's nothing to do about it. Shall we head inside?"

"After you."

I take a deep breath, then square my shoulders and face the crackling portal. Slowly, I draw out my Photonic Dagger and hold it in my left hand, placing my Diamond Dagger in my right. I bounce on the balls of my feet, then charge forward.

[ViperQueen: Go Jason!!!]

[ShadowDancer: Soloing a Rift! That's got to feel epic!!!]

[DarkCynic: He's not really soloing it.]

[LunarEclipse: I mean . . . Ali's good, but . . .]

[GoldenShield: Two of them together is still impressive!]

[DarkCynic: I'm not saying that it's not! I'm just saying he's not doing it solo.]

The argument in the chat continues for some time, but I mostly ignore it as I reach the portal and jump forward. I don't know why, but it's just sort of fun to jump through these things. I extend one of my feet forward, kind of like in those martial arts movies, and sail through the crackling energy with as much flair as I can manage.

Just like the last time I went through a Rift, the pain that explodes across me is *far* from pleasant. Lightning crackles up and down my body. It's like . . . Well . . . If going through a portal into a dungeon is like getting sucked through a straw, going through a Rift portal is like being sucked through one of those curly straws that you buy for kids—those ones that come up out of the cup and then wrap around the whole thing, and it's impossible to clean because there are so many bends. That's what this feels like. More or less.

Anyway, after shooting through the straw for a few moments, I get spit out the other side and find myself in a rocky cave. The ceiling is high and broad, while glowing crystals on the walls light up the area. I catch a glimpse of torches alongside the crystals, and my dagger blazes with light.

"*SCREEEEEEEE!*"

Something emerges from the darkness. Actually, several somethings. I spin toward them, taking them in as quickly as I can. Hobgoblins, I'm sure of it. Take an ordinary goblin, make it stooped over, and then add wings and fangs and longer claws. There are dozens of them, and they all scream and fly at me like a swarm of the ugliest locusts I've ever seen.

"*Screeeeeeeeeee* to you too!" I throw my Diamond Dagger into their midst, downing one, and then expand my Photonic Dagger into a sword and rush forward. The blade's light shines in the hobgoblins' eyes, and I slash forward.

The hobgoblins scream again as I dive into their midst, sword flashing and flaring. They're tough, but not so tough that my sword can't handle them. I cut off arms and legs, heads and wings, and body parts rain down around me. As I battle, though, they just keep coming. It seems like a whole hive of them, and with a *thump*, two substantially larger hobgoblins emerge from a hole in the roof and buzz down to land on the ground not far from me. These are equipped with large axes, and I grit my teeth.

"Alright, then! Time to show these things who the real master of this Rift is!"

I race forward, blade flashing like lightning, and cut through a dozen more of the monsters as I charge the two more advanced hobgoblins. They both cackle, then raise their axes to strike. Then, before I know what's happening, they *throw* the axes.

"Jason!"

Ali's voice cuts through the air, but I don't look away. I raise my sword and bat aside one of the axes, but I can't stop the second one from hitting me in the left leg. Pain flares through my whole body, it seems like, and the two larger monsters lumber forward, sensing blood. Well, probably just *seeing* blood, as a great deal of it is dripping down my leg. I snarl, then reach down, grab hold of the handle, and pull the weapon out.

"Here! You can have it back!"

I switch my sword to my left hand, draw back the axe, and fling it as hard as I can. It hits the closest larger hobgoblin in the face, and a loud *crack* echoes through the cavern. The thing stumbles and falls, but the second hobgoblin master spreads his wings and launches himself at me.

Wham!

His knobby, scratchy hands latch down on my arms, and his wings buzz furiously as he launches me into the air. I gasp as he takes me up to the top of the cavern, where he slams me quite forcefully—and rudely, I think—into the ceiling. I gasp with pain, and the thing cackles at me before drawing a rusty knife off his belt.

I grit my teeth, then smash my elbow into his face as hard as I can. It staggers the thing a bit, but he still hangs on and stabs me in the leg. The same one, I should add, that got hit by the axe. More pain lances through my body, and I fight to keep from screaming. Desperately, I grab the hand and hold it tight, preventing him from stabbing me again, and slowly, I start to bend his wrist.

Snick!
BOOM!

An arrow flashes past my neck and hits the hobgoblin in the air. He doesn't even have time to scream in pain before an explosion goes off inside his head, and we both plummet back to the floor. I crush another hobgoblin under my fall and climb back to my feet as Ali lets another arrow fly.

The hobgoblin horde is swarming upon her now, and she retreats, leaping up onto a small boulder with the agility of an elf. I take hold of my sword and lurch forward as quickly as I can, slashing and hacking at the monsters as I fight my way over to her. The hobgoblins around the boulder turn as I approach. Some of them flee, others lunge at me, but they leave her well enough alone.

"*Screee!*"

The scream echoes in my ear as another, smaller hobgoblin leaps onto my shoulder and sinks his fangs into my neck. I grit my teeth against the pain, and Ali adjusts her aim.

Snick!

Another arrow flashes past my ear and into the torso of the creature, and he slowly loses his grip and slides to the ground. With that, I spin around and decapitate three of the creatures in one blow, leaning against the stone for support.

The hobgoblins continue to come for the next several minutes until, finally, they slow and cease altogether. Ali shoots down the last few stragglers, and I sink to the ground. Blood—my blood—seeps across the stones. The hobgoblins weren't all that powerful, but there were so many of them. I start to notice other wounds as well, smaller ones that I hadn't even noticed at the time. Now, though, I feel as though my life itself is leaking out of me.

I have an entire Rift to get through, and already I feel as

though I'm getting beaten. If I'm going to beat this place, I need to buckle down. No mistakes. No errors.

I know I can do it. The only question is how much life I'll have left in me by the time I'm done.

CHAPTER TWENTY-FIVE

"Are you okay?" Ali rushes to my side and kneels down, looking at my assorted wounds.

"Peachy," I groan and open up my inventory. It takes me a moment to scroll through everything to what I'm looking for, and several bottles of Pumped! come tumbling down onto the ground. I grab a Grape version of the soda and chug it, watching as my skin heals over, and then take up a bottle of Lemon-Lime. As both energy drinks land in my stomach and churn rather uncomfortably, I groan and lean back, but my body heals, and my health bar ticks steadily upward.

"Do you seriously do *all* your healing with that stuff?" Ali raises an eyebrow.

"In fairness, I'd love some Pumped! hamburgers or fries, but it's been a while since I ran across a dungeon that had any." I grimace as the energy drinks churn once more, then fade away. "Healing items tend to be lower-level drops. I don't think I've picked up any in quite a while."

"Well, we're going to have to change that, if we get out of here alive." Ali holds out a hand and helps me to my feet. "Come on. We need to keep moving."

I glance around the area, locating a small exit. It's not large, maybe four feet in each dimension, and is covered in scratch marks. I grimace, then slip toward the exit and crouch down.

"So, quick question." I start slipping along through the narrow passage. There was a time when I wouldn't have batted an eye at such a crawl, but now, as my body physically enlarges from the powerful upgrades, I find that I can barely fit at all. "Just how many arrow types do you have?"

"Five," she answers quickly. "First is just a normal arrow. After that are exploding arrows. Those are fun but take a while to recharge once I use them up. Third would be penetrating arrows. They can shoot through a decent bit of damage resistance. Fourth are the bird arrows, like what Burnie shot down this morning. They're slower and don't deal quite as much damage, but you can use them to shoot around corners and things like that. Finally, I have soul arrows. They deal the same amount of damage as a normal arrow but can attack things like wraiths and ghosts. Incorporeal stuff."

"I could have used a couple of those earlier." I think back to the ice wraith in particular. "Well, if we encounter something like that now, I'll know that I don't need to run around looking like a fool anymore."

"Ahh, I'm sure you didn't look like a fool." Ali laughs softly.

"Don't be too . . ." My voice trails off, and I squint forward through the darkness. I can see a bit of light, and I carefully open up my portal just in front of me. "Krak, you're up."

Krak scampers out and runs back to my side.

What is it?

"I need to know what's ahead." I shrug. "Figured you might be able to give me a clue."

Krak nods, and in the darkness, I see him bend down and place his claws against the stone. His eyes flicker wide open, and he turns to look at me in amazement.

We're in a Rift, not a dungeon!

"That's right." I start creeping forward. "Is that a problem?"

Rift bosses are . . . mean.

"Do I detect a hint of jealousy," I raise a questioning eyebrow, "Krak?"

I tried for YEARS to get assigned to a Rift! Never was allowed.

Krak crosses his little arms and stomps forward, using his Shock Wave skill to make the tunnel rattle. I have to laugh as we continue to crawl forward, and soon, the tunnel widens into a small chamber. It's hardly large enough for Ali and me to crouch next to each other, but there, we're able to peer out into a larger, gloomy cavern.

There are a handful of torches flickering around the edge of the cavern, casting their pale light upon a large expanse of stone that looks something like Swiss cheese. The walls are pocked with nooks and crannies, and all across the floor, there are large domes that rise up, filled with the same. I can see things inside, but I can't quite tell what they are.

"Any ideas?" I glance down at Krak.

I've told you before, my perception is terrible. I can sense the odd thing about the location, such as the fact that we're in a Rift instead of a dungeon, and I know how to look for secrets, but that's a long way from actually being able to see through walls.

"Fair enough." I look over at Ali. "What about you?"

"I'm sensing a lot of bodies." Ali's voice is thoughtful. "At least one in each of those little nooks. If I had to guess, we're looking at a nesting ground of some sort. Hard to know for sure, but there are a *lot* of creatures in here."

"In that case, why don't you go light them up?" I nod forward. "Use an exploding arrow and hit that central one, and I'll follow behind. There will be a pretty good gap before anyone notices you're there, which will give you time to watch my back."

"Works for me."

Ali raises her bow and nocks an arrow. Krak scampers out of the way, and I draw out my sword, ready for whatever comes next.

When Ali lets her arrow fly, there's a brief pause and then a great flash of brilliant light. I find myself momentarily blinded and fight to keep from staggering backward. The shock wave hits me a moment later, thumping deep within my chest. As I regain my vision, I find a great deal of fire dying away and the interior of the chamber an absolute mess. Rubble rains down, body parts lay scattered, and I leap forward, holding my sword high as I lead the charge.

SCRAW!

A great *thump* echoes in front of me as one of the creatures launches itself from the walls and lands right in front of me. I find myself looking up at nothing other than a gargoyle, albeit a much larger and angrier looking one than the gargoyles I've fought previously. Smaller gargoyles stream out of the honeycomb and race away, and it suddenly dawns on me what we stumbled into.

"Wait. *Nesting* ground. This is a nursery!"

The baby gargoyles know enough to stream away. Meanwhile, the angry mama gargoyle lunges forward, claws raking through the air. She spins rapidly, her tail whistling as it slams into my body, lifts me clean off the ground, and smashes me quite forcefully into the wall nearby. I groan and look up as she charges forward, and I bring up my sword to block.

She slashes at me, and I do manage to block—just barely. That said, the effort bats me to the side, and I fight to keep my balance. Suddenly, fire wells up within the gargoyle's throat, and I remember some of the powers that Garg possessed.

FOOOOOOOM!!!

A great blast of flame and smoke rolls from the gargoyle, a great deal more than I'd ever seen Garg able to produce. I narrowly dodge out of the way, then charge the monster. I leap up into the air and slash my sword at her throat, and the blade connects with armored scales.

Clang!

The attack does almost no damage, and the sword actually falls from my grasp. As I land, the gargoyle raises a foot and stomps down at me, trying to smash me beneath *those* claws. I narrowly avoid that attack, but don't dodge the second strike, where she rakes me with the long claws coming off her hands. I'm knocked backward, bleeding down my arm, and grit my teeth.

"And you're not even a mini-boss! You're just a tank!" I pull out my Diamond Dagger and rush forward, then dodge to the side and leap up onto her back. She whacks me with her wings, but I do my best to shrug it off and grab hold of the monster at the base of said wings. As she flaps wildly, I pull back with all my might, forcing her to stand upright slightly.

"Ali! You're up!"

BOOOM!!

The explosion comes a moment later, hitting the gargoyle dead in the center of the chest. The monster is lifted off the ground and comes crashing down, directly on top of me. Scales and spines dig into my skin, and I wince in pain.

"Uhh . . . Maybe the armor-piercing ones?"

The gargoyle starts to roll, and I take a deep breath. We're not far from the wall, so I wait until she's righted herself. At that moment, I throw my weight at the wall as hard as I can, still holding onto her back. The thing wavers and stumbles, and as I get close enough, I let go with my left hand and grab hold of one of the nooks. There, for that moment, I hold the monster tight. She tries to stretch away, and my muscles strain as I keep her right there, in place.

Thwack-thwack-thwack-thwack-thwack-thwack!

Half a dozen arrows flash through the air and stick the thing like a pincushion. The gargoyle roars, then turns and stares at me with bloodshot, angry eyes.

"Uhh . . . Hello?"

FOOOOOOOOM!!!!

I lose my grip under the gargoyle's immense blast of flame, and as I stagger to my feet, I find the thing thundering across the room toward Ali. She, to her credit, doesn't panic and unleashes a flurry of arrows that stick through the thing's face. I grit my teeth and draw out my Diamond Dagger, along with my Shadow Dagger, and race forward.

"Krak, now would be a great time to chime in with any ideas!"

Krak doesn't give me anything, though, and I come up to

the back of the monster as she reaches Ali. I spring into the air and come down onto her back once again, driving my daggers into the gaps between her shoulder blades.

That makes the gargoyle howl, and she roars and staggers backward, spinning and batting her wings to swat at me. I smile as she turns her attention from Ali . . . but suddenly find her throwing herself backward against a nearby wall.

Crunch!

I suddenly find myself slammed between an immense, two-ton gargoyle and a great deal of thick wall. The stone crumbles around me, and tiny little fangs and fingers claw their way out, slashing at my shoulders and gnawing at my back. Dozens of small pinpricks flash up and down the length of my body. I cannot describe how much it hurts, and the gargoyle simply laughs. I have the feeling that she's feeding her young, and quite enjoying the fact that they're getting a good meal.

"All . . . right." I gasp out. "Guess we're doing this the hard way."

I yank out both daggers and, before she can do anything, plunge them into either side of her neck. She howls and presses back a bit harder, nearly crushing all my bones, but I hang on and drive my daggers a bit deeper into her throat. Blood, both my own and the gargoyle's, gushes down the front of the monster, and I take a deep breath.

"You . . . will . . ."

She slams her head backward once more, driving the last of the air from my lungs, and I snort, let go of the daggers, and wrap my arms around her neck in a great hug. Each hand latches onto the dagger opposite it, and with that, I pull as hard as I possibly can.

The two blades carve lines through the impossibly thick scales on the gargoyle's neck, and she staggers forward and collapses in a heap, dead before she hits the ground. I'm left in a pool of ooze on the back of the thing and slowly stagger to my feet.

"Are you alright?" Ali rushes out from cover to my side. I wave her back, looking at the assortment of smaller gargoyles still streaming out of their hatches and out through escape holes. She ignores me, though. "It's alright. Those are all a low enough level that they don't bother me."

"How . . . How did you fare there?" I gasp, slowly standing up and shaking my head to clear the cobwebs away.

"That thing was powerful. Rank B. Frankly, I'm surprised even you were able to kill it," she answers. "I . . . I couldn't affect it. All my skills that usually let me manipulate monsters, all their insides . . . They wouldn't work. It just kept telling me that the thing was too high of a level."

"And how powerful of a monster *can* you affect?" I ask as I check myself over. My wounds are already healing, thanks to the Pumped! that I took earlier.

"I think . . ." Her voice becomes quiet. "Rank D?"

"That's good to know." I sheath my daggers, then wipe off my hands and look around for an exit. There's a low archway on the other side, as well as a ladder of sorts, carved out of the stone by gargoyle claws, that leads straight upward. "Well, it looks like we have some options. Rifts are often a bit larger and have multiple paths you can take to get to the end. Any input on which way you want to go?"

[ChaosRider: Go straight!!! It's super dark and creepy!!!]

[IceQueen: No, go up! I bet the higher you get, the lower

the level of the monsters, which will make things easier for Ali!]

[DarkCynic: No, go down!]

I frown at the last comment and look around a bit for anywhere to go down. I find it after a few moments: a shadow that I almost didn't notice and likely would have mistaken for a simple hatching nook instead of an actual exit. Slowly, I walk over and kneel down, and Krak comes skittering over to my side.

"About time you showed up," I murmur, glancing at the little lizard. "And just where have you been?"

Sorry! I . . . I hid, and then I got distracted.

"Distracted with what?" A smile plays across my lips. "I don't suppose you found a secret horde of loot, or something like that?"

Not exactly. I . . . I was able to pick up some energy signals. Energy signals that I recognized.

"Is that so?" I smile at the small dungeon boss. "And what exactly are we talking about? A bomb, or a giant laser, or . . ."

I think I know the boss of this Rift.

Now that gives me pause. At the same moment, the chat explodes.

[ChaosRider: WHOA!!! That's super cool!!!]

[DarkCynic: Yeah! Krak will totally be able to know all the boss's weaknesses, and they'll just decimate him!]

[ShadowDancer: This is going to be the quickest Rift ever!]

"Generally, I would say that you knowing such a thing would be good." I pause. "Is that the case?"

That depends on how you define it.

"Is it going to be an easy fight?"

Far from it.

"Do you think we can win?"

Maybe?

I let out a long breath, then give a nod. "In that case . . ." I slowly rise up. "Maybe you had better tell us which way we should go."

CHAPTER TWENTY-SIX

Ali joins me near the tunnel that plunges downward. Meanwhile, Krak sits down and dangles his legs over the edge. His thoughts are projected to both of us, making it easier to have a conversation.

It's an old buddy of mine. We went back and forth. Sometimes I would be the superior; sometimes he would be. The last I heard of him he had just been promoted to dungeon boss in some bright, disgusting sort of overland dungeon. The assignment that none of us wanted.

"Then, if you're right and it is him, he somehow got promoted to a Rift boss." I stroke my chin. "What do you know about him? What is he?"

Krak sighs and shakes his head. *He's a troll, and a big one at that. He's slow, but he's incredibly powerful, and his damage threshold is extremely high. Trolls don't usually climb the ladder, so to speak, but he managed to rise above by infusing himself with magical crystals. The last I saw of him, he had crammed a fire crystal into his heart, making him both impervious to fire and able to generate infernos upon command. He's no one to mess with, and that's a fact.*

"What do we need to do to beat him, then?" I ask, my mind already whirling about how to take down a giant fire-troll.

Ali's skills would actually be incredibly useful if we could manage to raise her level a bit, even temporarily. Krak strokes his chin for a few long moments, seemingly lost in thought. *Rifts will usually have secret loot rooms, just like dungeons. Sometimes two or three. There's a specific magical item that's coming to my mind: a single-use item that will lower the requirements for a skill to work on an item or creature, or whatever.*

"Do you think we'd find that particular item hidden in here?" I ask, scarcely daring to hope.

Maybe. It has a pretty high drop rate, but of course, it's impossible to know for sure. The best thing I can do is take you to one of the loot rooms to see if we can find anything.

"Do you know how to get to the loot room here?" Ali looks at Krak as if he'd grown an extra head.

I can try. I know a few tricks. Krak stands up, and then points downward. *This is our best bet.*

"Then that's what we've got to do." I give a nod. "Lead the way."

Krak leaps into the hole without another word, vanishing into the darkness. I take a deep breath, then nod at Ali and jump down as well.

The darkness closes around me, and for a long moment, I simply hear the *whir* of walls that are altogether too close to me. The wind whistles in my ears, and then, without warning, I slam to the ground. I manage to tuck and roll, coming up out of it into a stance. Ali lands an instant later, and we look around.

The darkness thins a bit, letting me see a long, winding tunnel pocked with similar holes as what I noticed above. I transform my Photonic Dagger back into a sword, then slowly start to walk forward. Light comes from crystals jabbed into the ceiling, seemingly cemented in place using some sort of artificial sealant.

As we walk along, chittering noises begin to echo down the path, and Krak bends down and puts his head to the stone.

Yes! I do believe we're on the right path. This way!

He scampers onward, and I follow. Suddenly, I see shadows appear in the distance on the wall, and several hobgoblins walk into view. There are three of them, all of the larger variety. Then, behind them comes a fourth, one of even greater stature. All three of the "smaller" ones draw out hatchets, while the last one draws out a massive orcish war hammer.

"What is it with these hammers?" I scowl, readying myself. "I really, really hate fighting against hammers."

Ali raises her bow, nocking an arrow in the blink of an eye. "You ought to be more flexible, adapting your battle style as needed."

"I can adapt well enough." I shrug. "I'm not worried. I just don't like it. You want to open this party?"

"Sure."

Ali lets an arrow fly, and I race forward, pounding across the stone as fast as I can go. A massive explosion shakes the tunnel, filling it with fire and smoke, and with that, I leap into the midst of the monsters, jabbing with my sword as hard as I can.

By this point, I've pretty much accepted that slashing at the creatures won't do anything, but stabbing works more or less effectively. As the first of the hobgoblins emerges from the smoke, I slam the sword into his belly as hard as I can, and the sword sinks in all the way up to the hilt. The hobgoblin sways and gargles, and blood leaks out his mouth. I kick him hard in the gut, knocking him backward, and turn to the next one in line.

The second hobgoblin snarls and lunges forward, slashing with his hatchet. I duck backward, taking several steps back in rapid succession as he attacks. The third one joins in as well, chaining his attacks to that of the second. In the back, that last hobgoblin just stands there, watching . . . waiting. I don't know exactly what his plan is, but he's waiting on something, and I don't particularly like it.

In any event, the two smaller hobgoblins are giving me no quarter, pushing me steadily onward. When one of them pauses, the other attacks, making sure that I don't have any space to breathe. I quickly realize that if I keep getting pushed back, I'll eventually hit the wall, and . . . well . . . things aren't going to go well for me at that point.

"Ali! If you felt like shaking things up . . ."

There's a pause, and something flashes past my head and slams into the head of the hobgoblin on my right. No, not just the head. The eye. That girl is an *excellent* shot, there's no doubt about that. The hobgoblin rears backward, momentarily breaking the cycle. The other hobgoblin finishes his attack, momentarily over-extended, and I lunge forward, slamming my sword into his chest. The sword sinks in deep once again, and the hatchet falls to the ground with a clatter.

Before the hobgoblin with the arrow in his eye can recover, I bend down and scoop up the hatchet. With all my might, I spin and throw the weapon into the final smaller hobgoblin's chest. It doesn't penetrate very far, but it *does* break the skin, and the poor creature howls, drops his own hatchet, and throws himself at me.

I dive back out of the way, and the hobgoblin over-extends himself, exposing his back. I draw up my sword, flip it over, and stab it downward between the two wings. It sticks firmly between two vertebrae, refusing to budge another inch, and I let out a long breath.

"All . . . right." I brace myself, then draw back, pulling my sword out. The hobgoblin whirls faster than anything, snatches up another of the hatchets from the ground, and throws it at me. I respond accordingly, batting it out of the air with my sword, then come up to meet him as he launches himself at me like a bullet.

The two of us slam together with bone-crushing force. Something rather loud *crunches*, and I'm honestly not sure if it's me or him. In any case, I see something sharp and shiny protrude out his back, and I give a nod of satisfaction. He's dead—or will be within a few seconds. Slowly, I stagger back, pulling out my sword, and the hobgoblin sways, tilts, and comes crashing down on the ground.

A low chuffing noise echoes through the air, and I look up to find myself facing the final hobgoblin. He's so tall that his head scrapes the ceiling, and he smacks the hammer into his palm several times. Then, with blinding speed, he lunges forward, whirling like a top as he attempts to flatten me like a bug.

I duck, and the hammer *whooshes* over my head, so close

that I can feel the passing breeze. The hammer slams into the stone wall, sending cracks spiderwebbing across the nearby area, and he rips it out with extraordinary force. With that, he lifts the hammer high over his head and lunges forward again, bringing the weapon crashing down. I leap backward, narrowly avoiding the shock wave that rolls out from the point of impact.

"This guy . . . is . . . good," I pant as he rips the hammer out of the ground once more and slowly stalks forward.

[ChaosRider: You've got this, Jason! Just take him down like you do everything else!]

[DarkCynic: Try to get behind him! That seems to be where these things are the weakest!]

[ViperQueen: No, the belly! The belly!]

[LunarEclipse: I think you ought to try and throw one of the hatchets at it!]

The chat continues to suggest more and more solutions, and I shake my head. The hobgoblin lunges forward once more, then suddenly spreads his wings and blasts forward. Dust explodes up into the air behind him, and he slams into me an instant later. I'm driven to the ground with a rather extraordinary amount of force and groan as he passes me by and flashes off down the tunnel. Suddenly, though, I realize where he's headed and jump back to my feet.

"Ali!"

Ali draws back her bow and launches bolt after bolt into the face of the monster. She hits him in the eyes several times, then the nose and the mouth several times more. He drops to the ground and howls in pain but doesn't stop moving forward. Recovering from the surprise of it, I race forward.

Quickly, I draw out my Diamond Dagger, twirl it in my palm, and throw it as hard as I can. The blade cleaves through the air and slams into his back, right between his wings, and the monster yelps. The dagger sinks in about halfway—not as much as I'd like, but enough. He turns back to me, and I charge forward at the thing.

"*RRRRRRRARG!!!*"

His call echoes through the tunnel, and the monster throws his hammer at me. I'm caught utterly unawares and drop to the ground as it sails over my head, smashing into the ground not far behind. As I come up, I find the thing turning around and leaping into the alcove with Ali. She screams, followed by a loud *smack*.

With a loud crash, Ali is flung out of the entryway and lands on the ground not far from me. The hobgoblin appears once more, flying through the air again, and I duck out of the way as he flashes overhead. As he comes down for a landing, his claws bite through the stone, and he picks up the hammer once more and lunges forward.

Ali, on the ground, seems terrified. Her mouth opens in a silent scream as the hobgoblin sets his sights dead on her. He raises the hammer and starts to bring it down, and I do the only thing I can.

I step into its path.

I plant myself over top of Ali and raise my hands, catching the shaft of the weapon on my palms. The hammer is stopped, though I'm driven to my knees in the process. The hobgoblin snarls and snorts, scratching at the ground with his feet, and I slowly let out a long breath and force my way back upward, pushing the hammer higher along with me.

"You . . . will . . . not . . . hurt . . . her."

The hobgoblin snorts and tries to pull back, but I brace myself and yank. Not expecting it, the war hammer is pulled from his palms, and I grip the weapon with every last ounce of strength I have in me. Desperately, wildly, I swing it around and smash the thing into the face of the hobgoblin.

Bone crunches loudly under the impact, and he stumbles backward, quite injured. I don't pause but follow up the attack with another, this time swinging the hammer around me and throwing it into the monster. It hits the creature in the chest and knocks him backward into a wall, where the weapon drops to the ground. I rush forward, preparing my sword, and stab him deep in the gut. The blade can only penetrate about halfway, but I reckon that's enough.

My reckoning is proved wrong as the creature straightens and starts to pull backward. Quickly, I stab him again, this time in the chest. He howls, and I stab him again, then again. As he staggers and reels about, I take a deep breath, then bring the sword back and whack the creature's neck with all my might.

The blade doesn't sink in far, but it's enough, and blood spurts down his shoulders. Before he can recover, I draw the blade back, then strike again, then again. The blade flies fast and furious, and after half a dozen strikes, I'm gratified to see the head of the monster slowly fall off and land on the stone with a dull *thump*. The rest of the body follows an instant later, this time with an impossibly loud *crash*, and I wipe off my sword and sheath it.

"Are you alright?" I kneel down next to Ali, but she simply nods and sits up.

"He hit me, but not badly." She shakes her head and rises. "You know, I hate to say it, but it does get sort of old for every fight to end with one of us running to the other to ask if they're alright."

I have to laugh as I help Ali get steady. "Fair enough." I turn and give a nod down the tunnel. Krak sticks his head out from one of the little holes, and I square my shoulders. "It looks to me like Krak either found something or is waiting on us." I start off down the hall, then glance over my shoulder with a grin. "Let's make sure that the next fight ends differently, shall we?"

CHAPTER TWENTY-SEVEN

K rak leads Ali and I along through the winding passages. During the time we were fighting those three hobgoblins, he managed to figure out the pattern of the creatures, though I don't understand quite how. In any case, we duck into the little nooks at regular intervals and manage to slip along almost completely undetected as we make our way steadily toward the mysterious loot room that Krak is promising. I have to say I'm grateful for his help. I like fighting monsters, but these guys are tanks, and trying to protect Ali isn't the easiest thing in the world.

After half an hour or so of quietly working our way along, Krak brings us to a section of wall that seems slightly different. It doesn't have any of the holes present in the other rooms and almost seems made of a different material. Don't get me wrong, I'd likely have missed it altogether if Krak hadn't pointed it out, but once you saw it, you couldn't un-see it. I suppose I'm digressing. Anyway, Krak quickly climbs up the thing—it's made of a rough material filled with little places for his claws to latch onto—and starts pressing different knobs all along it. Light flares underneath the surface, and after a moment, he jumps down and gives a nod.

"And there we go!"

There's a rumble, and the door slowly grates inward, revealing a darkened tunnel. Torches flicker to life, and I climb inside. The tunnel isn't long, thankfully, and I soon reach the end to look out over the storage room.

[ShadowDancer: WHOA!!! That's really cool!!!!]

[DarkCynic: Yeah, but what sort of monster guards a place like this?]

[FireStorm: I'm sure we're about to find out!]

[RazorEdge: Jason is going to LOVE this!]

[ChaosRider: Yeah, but Ali is going to hate it.]

I have to laugh at that final comment as I slowly step through. I'm in a root cellar, a really big one. It must stretch for a hundred feet in front of me, maybe fifty feet on either side of me, and is a good thirty feet tall. Large wooden beams run up from the center of the floor to support the ceiling, but that isn't the best part. No, the best part is the shelves and the items resting atop them.

In one section, off to my right, I can see a large number of healing items: bandages, gauze pads, medicines, and other such things. Just to the left of that, there are some weapons and valuable loot, including gemstones and gold. Then, to the left of that, and filling the rest of the room, are a great, *great* many cans and bottles of Pumped!

To be sure, I've never seen so much Pumped! in one place before. There have to be hundreds of them, in more flavors than I'd ever dreamed existed. There are flavors that seem normal, like Orange, Strawberry, Cherry, and all the ones I already have. There are flavors that sound more than slightly outlandish, including BBQ, Ketchup, Pickle Relish, and Hot Dog. There are some that don't necessarily sound *terrible*, like Marshmallow and Chocolate, and there are some that I likely would only touch if I were desperate to survive, like Goblin Liver, Slime, and Octopus Eye. In any case, ignoring the last category, I quickly rush through, snatching up as many as I can stuff into my inventory.

"I know those taste good. Theoretically." Ali slowly walks into the room behind me. "They might heal you, but you're also still getting all the sugar and other gross stuff they put in there. You might wind up healing yourself, but you're only going to pack on the pounds. In a year, you'll have a full health bar and three hundred pounds of blubber to show for it."

"Meh. I make up for it by not eating real calories." I dump in a great many Cottage Cheese cans. It doesn't sound like the best combination to me, but I rather like Cottage Cheese, so I'm willing to give it a whirl.

"That's not how that works."

"Sure it is." I turn around and nod to Krak. "Now, why don't you show us what we're actually here looking for?"

It'll be right over here.

Krak scampers to the medical stuff that actually looks somewhat normal, and I follow. There, I find myself looking at a wide array of things that look like they belong in a hospital. None of it makes a great deal of sense to me, so I pull up a list of descriptions and start working my way through them all.

"Mmmm . . . Fill your health bar twice." I pick up a small bottle of pills. "That sounds useful."

"And look at this! More powerful projectiles!" Ali snags up a bottle of carrot pills. "As well as better perception!"

"Your perception already has to be close to S-Ranked." I mutter absently as I scan over the rest of the items.

"D, but I'll take it as a compliment." Ali smiles and bows, then crouches down. "Krak, is this it?"

Uhh . . . Yes! Krak bounces down to the bottom rack, where there are three small emergency medical kits. *They're loot boxes, of course, but they'll generate something pretty high level.*

"Alright, then." I nod to Ali. "Want to give it a whirl?"

Ali lets out a long breath, then reaches out and takes hold of the first one. There's a flash of light, and a small bottle appears in her hand.

"'Anti-aging pills.'" Ali blinks in amazement. "'For the elderly warrior. Feeling blue that you can't keep up with the rest of your squad? Then try one of these patented anti-aging pills! It'll turn back the clock ten years, guaranteed, for a duration of about a day. Taking a second pill will turn back the clock another ten years. Do not turn backward beyond zero. Side effects include more rapid aging after reversal, stomach pains, ulcers, cancer . . .'"

She stops reading, and I reach past her for the next kit. "We'll just try this one. Here goes nothing!"

With a flash of light, the second kit dissolves in my hand, and I find myself looking at a bottle of Amped! soda. I blink in surprise, then glance at the label.

"'When Pumped! just won't do, go for Amped! instead. Higher concentrations of health crystal, stamina crystal, sugar, and caffeine ensure that your health bar will increase to almost five times your ordinary health bar and that you'll be healed all the way as soon as you consume it!'"

The bottle is accompanied by a great many warnings and disclosures, but I tuck the bottle away without reading any further. Krak scampers up and reaches for the shelf.

Perhaps I should take a turn?

I don't object, and Krak quickly snags the lowest medical pack. There's one final burst of light, and in his hand, a small bottle takes form. He shakes it a few times, then tosses it to Ali.

Here you go! Just needed the magic touch!

Ali catches the bottle, then starts to read, "'All requirements for using and targeting skills, weapons, enchantments, and other such things are lowered by a significant margin. Duration: 15 minutes.'"

"Just long enough for a single boss fight," I murmur. "Interesting."

You might let me carry it for you, Master. Krak holds out his hands. *I don't know for sure, but it's possible that there will be scanners or detectors in place that would sense it. At that point, if it's within his power, the boss would simply make sure to raise his requirements to offset it. I mean, there are some things he can't do, like changing his own level, but he could shuffle around his minions, change up his attacks, that sort of thing. Not a necessity—you can carry it—but it might be what we need to sneak by.*

"That works for me." I nod to Ali. "What do you think?"

Ali pauses, then nods and tosses the small bottle down to Krak. "Keep it safe and give it to me as soon as we get into the room."

"Will do." Krak nods and turns. "Now, let's get—"
Boom!

There's a loud crash, and a creature drops down from the ceiling of the root cellar, passing through a trap door that I just didn't notice. It lands in front of the exit with a snarl and a thud and slowly rises up to look at us.

It's a minotaur.

The thing stands at least seven feet tall and is rippling with muscle. He carries a double-bladed axe, and steam and smoke drift out of his ears as he snarls and stamps his foot.

"I guess we're going to have to do this the hard way." I draw out my Shadow Dagger and give it a spin.

"Do we ever *not* do things the hard way?" Ali takes out her bow and steps backward.

"Without challenge, there's no glory." I shrug and throw the dagger as hard as I can. The weapon slams into his chest, and he snarls and charges forward, snorting and stamping his feet and sending up sparks from his hooves.

"I suppose that's one way to look at it." Ali fires a penetrating arrow into the right eye of the monster, making him stumble. Desperate, the minotaur changes direction and charges at me, lowering his head to gore me with his horns. I dive out of the way, and he crashes into a wall of Pumped! right behind me. Gouts of soda spew across the floor, the minotaur, and me, and I find myself soaked to the bone. Sticky, to be certain, and soaked.

"It's the only way of looking at it." I brace myself as the minotaur swings around. He lunges once more and swings a mighty fist but misses me by a mile. With that, he grabs his axe, twirls it, and lunges once more. This time, he overextends, and I'm easily able to sidestep as the weapon *thunks* down and sticks in the dirt floor below. With that, I flash my sword through the air, cutting off his head. "See? Not a problem. That was painfully easy. Hardly even worth a—"

Wham!

I'm driven to the ground as a second minotaur appears out of the darkness and smashes a fist into the side of my head. Where the first one had lost his depth perception with only one eye, this one still has both eyes fully intact and is more than capable of using them to his advantage. I'm hardly able to rise up off the floor before he kicks me in the ribs, knocking me sideways into another shelf. Gallons of Pumped! soda pour down across me, which—thankfully—raises my health bar—albeit not a great deal, given that I don't actually consume it—and gives me a handful of minor buffs. I rise back to my feet, dodge to the left as he throws another punch, and try to stab at him with my sword.

Which, of course, is when I notice that it's lying on the ground on the other side of the room.

Quickly, as this minotaur draws out a battle axe, I dive forward, and he narrowly slices over my head. I can feel the breeze of the weapon going just over my back. As I come up, he snorts and charges, and I desperately climb to my feet and draw out my Shadow Dagger.

"Heads up!"

I blink, and an arrow flashes past my head, so close that I'm pretty sure it shaves a few hairs off. The arrow sticks firmly in the face of the minotaur, right between his eyes, and he bellows and staggers backward. I spin and stab him in the gut several times with my dagger, then step back and throw the weapon into his neck. The minotaur gargles and reaches up to grab hold of his throat, staggers once more, and falls to his knees.

"Wait," Ali calls out as I start to walk toward it. "I've got it."

"Alright." I take a step back. "Go for it."

Ali nods, then draws back her bow once more. The minotaur snorts and starts to rise, and she fires an arrow straight into his heart. That staggers him, though he takes three more arrows—all to the heart—before he slowly topples to the side and lands with a *thud*.

"Sorry." She lowers her bow and shrugs. "I thought it would give the fans something to cheer for."

"I'm not complaining." I shrug as I walk over and retrieve my sword, then glance around the room. Most of the loot items have been destroyed now, though there are still a few odds and ends lying about. I grab a few more cans of Pumped!, snag a few of the actual medical supplies, and then nod to Krak, who had hidden himself up on the top shelf behind a gallon jug of Pumped! drink. "Alright. If we have what we came for, I think it's high time we got moving."

Then I shall lead the way. Krak hops down and lands on the ground, somersaulting forward as he does so. *I've been listening and watching, and I'm pretty sure I know how to get us there. This guy . . . He always does things in a predictable manner. Makes me wonder why he got the job instead of me, but I suppose it's who you know, not what you know. He was always good friends with that trickster guy, which probably made him good for a promotion or two.*

I don't have a clue what Krak is talking about, but by this point, I've pretty much decided that I don't want to know. Ali and I fall in step behind him, and we follow as he leads us out into the tunnel once again.

We're on the move, on the hunt for the Rift boss. Once Krak takes us to him, well . . . all we'll have to do is cut him down.

CHAPTER TWENTY-EIGHT

K rak skitters to the entrance of the tunnels once more. I follow closely, and Ali comes up just behind me. We pause in the entry way and peer out but see nothing. If there are any patrols in the area, they're lying in wait. Krak presses his ear to the ground, as if to search out that very thing, then lifts his ear and nods.

We're safe. Come on! It won't be long now.

I nod and come after him as he enters the hall and turns to our left. From here, the tunnel becomes shorter, so much so that I have to stoop over. The walls become rougher and more jagged, with the glowing crystals often scratching along my arms and legs. As we make our way along, the chat begins to fill with speculation.

[RazorEdge: I bet he's going to have to crawl through a pit of slime to get to the boss room!]

[LunarEclipse: Nah, they're totally going to have to go through a snake pit!]

[IceQueen: The final boss is a troll, so maybe there will be an army of golems or something standing in the way.]

I chuckle a bit at the chat but mostly ignore it. Krak drops to all fours and moves in bursts now, flashing forward a dozen feet and then stopping, only to turn and dart to one side of the path, then the other. Finally, he comes up to a small, darkened hole that I might have crawled past entirely.

Through here.

He vanishes into the darkness, and I lay down to crawl through. My shoulders have grown so wide that I barely fit, but I do my best to wiggle after him. "How does he expect anyone to get to him if *this* is the way to his boss chamber?"

This is what you might call a shortcut! It will lead us there in . . . well . . . right about . . .

A loud *crack* echoes through the air, and I feel the ground underneath me starting to crumble. Frantically, I start trying to back up, but Ali is already in the tunnel, preventing that from happening. The floor gives way, and all three of us tumble down into a vast, open space.

A *wet* space.

We fall through the top of a massive cave ceiling, and for a moment, I find myself looking upon what seems to be a subterranean lake. The cavern is vast, hundreds of feet long in every direction, and is marked by small islands here and there. Thankfully, and probably by design, one of the small chunks of stone is located directly beneath us, and we land with a loud *thud*. I, of course, form the cushion that both Ali and Krak land upon. We all groan and climb back to our feet, and I take a good, long look around.

We're near the start of the chamber, far as I can tell. The

islands, dozens of them, are strung out in a long chain, leading from one side of the lake to the other. There are two islands between us and a large, gaping cave, through which I can see a number of trolls marching back and forth. Stretching out in the other direction, the rest of the islands lead to a massive set of iron doors engraved with an angry-looking face. The boss chamber.

"So, all we have to do is get from one side of this lake to the other?" Ali draws out her bow and nocks an arrow. "Seems easy enough."

You do realize that there are monsters in the water, right? Krak leaps up onto her shoulders, then perches on her head. *And unless your legs are a lot more powerful than I give them credit for, you're not going to be able to jump from one island to the next.*

I grimace as I notice that he's right. The islands are a good twenty, maybe even thirty, feet apart. If I had room to back up and take a good run at it, I could probably make some of the jumps, but even I would be hard pressed to make most of them, and Ali's level is a good bit lower than mine. The question then becomes . . . just how are we intended to cross?

"I assume there's a way to get there, then." I glance down at Krak. "My guess is that dungeon and Rift bosses are prevented from creating an impossible scenario."

Technically, no, but . . . Well . . . it's complicated. Krak leaps down from Ali's head and paces up to the water. He dips a toe into the drink, then pulls it back out. *If I had to guess, there's probably a hidden boat somewhere along the main path that we could have found if we had been patient.*

"And whose fault is *that?*" Ali glares down at him.

I'm sure we shouldn't put blame on anyone. Now . . . Krak crosses his arms. *I would say that you'll just have to swim. Quickly.*

I take a deep breath and nod, slowly taking a few steps back. I bounce on the balls of my feet to take a running start, at least as much as I can manage, but Ali holds up a hand.

"One moment, first." A small grin comes across her face. "Have you ever heard of blast fishing?"

I shake my head. "What's that?"

"Most commonly attributed to rednecks, it's a practice that actually still takes place around the world." Ali draws back her bow and aims the arrow down into the water. "Hold on tight, please."

She lets the arrow fly, and it streaks into the depths of the pool. There's a brief pause, followed by a massive, though muffled, *BOOM!* Fire and light flare up beneath the waves, though the only things that reach the surface are a few bubbles. A moment passes, and a great many large fish bob to the surface as well, dead or stunned. Krak reaches out and grabs one, holding it up to examine the thing.

Piranhas!

"Good to know!" With that, I race forward and leap into the air, sailing out across the water. I come down about ten feet short of the next island, and swim quickly through the school of dead—or at least stunned—fish, and soon splash up onto the shore. As I do, Ali jumps as well, along with Krak. I make sure they're okay, then race to the next island.

By the time I get to the next island, the waters are starting to churn, and I draw up short as a tentacle—not a big one, thankfully—erupts from the water between this island and the one beyond it. I bounce on the balls of my feet as Ali and Krak join me. In addition to the tentacles, I see several more piranhas swimming up as well. They don't look quite like normal piranhas, to be certain. They're quite a bit bigger and have a lot more teeth. More like barracudas, really. In any event, they look quite hungry, and I'm made of meat.

"Another blast charge, please." I glance over at Ali, who nocks an arrow.

"With pleasure."

She fires another bolt into the depths, and another boom shakes the cave. Dozens more piranhas float to the surface, and the tentacle flops limp. The three of us begin frantically making our way along the deadly stepping stones. Ali continues to let off more blasts every couple islands, stunning the fish and tentacles, and I have to admit, I'm surprised as we make fairly good time. Soon, though, we come up to one final stretch, three more islands left, and Ali grimaces.

"Out of exploding arrows?" I venture.

"Yeah." She nods. "I'll generate more in a couple hours, but that doesn't help us here and now."

[ShadowDancer: Poison the waters! That seems like it would work!]

[IceQueen: They don't have poison, unless they've picked up drops without the live stream seeing it.]

[LunarEclipse: Besides, if they poison the waters, they'll poison *themselves* when they get in it!]

[ShadowDancer: Oh. Right. Umm . . . Electricity?]

I laugh at the last one, and bend down. "First off, electricity will only work against the piranhas. Octopuses are resistant to it, remember? Secondly, I don't exactly have a way to generate electricity." I take a deep breath, then nod. "We'll just have to hitch a ride."

"What exactly do you mean by that?" Ali asks quietly, a hint of nervousness in her voice. I have to give her credit; she hides her fear well, though I can tell that she has a good hint for what I'm about to do.

"I mean . . ." I slowly take a step out into the pool onto a rock just below the water's surface. "I'm calling up someone to help us."

The water swirls all around me. Dozens of the toothy fish swarm up to eat me, but before they can get there, several tentacles explode upward from the depths. I brace myself and step back onto land as two great, slimy tentacles erupt from the water and latch down around my arms. A third wraps around my right leg, and I grit my teeth.

"Alright, kraken! Octopus! Whatever you are . . ." I start to pull with all my might. "Time . . . to . . . come out!"

I start walking backward, slowly and surely. For a moment, the underwater creature and I strain against one another. I fight to drag it up from the depths; it fights to pull me down. I take a deep breath and pull it backward one more step, then another.

Master? I'm a bit confused as to how exactly this will help us.

"Just you wait." I smile grimly. "This . . . is," I let out a long breath, "not nearly as easy as it looks."

With one mighty heave, I take two more steps backward, and the body of the beast is dragged up into view. The great, fleshy bulk of the creature seems to be about five feet across, give or take a few inches. Tentacles writhe about the surface of the water as it fights to get free, and I give it one last tug.

The creature is pulled up onto the island, and with that, it lunges forward at me, abandoning its plan to drag me into the depths. Ali and Krak both step back out of the way, and I ball my hand into a fist and lunge forward to meet it. We come together in the middle of the small island, human skin meeting octopus-fish.

WHAM!

It's hard to describe that conflict precisely. Tentacles wrap all around me, lashing at my face and tearing at my skin. The great beak of the creature chomps down on my arm, and I grit my teeth to avoid hollering in pain. I punch the creature between the eyes, just as hard as I can, and it reels back slightly.

"Skill: Monster Trainer."

Energy wells up in my palm, and the octopus suddenly realizes its precarious state. It turns to try and escape, but the surge of energy pours across it an instant later. It freezes in its tracks, and the familiar messages begin to appear.

[Giant Octopus is resisting your efforts to tame it.]

"I know, I know," I murmur as I pour a bit more effort into the stream of energy. It sounds weird, but I can imagine a prompt like "Push B" appearing in the air, and I rather wish that I had a button I could push incessantly just for the sake of feeling like I was doing something more.

[Giant Octopus is still resisting your efforts to tame it.]

"Yeah, yeah." I let out a long breath. "Just . . ."

[Giant Octopus has successfully resisted.]

"What?" I blink in surprise. That's never happened before. "What does that—"

Crunch!

The thing jumps upon me once more. Caught off guard, I'm smashed back against the ground, groaning in pain as it wraps all its tentacles around me and begins to squeeze. The beak tears at my chest, ripping through my shirt, and I bite my lip. The pain is extraordinary, and I take a deep breath and elbow the creature with all my might. Being a blubbery blob of flesh, the action doesn't do much, save to make a little ripple flicker across its body.

And then, suddenly, it goes still.

[Skill: Random Strikes has randomly tamed a Kraken.]

"A what?" I blink in surprise. The octopus quickly lets go of me and scrambles to escape, but it's too late. A much larger tentacle erupts from the water and snatches up the octopus, then vanishes back into the depths, dragging the creature along with it. The water turns inky black . . . And then a great tentacle floats up to the surface, forming a bridge between the island where I'm standing and the next one.

"I . . . Thank you." I dip my head and slowly step out onto the tentacle. It's about a foot wide, which isn't the *easiest* thing to walk on, but I make do.

You are welcome, Master. The voice is deep and resonant. *Allow me to serve you however I can.*

"I will certainly do so." I nod as I reach the next island. Another tentacle rises up to connect that particular island to the next one, and I make my way down *that* path as well. "I don't suppose you know anything about this particular boss that would help us?"

I'm afraid I'm rather new here. I was just transferred from a jungle dungeon after the boss was taken down by a group of humans.

"That's alright." I come up to the small stone platform just in front of the door, reach out, and press my palm against the metal. There's a rumble, and it slowly swings inward. "Can you find your way into my pocket dimension?"

I can! Let me know if you need anything at all, Master.

With that, as Ali and Krak step off the makeshift path, the tentacle sinks back into the water with a ripple. I glance at the other two, then shrug.

"Not exactly what I intended, but I'm pretty happy with that result."

"I'm not complaining. It looks epic, in any case." Ali takes out her bow and nods forward, into the darkness of the boss chamber. "Well, shall we?"

I glance down at Krak, who's eagerly staring ahead. "Are you ready to meet up with an old friend?"

Krak gives a quick nod of his head, and he scampers forward. *Yes, Master. I most certainly am.*

CHAPTER TWENTY-NINE

A s we enter the chamber, the doors slowly swing closed behind us. They slam together with a hollow boom that echoes over and over and over, and slowly, lights begin to come on. First, a dozen flickering torches light up the area, revealing a large, domed sort of cave a hundred feet long on any side. There are hundreds of crystals set in the walls, which begin to glow as well after a few moments of only the torches burning. The floor is uneven and scattered with a great many boulders and stones and such things. Really, it looks like sort of a mess, and Krak seems to agree.

I still don't get it! This place is a disaster. No reason he should have been given this assignment. I suppose some people just have everything, and others just don't.

I snort. "You know, you *are* tamed now. You don't have to keep lamenting about how poorly you were treated when you were still a dungeon boss."

Hey! I'm sure you still have grievances from whatever you used

*to do before this whole apocalypse kicked off for you. Doesn't nec-
essarily mean I want to go back to it. Just means that I feel like
I would have been more qualified for certain promotions than I
was given credit for.*

"Fair enough." I chuckle as I look around the room.
There's a large pile of rocks near the back of the chamber that
I suspect is likely the troll we'll be fighting, but it's hard to
know for sure. "Well, Krak, what should we do to ensure that
we take this guy down?"

As if in answer to my question, the aforementioned pile of
rocks begins to rumble and shake. Slowly, it starts to rise . . .
Or rather, something underneath it rises up. Stones comes
crashing to the ground, and a few moments later, I find myself
looking at a massive troll. It's a good forty feet tall, at the
least, and has not one but *two* crystals planted firmly in its
chest. One is red, and through cracks in the tough skin, a
fiery energy seems to radiate outward rather like blood vessels.
Right next to it, though, is a blue crystal, and more streams of
energy crackle out in the other direction. This thing is a beast,
that's for sure, and I draw out my sword and take my stance.

"Krak!" The voice is low and deep, and the troll thumps its
chest. "I thought that was you! I'd know your smell anywhere."

*Tornak! It's been a while! Last time I saw you, you were sink-
ing down into the depths of a swamp after you got punched by
an orc!*

"As I recall, I asked you for help, and you let me sink." The
troll, Tornak, scowls down at Krak.

*Can you blame me? You must have weighed three tons, and you
don't exactly need to breathe. I knew you'd get out. I wasn't going
to be able to help you, and I do need a bit of air now and again.*

"Fair." Tornak thumps his chest again. "It's good to see you, Krak." He turns toward Ali and me. "So, what have you brought me to eat today?"

I flash a smile and lift the sword. "He hasn't brought you anything to eat. He's with me."

"Working with humans?" Tornak begins to laugh. The deep, booming noise echoes throughout the room like a series of thunderclaps. "No, no! You've got it all wrong!" He slaps his thigh, then shakes his head. "You're a beast tamer! Did you . . . Did you actually think you had *tamed* him?"

I glance over at Ali, whose face is becoming rather terrified. I frankly can't say that I blame her.

"Uhh . . . Yes." I nod. "He's been very helpful."

"He led you right to me!" Tornak continues to laugh. "I mean . . . you should know," he can barely speak around his laughter, "bosses are immune to taming! It's one of the best perks of getting this sort of gig! He probably just sent you a private message that said that he had been tamed, or something like that, and then has been playing along ever since!"

I even got him to heal me after he cut off my head. Krak flashes along the ground, and Ali lets off an arrow, which he narrowly dodges. He reaches Tornak's leg and climbs up to the shoulder of the great troll. *And give me some medicines . . . and a potion that will cause me to grow . . . and some dragon eggs . . .*

Krak suddenly opens his inventory and pulls out the bottle of pills that we had procured for Ali. He gulps them all down, then pulls out a large flask full of a purplish liquid—my mind flashes back to the tower where I fought Simon—and he gulps that down as well. With that, he jumps down from Tornak's shoulder, growing nearly to his former size in the blink of an eye. The ground shakes under the impact, and he tilts his head from side to side, cracking his neck.

"Krak?" I take a step back. "Don't do this. You have a chance to join our side."

"And why would I?" Krak speaks out loud for the first time, likely due to his vocal cords coming in. "You come into our home, you kill all our people, you use us for sport and mount our heads on your walls, and you proudly display the very items that you use to kill us. I'm not the evil one here, and it's time that I—we—eliminated this particular threat to our world."

[ChaosRider: AHHHHHH! I did NOT see this coming!]

[RazorEdge: I sorta did.]

[GrendleH8tr: Stay solid and you'll get through this. Don't get excited.]

[Originalgoth: HAHAHAHA!!! BURN!!!!!]

I glance over at Ali, but we're given no time to put together any sort of a plan. A massive sword appears in Krak's hands, and he lunges forward, slashing down at me with all his might. At the same time, Tornak's crystals flare up, and he claps his hands.

FOOOZZZZZZZAK!!!

A blast of fire mixed with lightning erupts across the battle arena. I really can't stress enough just how awful this particular scene is: a great ball of fire flickering with lightning erupting all around the inside. Positively terrifying, I can assure you of that. Anyway, I dive out of the way of Krak's blade, get picked up by the shock wave of the impact, and wind up being thrown right into the path of Tornak's attack. Fire and lightning course all around me, and I'm blasted into a nearby wall hard enough to crack the stone.

"Ow." I slide to the ground and take my stance once more. The electricity is still making my limbs twitch, and my clothes—what's left of them, at least—are smoking from the intense heat. "This is going to be rough. I can sense it now."

I spare a single glance at Ali, who's frantically hiding behind some of the rocks, and charge forward. I have to keep the monsters away from her, that much I know. Krak slashes out with his sword again, trying to drive me toward Tornak. Instead of obeying, I fall flat on my face, allowing the weapon to pass harmlessly over me, and then leap to my feet and charge at him once again. He lets out a hiss and lifts a foot to try and stomp on me, and I leap into the air.

Crash!

The foot comes down and sends out a shock wave, a powerful one, but I pass harmlessly over it. When I come down, I leap at the lizardman, stabbing the weapon deep into his calf. To his credit, he doesn't scream but simply bends down and slashes at me with his massive, oversized claws. I'm batted aside rather easily and slam into a nearby wall. My sword remains lodged in his leg, though it doesn't seem to bother him too much.

"Pathetic human." Tornak turns around and throws a punch at me. I dodge out of the way. Fire and lightning explode outward from the point of impact, blasting me to the ground. I hear something whistling through the air and roll out of the way as fast as possible.

Wham!

Krak's sword catches me right in the gut, and I'm lifted off the ground and flung across the cave, where I smash into a wall once more. This time, as I fall to the ground, I hear something snap inside of me. Unfortunately, I'm given no time to think about it, as Tornak thunders forward, bounding across the ground with more agility than I really think is proper for a troll to have.

"Die, human!"

"Die, troll!" I draw out my Diamond Dagger and fling it up at the creature. It hits him in the neck but merely sticks in the rolls of blubber there. He lifts his foot and stomps down just in front of me, so the shock wave blasts me back into the wall. He follows it with a killer punch, his fist the size of my entire body, crackling and brimming with both fire and electricity.

Desperate, I launch myself upward, and the fist slams into the wall just beneath me. Once more, I'm caught in the resulting explosion and come down with a *thud* not far from Ali, who is holding an arrow in her hands and looking at it rather intently.

"Something wrong?" I groan as I slowly stand back up.

"Not exactly," Ali murmurs and shakes her head. "I have an idea. I can't say for sure that it'll work, but it's the best solution I can see."

"Hit me with it." I smile and nod. "Long shots are some of the best shots. And these guys are . . . tough."

"Then take this." Ali hands me the arrow, then her bow. "It's true my power level is too low for some of my skills to work on such high-level monsters. *However*, I do have an ability to infuse a skill or effect into a plain arrow. At that point, if *you* fire it . . ."

"I might be able to make it work." I give a nod and stand up. "Like you said, worth a shot."

Krak lunges forward before I have a chance to take aim, and I'm forced to dive to the side. Ali screams as the sword smashes the rock she was hiding behind. I race to the side, pounding toward an open line of sight, while Ali simply flees for more cover.

"That won't help you!" Krak gloats. He lifts a foot and stomps down, sending out a massive shock wave that pulverizes a great many of the stones. Ali is knocked to the ground and groans as she sits back up. "You're dead meat, girl!"

I grit my teeth, then sling the bow onto my back as Krak approaches Ali. Tornak turns toward me, and I know he'll flatten me the moment he gets a chance, but I have to save Ali before I can deal with him. Quickly, I race for Krak, dodge another blast from Tornak, and jump upward.

Krak's clothes, as he grew, grew with him. I snag the hem of his loincloth, brace myself, and swing up onto the base of his tail. There, I draw out my Shadow Dagger and stab it into the base of his spine, cutting between two vertebrae, and he howls in pain and draws up short, staggering a bit. An instant later, Tornak lunges forward to try and hit me, and I leap out of the way. Tornak's fist hits Krak and blasts him into a wall, and I chuckle.

"Now why," Krak turns around, hissing, "did you do that?"

"Accident." Tornak shrugs, though I get the feeling that the troll didn't exactly mind the attack. "Come on. These guys are almost dead."

I quickly try to fit the arrow to the string, but I'm not exactly used to shooting bows and arrows, so I'm not able to get it before the two of them are upon me. I turn and race back out of the way as they lunge forward, punching, slashing, and launching blasts of fire and magic at me. I don't see Ali anymore, so I hope she's alright. Without any other options, I back up, and Krak lunges forward one more time.

This time, as the overhand strike hits home, I jump forward and race up the sword. Krak seems as surprised as I am, and I quickly reach his shoulders and jump around behind his head. There, I draw out my light sword, change it into a dagger, and drive *that* between the bones of his neck right at the base of his skull. He howls and falls to his knees, and I turn to Tornak.

BLAM!

I'm hit full force by his massive fist and am launched backward with all the speed and might that the troll can manage. My health bar drops to a sliver of what it once was, and I glimpse the wall flashing toward me at an impossible speed. A single thought goes through my mind, and I stretch out a hand.

Splat.

A tentacle wraps around my wrist, and I come up just a few feet short of hitting the wall. Down on the floor, my pocket dimension crackles and flickers with my Kraken's tentacle sticking out. I drop back to the ground, and the tentacle sucks itself back inside as it closes.

"That's—"

With a *slurp,* the portal opens again just above my head, and another tentacle reaches out and grabs me. I have a moment to think about it before it tosses me into the air, up over the heads of the two monsters. I come down on Tornak's back, where I grab hold of his knobby flesh. Almost instantly, fire and lightning explode up and down my body, and I grit my teeth.

"I . . . will . . . not . . . fall!"

With that, I open up my inventory and pull out Ali's arrow. I don't really have time to figure out how to shoot it, but I can certainly just jab it into the beast. I slam it into his back as hard as I can, then let go and fall to the ground.

[Skill: Fusion.]

[Would you like to fuse together part of this monster's body?]

"Yes!" I nod as a diagram appears in front of me. I don't really have time to look it over, but I know from experience what I need to do. "The lightning crystal! Fuse it into his heart!"

There's a pause, and a blast of lightning flares through the cave. It arcs from crystal to crystal, from Tornak to Krak, and everyone inside screams in momentary pain. As the chaos dies down, Tornak turns to face me.

"You'll pay for that! You've made me more powerful than ever!"

Lightning flares down his arms and legs, through his chest, and in his eyes. I take a deep breath, then issue one more command.

"Kraken? I could use you right about now."

My pocket dimension opens, and a great many tentacles swirl out, forming a Faraday cage around me. Another tentacle snakes across the cave, snags Ali, and drops her inside as well.

Lightning seems to split the air itself, resounding here and there and everywhere. Here inside our cage, though, Ali and I are perfectly safe.

"Told you that octopuses are resistant to electricity." I glance at Ali with a smile.

"I never doubted you for a second."

Outside the cage, Tornak is starting to shake. He seems to have lost control of the attack, of the blast, and falls to his knees. His flesh blackens and cracks, exposing veins of pure, crackling energy beneath . . .

And with that, he explodes.

A great many sparks shower through the room, along with bits and pieces of ash. The tentacles all withdraw, and Ali and I stand back up.

"I . . . Wow," Ali whispers. "That was cool."

"And, unfortunately for Burnie, I never would have known it was possible without his sacrifice." I sigh, then turn toward Krak, who's lying not far from there. He groans and starts to rise, only to start shrinking. A few moments later, he's returned to his hatchling size, and Ali and I stand over him. I pull out my sword and press it against his throat, and he winces.

"Give me one good reason why I shouldn't kill you, right here, right now."

"Human sentiment!" His voice is high-pitched and squeaky, but he seems to prefer it to the telepathic speech I'm used to hearing from him. "If I was just a boss, you'd kill me without hesitation. But because I deceived you and pretended to be your friend, some sense of justice, some sense that I'm not worth just killing outright, still lingers inside you."

"And what will you do if I leave you alive?" My eyes narrow.

"Exactly what I've been planning to do!" Krak draws himself up. "Take over this Rift. Become its master. You did exactly what I needed you to do, securing the promotion that I knew I could never get for myself. Now that you've served your purpose, well . . ."

Krak waves his hand, and a blast of interdimensional energy flares around my feet. I suddenly find myself falling . . . falling . . . sucked down that long, twisty straw and back to Earth once more.

CHAPTER THIRTY

When Ali and I come tumbling out back onto the floor of the sub-basement, I find a great many messages pouring across my vision.

[Congratulations! You have defeated a Rift!]

[You have leveled up!]

[Congratulations! You are now Level 25!]

"Twenty-five?" I have to smile at that. "Leveled up twice! Not going to complain about that."

"I leveled up three times!" Ali beams as she climbs to her feet and helps me up. "And we would have leveled up even more if we had managed to take down Krak."

"That's the second time I've fought him in a boss fight and he's managed to get away," I mutter. "Probably why I've hardly leveled up recently. Oh, well. That's the way it goes, sometimes."

[LunarEclipse: Hey, you're still great, Jason!]

[ShadowDancer: Yeah! And hey, that just makes for a more epic rematch later, you know?]

[ViperQueen: Exactly! He's in charge of the Rift now, so you're sure to see him again!]

As if in answer, the Rift portal flickers and closes, and I let out a long breath. My body aches, and my stomach rumbles. I'm glad to be back, that's for sure. Across the room, the elevator dings, and Ali and I both turn and walk toward it.

Neither of us say much as we make our way back out through the lobby and into the street. There are several news reporters waiting to interview us, and I say a few words here and there, but I'm so overwhelmed by it all that I mostly just want to get away. I'm quite thankful when Mr. Wang's helicopter appears, and soon, the two of us are borne away upon the winds.

"Wow, wow, wow!" Mr. Wang shakes his head in amazement. "I just can't figure the two of you out! So good! And the way the tentacles made a Faraday cage, and the way you fought those things . . . Wow! You're making me a ton of money, Jason. I do hope you know that."

I snort. "Trust me, you've made that abundantly clear."

Mr. Wang smiles, then turns to Ali. Before he can say a word, she shakes her head.

"I have absolutely no interest in doing work like this for you."

"Fair, fair." Mr. Wang holds up his hands and chuckles. "I won't push. For what it's worth, that seven hundred million has been placed in your bank account, ready for you to use to your heart's content. Go hire a construction crew to build a new apartment building, or squander it all on a mansion, or buy a skyscraper. I don't care! You do you."

Ali's jaw drops. "Seven hundred million?"

"There were some charitable donations that came in as people watched you struggling through the dungeon." Mr. Wang shrugs. "Apparently a lot of people sympathize with your plight! None of them are landlords, mind you, but you've got a lot of people watching your back."

Ali's eyes fill with tears. "Thank you."

"Not a problem whatsoever!" Mr. Wang beams. "I'm here to help just as much as I can!"

I smile and nod. Mr. Wang certainly is something else, though I do question how much of his charity is motivated by true generosity and how much is motivated by a simple desire for money. In any event, I'm definitely thankful for all his help, so I'm not going to complain. To be certain, getting flown from dungeon to dungeon *is* a lot nicer than simply running through the streets looking for them, especially now that the world is, at least somewhat, returning to normal.

"Oh! Jason." Mr. Wang turns to me as the helicopter slowly comes down for a landing. "I meant to tell you. I've been doing some research on Burnie, and I have some ideas. To start with, there are some rather powerful necromancers who have popped up and have voiced their support in attempting to revive him that way."

"Not a chance." I shake my head firmly. "I've never seen a scenario where necromancy doesn't come back to bite you somehow."

"Indeed. I was hoping you'd say that, but I felt duty-bound to offer it." Mr. Wang crosses his arms, then pulls a small token out of his inventory. "In that case, here's the only other option I've seen. Those anti-aging pills you pulled out of the dungeon?"

Ali frowns, then opens her inventory and pulls out the small bottle. "What about them?"

"I've been speaking to some experts in the chats, and someone suggested you try to use one of them to turn Burnie back into a Phoenix and then cure him before he turns to ice again." Mr. Wang shrugs. "I don't know if it'll work, but I'd really like to see Burnie back in the mix of things."

"Let me guess." I raise an eyebrow. "People are willing to pay more if he's on my team?"

"Near as I can tell, almost twenty-five percent more." Mr. Wang smiles broadly. "Of course, with your new Kraken, who knows how it'll all come together? We'll just have to see. I'll have a new assignment for you in the morning."

The helicopter comes down to land on my helipad, and he opens the door. "Go get some well-deserved rest and get ready for your next adventure!"

A few moments later, as Ali and I touch down on the concrete, the helicopter blades roar even more fiercely, and the chopper flashes off through the sky.

"What do you think he'll be up to next?" Ali glances at me.

"Please believe me when I say that I don't have the faintest idea." I sigh, then shrug. "Well, shall we go see if we can bring Burnie back?"

We quickly make our way inside, where we take out Burnie and set him on the counter. Bjorn comes out as well and uses his cold powers to keep the ice sculpture from melting. Carefully, Ali hands me the anti-aging pills, and I dump several of them out onto the counter. I only need to turn him back a day or so, not ten years, so I quickly do the math, break off a little fleck of one pill, crush it up, and dissolve it in a glass of water. That done, with few other options, I pour it over the icy form of my Phoenix.

[ChaosRider: I HOPE THIS WORKS!!!!]

[ShadowDancer: It's sure to work!!!]

[Originalgoth: That's just going to melt it even faster.]

[DarkCynic: Put a lid on it, lady.]

I laugh, then sit back to wait. Frankly, I don't have the faintest idea if this will work or if all I'm doing is pouring water on a statue. The whole world seems to pause; even my chat goes quiet . . .

And then the faintest breath of color spreads across the edges of his feathers.

I gasp in relief and joy as the blue tips of his fiery wings appear on the ice, then sweep upward with a great rush of color. Within a moment, all the feathers have taken form, the legs have taken flesh, and his eyes blink several times and turn to look at me.

Master?

"Burnie!" I beam and lean forward to give the Phoenix a hug. "You're alive!"

I am! Though, Burnie twists his head around to look at his feathers, *I do appear to be somewhat blue.*

I have to nod and laugh in agreement. Burnie's feathers, instead of returning to their ordinary colors, have become entirely blue. I don't really have any idea what that means, but my guess is that it means he can generate ice instead of fire. Perhaps it means he doesn't have to worry about turning to ice any longer? In any case, Ali leans forward and begins to scan him, while I simply stroke his back.

Master? I . . . I think I need to warn you about something.

Burnie scratches at the counter. *I don't know how to say this, exactly, but . . . I think Krak may be planning to betray you. The reason I shot that last blast of ice was because he triggered me to do it. There's a pressure point on my neck. He just reached up and . . . and then the next thing I know, I'm here.*

"Yeah, we sort of picked up on his true nature." I grimace. "He betrayed us and tried to tag-team us with another dungeon boss. And then took over the Rift when we managed to kill the other guy."

That sounds about right.

"And . . . Done!" Ali steps back from Burnie. "It looks to me like the ice crystal has been fully integrated throughout your entire body. You shouldn't have to worry about freezing up any longer."

Burnie spreads his wings and launches himself upward. I should mention that my living room has an incredibly high ceiling, and Burnie simply swirls and glides around through the lofty area. Finally, he comes down to land on my arm and gives me a peck on the ear.

Can we go outside?

I give him a nod, and the group of us slowly goes out onto the helipad. By now, the sun has set, with only a faint halo of orange light still visible on the western horizon. The night sky is black as coal, with the stars shining down brilliantly. Distant roars and grunts echo across the city, intermingled with the *beep* of car horns and the wail of sirens. Burnie stretches his wings and launches himself up into the sky, sailing and looping, and I smile broadly.

"It looks like he's loving it!" Ali grins. "Burnie! Try out your new powers!"

Burnie flips around, then looses a massive gout of flame. It's a blue flame, so hot that I can feel the heat from where I'm standing. As he swoops back and forth and lets out more blasts, I have to admit that I'm more than impressed. I don't know what that ice crystal did, but it really doesn't seem to have cooled him off at all. When Burnie comes back down and lands on my shoulder, I give him a nod.

[ShadowDancer: That was so epic!!!]

[IceQueen: So, he's even hotter than he used to be??? I don't know how that works, but I love it!!!]

[RazorEdge: I mean . . . blue flame *is* hotter than orange flame. Maybe . . . I dunno.]

I don't know either, but I also don't care. Suddenly, I remember that I need to level up and glance at Ali. She's already a step ahead of me and is beaming from ear to ear.

"I have a new arrow type!" A small, wooden shaft appears in her hand, and she shows it to me. "It's a teleporter arrow! I'll teleport wherever I shoot it!"

"Now *that* seems helpful." I chuckle softly, then open up my own interface. "I have two to choose from. Weapon, creature, or skill?"

"Weapon." Ali nods. "One weapon, one skill. You don't need any new creatures, I think."

I can't really disagree, and I make the selections. There's a pause, and with a flash, a dagger with a bluish blade appears in my hands.

[Weapon Acquired: Dagger of Damage]

[Level: C]

[Details: Deals an increasing amount of damage based on the number of times the creature has been attacked.]

I whistle softly. "That'll help with stabbing things lots of times! It'll be interesting to see how fast it scales, exactly, but—"

"But it seems right up your alley." Ali nods. "Now, what about the skill?"

[Skill Acquired!]

[Bonus XP (passive): Earn extra XP per kill and level up faster!]

"That's something I can get behind." I smile as I look the skill over.

"Yeah, because *you* need to get more powerful." Ali snorts, then smiles and starts walking toward the edge of the roof. "Well, thank you for everything, Jason. I'm going to get going, I think. I need to get some rest and then get to work providing housing for my warriors tomorrow. That's going to be quite a task, I think."

"You're more than welcome to stay here, you know." I shrug. "It'd be a lot more comfortable than sleeping down in the park. I can use the couch."

"Yeah, but what would that say? I can't have better living conditions than the people I'm trying to help." Ali draws out her bow and fits a new arrow into it. "Besides . . . I really, *really* want to try this out."

She draws back the string and lets fly. There's a long pause, and the wind blows a bit harder. Her hair streams out behind her as she stares off into the distance . . . And then, with a flash of light, she vanishes, as if she'd never been standing there at all.

"Huh," I murmur. "Looks like those teleporter arrows really are handy." I wave my hand, and Burnie flies down to land on my arm. "Well, come on. We'd best head inside. We need to get some good sleep too, and—"

A loud scream echoes from below, and I frown and walk over to the edge of the roof. Down below, at the base of the tower, a large portal seems to have formed. It looks to me like giant rat-people are streaming out, each one a good six feet tall, and all wielding large swords and battle axes. Wealthy residents of the tower race away down the street, even running out into traffic. Some of the rats chase after them, but most of them turn and charge up into the complex itself. I frown and stroke my chin, then turn and glance at Burnie.

"If I can't even protect the very building where I live, no one is going to hire me."

That's a logical conclusion, Master.

"Then it would make sense that I should go take care of that dungeon. It can't be long, maybe an hour, and *then* I can get sleep."

If that's what you want, I'll be right behind you.

"Wonderful." I take a deep breath, turn, and walk toward the glass doors . . . and then turn around and charge toward the edge of the roof. A moment later, I leap out into space and spread my arms and legs as I drop down toward the distant street below.

[RazorEdge: Uhh . . . Jason? You do realize that you can't fly, right?]

[FireStorm: Don't you nag him! He's got this under control!]

[Originalgoth: I sincerely hope that he doesn't.]

I laugh, then glance to the side of me, where Burnie has his wings folded against his sides, falling just as fast as I am.

"Burnie, get ready to burn!" I call out, then draw out my Photonic Dagger in one hand and my Dagger of Damage in the other. "Kraken! First, find a better name for yourself! Second, get me a place to land!"

In response, my pocket dimension flickers open, and a number of tentacles emerge to form a landing mat.

This is my job now, and—even still aching from the Rift—I feel myself fluttering with excitement. This dungeon is going *down* . . . And then, after that, the rest will fall in turn.

ABOUT THE AUTHOR

Kaz Hunter is the author of the Apocalypse Reincarnation, System Bound, and Rise of the Strongest Sovereign series. A graduate of Texas A&M University (go, Aggies!), he started writing on Wuxiaworld and Webnovel. He has since moved on.

DISCOVER
STORIES UNBOUND

PodiumAudio.com

Printed in the USA
CPSIA information can be obtained
at www.ICGtesting.com
JSHW022004270524
63875JS00001B/5